Praise for the Author

'Mary Morrissy always writes with great insight, deep humanity and an oftentimes acerbic eye. These stories are assured little portraits of very ordinary people finding pathos, beauty and profundity in their very ordinary lives. I challenge you not to see something of yourself reflected here.' **Jan Carson**

'I adore Mary Morrissy's stories. Fresh, deft, succinct, each one is like a dart to the heart. There is also the particular pleasure, here as in *Prosperity Drive*, of encountering the same characters in different ways, sometimes fleetingly, sometimes from a completely opposing perspective, complicating and deepening our relationships with them and giving an additional, satisfying and heartbreaking unity to this collection as a whole.' **Lucy Caldwell**

'"During that time with you I was more alive and more unhappy than I had ever been" says a woman speaking of her affair with a married man in this collection of interlinking short stories. The line is sharp, pitiless and heartbreaking, just like everything else in this marvellous book.' **Carlo Gébler**

'…a novel of great brilliance and inventiveness … Penelope Unbound is a masterwork'. **John Banville,** *The Observer*

'Mary Morrissy [is] one of the brightest, most original stars in the firmament of Irish writing' **Nuala O'Connor**

Also by the Author

A Lazy Eye
Mother of Pearl
The Pretender
The Rising of Bella Casey
Prosperity Drive
Penelope Unbound

TWENTY-TWENTY VISION

Stories

Mary Morrissy

THE LILLIPUT PRESS
DUBLIN

First published 2025 by
THE LILLIPUT PRESS

62–63 Sitric Road,
Arbour Hill,
Dublin 7,
Ireland
www.lilliputpress.ie

Copyright © Mary Morrissy, 2025

10 9 8 7 6 5 4 3 2 1

All rights reserved. No part of this publication may be reproduced in any form or by any means without the prior permission of the publisher.

A CIP record for this title is available from The British Library.

Paperback ISBN 978 1 84351 916 4
eBook ISBN 978 1 84351 933 1

Set in 11.5 pt on 16 pt in Perpetua and Chap Regular by Compuscript
Printed and bound in Czechia, by Finidr

Life can only be understood backwards but it must be lived forwards.
— **Søren Kierkegaard**

For Joanne Carroll

CONTENTS

Onset	1
Remission	5
Fingerpost	16
Property	33
Repossession	48
Mortification	61
Heartburn	75
Notes on Biology	86
Seize the Day	99
Lost Property	115
Kiss of Life	128
Survivors	140
Husbandry	144
Twenty-Twenty Vision	159
Done Deal	177
Weight	194
Mature People	198
Curriculum Vitae	220

ONSET

When Chris told Delma that her husband, Jim, had been the victim of a beasting, Delma felt, unexpectedly, a rush of emotion for him. It took her completely by surprise. In the forty years Chris and Jim had been married, Delma hadn't felt anything much for Jim, one way or the other. She'd always suspected that he found her a bit full-on – well, she was! – and too loud for his taste. He liked his women more pliable than her. But look, he might have been a dryballs, but he was decent and honourable, a good provider and he'd stuck with Chris through thick and thin. But that was because Chris had kept things from him, things that Delma knew and probably shouldn't.

For instance ... his daughter Trudy, aged seventeen, had made him a grandfather, but he had no idea because Chris had hushed it up. She and Trudy had concocted this daft fiction that she'd got work experience in Dublin for four months even when she was clearly showing. She'd gone away, had the baby, put her up for adoption and Jim was none the wiser.

The pair of them had made a complete fool out of him and Delma had been party to it. She'd pitied him then, but pity was a debased emotion, so she'd parked it. Now she found herself blushing fiercely as if an old crush had suddenly been triggered. What was wrong with her, she wondered. Lately, she'd been prey to waves of nameless emotions that came over her like a blanching sweat.

'He went out on the beach,' Chris was saying, 'he didn't even put on sun block though I'd warned him ...'

Chris was just back from holiday with Trudy, her American husband, Mike, the kids and Jim, all squashed together in a cramped holiday let by the sea in Wexford and Delma had guessed – rightly – that she would need a debriefing. She'd opened a bottle of white even though it was just after lunch. Since her retirement she'd got into the habit of ritualising occasions, because there were so few of them.

'Isn't it a bit early?' Chris had said

'Live dangerously,' she'd said.

Truth was she'd missed Chris; when you're old, two whole weeks is a long time to be friendless.

They were sitting in Delma's conservatory, which she'd had built with her lump sum. She'd had visions of herself, regal on the faux rattan furniture, reading in the long afternoons just like this one. But the conservatory had been a total disaster. In winter it was Baltic and the windows clouded up murkily with condensation. In summer it was a house of mortifying sweat, even with the sliding door propped open.

'Honestly,' Chris was saying, 'he looked like he'd gone three rounds in the ring with Mike Tyson ...'

Delma didn't understand. What in God's name was a beasting? She imagined a bestial mugging – young turks beating Jim up leaving him battered and bruised.

Or was it some kind of monstering – that was a term she *had* heard of. She might not have had children like Chris, but she'd spent most of her working life in an office through which several generations of young people had passed, and she prided herself on being *au fait* with the issues of the day. Perhaps Jim had some dark sexual past of his own? Was this a Me Too thing?

Of late, though, Delma had found herself slower on the uptake, so she let Chris go on and hoped it would all become clear.

'We were getting worried he was gone so long. Mike even offered to go look for him, but I knew Jim wouldn't have liked that ...'

Chris always knew better.

Delma went back to that word – beasting – but the more she fixated on it, the more senseless it became. She remembered a game she and Chris used to play as girls, using paper origami and some complicated numerical formula she couldn't now remember to uncover their animal spirits. Delma was a tiger; Chris, she remembered, was a fox. She tried to imagine what Jim's would be. A guinea pig came to mind, nimble and nibbly and fastidious. It made her smile.

'It's not funny,' Chris said.

'Sorry,' Delma said.

'He could have died.'

In her mind's eye Delma saw the young men jostling with Jim out on the dunes. She saw them raising a bat and bringing it down on his defenceless skull; suddenly, she got impatient with Chris and how unclear everything was.

'Did they find the men who did it?' she interrupted.

'What?'

Delma knew from Chris's tone not to repeat the question.

'Have you been listening to a single word I've said?'

You've no idea how hard I've been listening, Delma wanted to say, and still I can't make sense of it. Your husband went AWOL for hours on the beach and when he returned he had a disfigured face as if he'd been in a fight and yet no one asked the obvious question ...

'What the hell happened to him, Chris?'

The silence between them ticked.

'I told you, Del,' Chris said speaking very deliberately. 'It was ... a ... bee sting.'

Suddenly, the words fell into place like the waterfall rush of Scrabble tiles being returned to the box after a game. The florid images of the thugs on the beach melted away.

'Oh, I see,' Delma said, relieved for Jim. 'Thank God, he's safe!'

If he was here, she believed she might even have hugged him.

But she saw a perplexed expression cross Chris's face, as if Delma had inadvertently revealed a hidden vein of love, a dirty secret of her own.

REMISSION

The treatment doesn't make me sick, it makes me dazed. And tired. Dog-tired. Fatigue strikes like a power cut and I have to sit down – *now!* The hospital is a stone's throw from Suesey Street, the part of town I used to frequent two decades ago, when we were an item. Last week, after my session, I found myself wandering there when I had one of my turns. It was a thundery kind of day; the sun was spiteful. There I was, passing 'our' pub. Where we would meet on days like this one, hot and humid, or on brown afternoons threatening rain. Either way, this was where we would meet in secret and hide from the prevailing climate of prying eyes.

As I halted in front of the pub, I wondered if I could still rightfully call it ours, since on the outside it had clearly been made over. The masonry is now a fuchsia red and there's a new name over the door – it's called Billy Pilgrim's. I suspected that inside would be similarly altered – primary colours, stainless steel, loud music, themed. Superstitiously, I've never gone back there. But needs must. Migrainous from the sun, I knew if I didn't take the weight off my feet soon, I would fall down on the street. I pushed through the pub's double doors with the same milky glass panels from before, and became a visitor in my own past.

The inside hadn't changed. The same polished oak, marble-topped counter, partitions of dimpled glass, brass rail to lean your feet on, a snug in the front of the shop, a back

Twenty-Twenty Vision

room and a mirror behind the bar so that even before you've got drunk you're seeing double. The smell was just the same too. An oozing mix of stale porter and pungent urinal. I made my way through the outer bar to our spot in the long back room, under the big station clock, so, you said, we wouldn't be reminded of how little time we had. The relief of sinking into pub leatherette! I looked around furtively in case I had expressed my ecstasy aloud. But even if I had, there was no one in the pub except for the bar-tender, a blocky, shaven-headed young man, with his sleeves rolled up and nothing to do. Apart from him — and he was probably still in short trousers when we were meeting in here — the rest of the pub was unchanged. I sat in our corner gratefully and ordered a mineral water. (A bald woman wearing a wig and downing vodkas alone at four in the afternoon would have seemed as big a cliché as our affair — the older married man and the youngish single woman trysting in a pub. These days I'm trying to avoid clichés, even age-appropriate ones.) The electively bald barman landed the glass on the low table with a clink-clunk and obligingly opened the bottle and poured. I drank thirstily. The flinty taste of the carbonated water set my teeth on edge — funny aversions afflict you with chemo. I pushed the glass to one side where it spat effervescently still trying to be the life and soul of the party.

I confirmed the barman's suspicions that I was a mad old bat when I called him back and ordered coffee instead. It came in a thick cream catering cup, slopped in the saucer. It was thin and bad, from a jug stewed for hours. But it was like a madeleine to our long-lost affair. With each sour sip, I was no longer visiting my past, I was right back in it.

After treatment, most sensible people would go home and crawl into bed. But the last thing I want to do is to give in to sleep during the day. If I do, it means I'll be awake – and alone in the graveyard hours. Ironically, I live alone, or should that be I live alone ironically? I have made it a practice to call out 'Honey, I'm home' when I let myself in as a joke to myself, on myself, and to puncture the squeamish silence of a house undisturbed since I left it. I try to imagine the existence that would match my smooth and hearty greeting. The set of *I Love Lucy* comes to mind, a gleaming kitchen rich in appliances, a brave suburban light. Not my dim and over-shadowed household. I use all the tricks of wolfish loners to combat solitude. I talk my way through tasks aloud. 'Triona,' I say, 'time to sluice the tub.' And so I set to, wiping down the surfaces, the tiles, the wash-hand basin and colouring the bowl with a squirt of lemony liquid. And because I can never manage to keep the towel wrapped around me – and now my body geometry can't support it – I end up naked and sweating amidst the disinfectant fumes, the closest I get to a sexual glow these days.

This was the time of day we used to meet. It annoyed me that you would arrive breathlessly as if you were just managing to squeeze me in. But once you sat and calmed, we entered another time zone where all other pre-occupations fell away. So absorbed would we become that a parade of our nearest and dearest could have passed by and we wouldn't have noticed. This place absolved us from being furtive; it was the only time we were not mindful of our situation, where it became just the pair of us, alone in the world. Perhaps that's why it was so intense; for an hour-and-a-half twice a week we played ourselves. No wonder I hadn't wanted to come back. But as I sat there, I found myself soothed by the atmosphere, not haunted by it. In the torpor of an empty afternoon pub, I realized I'd found the perfect asylum for the chemically blasted.

It didn't stay empty for long, of course. Students started trickling in. There was a trio of men in soiled overalls and mud-caked boots who sat at the bar like starlings on a wire. A family of tourists, Italians, guide book in hand, joined me in the back room. Mama, Papa, Silvio and Chiara. They took photos of themselves with their phones. Papa tried a pint and didn't like it; the children bought crisps and released salt and vinegar into the air. I ordered another coffee and settled in. Not out of nostalgia. I cannot be nostalgic for something I destroyed myself; I am not *that* perverse. I stayed because it was easier than going home. And then, coming up for five, when I was totally off-guard, when I had made my own of the place, you arrived.

Really, it *was* you. You, as a boy, that is. Slender – you always said you'd been a beanpole in your youth – a thin, hollowed-out face, gaunt almost, a mop of black curls and eyes to match. It was uncanny. The boy wore a sludge-coloured rain mac over a faded T-shirt, a pair of navy drainpipe jeans, dilapidated Beatle boots with pointed toes. If it wasn't you, this boy must have raided your youthful wardrobe. He sat in the outer bar in the corner but right in my line of vision. He – you, what pronoun to use? – nodded at the barman. He was a regular, it seemed. (Did you have a life in this bar before it became our haunt, I wondered? I'd never thought to ask.) He fished a paperback out of a canvas satchel and began to read. When the barman steered a pint towards him, he raised his eyes to say thanks and his gaze met mine. Well, I *was* staring. He brought the pint to his lips – I almost expected him to raise it in a toast – and then over a moustache of foam he smiled directly at me. Then I *knew*. Knew it was you, because that crease appeared between your eyebrows (the one I thought had come only in middle-age from too much worry) and your mouth turned downwards. You don't smile up like most people. It isn't, wasn't, a mirthless smile, just one tempered with a clownish sadness. I felt myself weaken all over again. Shyly, I smiled back. Why shyly? Because I felt all my old uncertainties return as if I too had been spun back in time. To a time before I met you. To a 'you' I'd never known.

You settled into your book. By right it should have been one of those orange-covered Penguins — Evelyn Waugh or Graham Greene — but without my specs, I couldn't work out what it was. After the initial startlement, I felt invisible and pleasantly voyeuristic. I was happy to sit and watch. After all these years, I finally had you all to myself.

Sharing. That's what usually dooms an illicit affair in the end. The mistress not wanting to share. But I didn't care about that. In truth, I didn't feel I was sharing you with anyone. She was just the silent partner as far as I was concerned. I just didn't want anything broken because of our association. I hated it when you talked about your past. Not because it contained her, but because it contained you. You blamed the past for our predicament. *Bad timing*, you would say. *If I'd met you when I was younger we could have ...* We could have what? Obliterated your mistakes? Had children? When I still could. You could have brought out the maternal in me. *If you'd known me then you'd understand ...*

Understand what, though? That you weren't always this rueful self? The trouble was I couldn't imagine you younger; I could only see you as you were. Acting old, your role to impart wisdom, already writing me out. *Don't do what I did*, you used to say, *don't marry for gratitude*. As if I were inundated with suitors seeking my hand. I was thirty-seven and considered past it. Worse than past it, because I was engaged in a fantasy relationship that couldn't stand the light of day. That's what my girlfriends told me. Even if you had managed to leave the silent partner, I'd have got the worst of you, an old man with sagging dugs and slowing walk, enduring a guilty superannuation trying to win back his wounded off-spring. I would get compromise while the silent partner would have had the wholehearted best of you. That ardent, warrior youth you seemed so nostalgic for. I would become the bath-chair pusher, the caretaker, witness to your decline. That was never my style.

For one thing, I've always been careless. Careless with people. Other people might mistake it for carefree; not the same thing at all. I am free of care because I care less. I was not vigilant enough even about myself, as it turned out. If I had been, I might have noticed the giveaway pellet on the underside of my breast, right over my heart.

The clock struck six and a girl breezed in. She had long, sand-coloured hair and a gapped fringe. She wore something filmy and floral. Not your type at all, but then that's presuming *I* was your type. She looked like the kind of girl who'd stand on the shore with a towel to dry you off if you were in swimming. Girlie was territorial about you, fixed you with her big eyes and talked – a lot – some breathless account during which she would snatch your hand for emphasis, or poke you playfully on the arm. I caught snatches of her conversation.

'And then he asked me if I'd cover the late shift ...' She exhaled indignation. 'I mean, really!'

You played with the ends of her hair and gazed at her with an unseemly kind of yearning that made me look away. Then you leaned in and kissed her. She was bruised into silence by your lips. That was something you used to do with me.

Remission

In mid-flight I would find my words smothered by your mouth. It used to infuriate me that you couldn't bear my small talk. Looking at it now, I recognized desire. As you disengaged, another person joined you, a boy this time. I thought maybe I'd be able to identify him. Maybe he'd be someone who had survived into my time? But I couldn't. His features seemed in untimely progression. He had a boy's eyes and soft chin, but a man's brow and nose. His mane of nondescript hair grazed his dejected-looking shoulders. I christened him Lionheart, but it was you, with your dark looks, that consumed my attention.

I kept you constantly in my sight-lines and every so often our eyes would meet and lock for a moment, though as the pub filled up with office workers, it was harder to maintain a clear line of vision. Girlie produced a phone and I could hear you planning the rest of your night. You wanted to go to a gig with a band called Methuselah, Girlie wanted to go for something to eat. Lionheart eyed Girlie, then you – he seemed to have the casting vote. I wasn't sure who he was most in love with, you or Girlie. Between the standing army of drinkers, I kept on catching your eye. A quizzical eye, at first, lightly sardonic, then more calculating, curious. This is how it was when we met. Even with age you couldn't cloak your emotions so everything got played out on your face. I felt, somehow, you were communicating with me, over the heads of your friends and the Friday night crowd. But what were you saying?

I hadn't thought of you in years. Really! Not in that way, I mean. Not in the pained malignant way of the unrequited. But no, that's not true. I *was* requited. During that time with you I was more alive and more unhappy than I had ever been. Maybe the two go together. Now I am chronically content and half-dead. Though even at the time I knew what we were doing was a recipe for heartbreak – someone's. Yours, as it turned out.

In the end, I couldn't stand the tension of waiting to see who would break first. You? Me? Or the silent partner? I wasn't slave enough to the cliché to wait for you to say – I can't leave my wife. So I ended it. Chop chop. A swift guillotine. I remember your face when I said it – here on this very spot. Everything fell, as if I'd struck you. You started bargaining furiously.

'Here, I'll phone her,' you said, lifting the mobile like it was a brick with which you were going to smash your life to pieces. On my account. A gesture. Our gestures give us away. 'I'll do it, right now.'

'Put it away,' I said. 'It's over.'

It's not every day you get a chance to see the prequel to love. That's what kept me in a sticky, airless Friday night pub sipping cold coffee. I've never liked being alone in a pub – call me old-fashioned. Even when we were together, I hated being early. Waiting for someone I was never sure of, full of dread about being hit upon by amateur predators. That wasn't a problem now. If anyone was a predator in this situation it was me. But I couldn't bear to leave before you. It seemed important this time around that you leave me.

Finally at half seven, the three of you rose, gathering up your stuff and pushed out into the main thoroughfare of the pub. Immediately, in a pincer movement, three of the suited ones moved in to claim your space. I felt the betraying heave of disappointment that goes with the slow withdrawing of love. You turned to go; then you stopped and whispered in Girlie's ear. She looked back at you briefly then bounced towards the exit where Lionheart was waiting patiently. I could see his face lighting up as she approached. Ah, so it was her he was after. He pulled open the door and she darted through it. He followed.

You turned towards me. I felt panicky but told myself to stop. You were going to the toilets, maybe, or using the side-door, the one that opened out on to a laneway, the one I used to favour when we were together. I could see your head bobbing up and down as you weaved your way around the crowd that stood between us. This was too close for comfort. I hadn't banked on our worlds actually colliding like this. You stopped in front of me.

Chemo fugue, my friends say. It was your ex-lover's son you saw. But no, I knew you had fathered only daughters. A trick of the mind, the light. But no, it was none of that.

'Do I know you?' he demanded.

When I didn't answer – well, how could I answer? – he rephrased it.

'Do you know me?'

He was more earnest than I expected. You were never earnest; had it beaten out of you, you said, in the rough justice of boarding school. You were playful in company, serious in bed.

'It's just that ...' he started. A lighter voice than yours; age makes us growl and grate.

'Yes?' I said, feeling the bloom of ambiguous trepidation show on my face.

'Can I ...?'

I nodded.

He folded himself on to the small stool opposite me that had remained empty except as a repository for bags and jackets. He laid these carefully on the banquette seat beside me. This careful piling gave me time to wonder. What was he going to say? Could he do me for harassment? Young people are touchy about this sort of thing and I had not kept custody of the eyes, as we were instructed in convent school.

'You've been staring at me all night,' he said simply. No outlandish accusations, then.

'I'm sorry,' I said, rising to go. I had been a bad voyeur; I'd attracted attention by the focus of my own. 'I have to go …'

I tried to squeeze by him but he grabbed my arm.

'Why is that?' he demanded. 'What do you want?'

To turn the clock back, I wanted to say.

He gripped my wrist and looked up at me imploringly. 'Are you my mother?'

That broke the spell, the chemo fog.

'What? No!!'

'Are you my mother?' he repeated and stood up, staring at me. There was the steel I knew from your eyes, the grit of refusal. I shook him off, my folly made manifest.

'My natural mother,' he hissed in my ear. When I tried to wriggle out of our awkward embrace he raised his voice. 'Are you the woman who gave me up? Who gave up on me? Who refused to meet me but feels free to spy on me? Are you?'

There was a ripple of anticipation in those around us; a pub crowd recognises when there is a row brewing. What I wanted to say was yes. Yes to everything. Except to the accusation of motherhood. To that I wanted to say – do you think, dear boy, that if I were your mother, I wouldn't rush bald-headed to claim you?

'Is it you?' he pleaded, 'come for me?'

Oh God, I couldn't bear the interrogative. I *had* come for you. But the wrong you. I yanked my hand away and ploughed my way through the crowds of drinkers, jogging elbows and upsetting drinks as I went. A couple of aggrieved 'heys' followed in my wake. I stepped out into the laneway where more shirt-sleeved drinkers had spilled out into the golden evening. Once clear of them, I ran. I ran, clutching my false hair in case I should lose it too. In my haste I crashed into a stack of shopping trolleys parked in a bay outside one of those late-opening supermarkets. I ducked in and found myself in the refrigerated aisle. He didn't follow me, or if he did, he didn't find me. I counted it as a lucky escape, a remission of sorts.

FINGERPOST

Christine is sitting in her car having a panic attack. At least, that's what she thinks is happening. It's both more and less frightening than she expected. No gasping for breath or throat closing up, or heart going like the clappers. No, it's just this. It's 4:30 pm, a mild February afternoon, the bare trees shrouded in a blurred light and she hasn't a clue where she is. There's no one about. Even though the street where she has parked, or abandoned herself, is homely with a cottage-style terrace on one side facing a large green, the houses have a stand-offish air, curtains drawn, no cars in the driveway and no evident signs of life.

Enter the Mount Helicon Demesne, the Google directions she'd printed out had instructed. When she drove in, it was like entering an alternate universe. Each development led into another and she felt like she was trapped in a Rubik's Cube. Enormous, detached McMansions with mock Tudor beams and double garages gave way to more modest gingerbready two-storeys with dormer windows and faux shutters. Then came little courts of maisonettes that were boxy and Swedish-looking, or what Christine imagined as Swedish from browsing Ikea catalogues. She'd driven past a dozen landscaped green spaces, some flat and planted with single, spindly-looking trees, others sloping like the grassy knolls of a golf course. *Take a right on to Granary Hill* was the next direction on the Google sheet. But nothing appeared that looked like a granary, not to speak of a proper hill. It was as if she'd entered a world where the names had no relationship to the landmarks. And it was totally deserted. Not a sinner about. She might as well be in the Gobi Desert.

She'd been smug starting out. *Head south on Empress Avenue towards Marine Road.* I know how to get to the end of my own road, she'd muttered to herself. When they'd bought the car, Jim had suggested a sat nav, but she didn't like the idea of a woman in the car (they're always women, aren't they?) barking instructions at her. Don't I have you for that, she'd said to Jim. Jim's specialty is telling her to turn when it's too late and then getting impatient with her as if she's some kind of dimwit. So she savours the experience of driving alone, because she neither has to speak nor listen. It's a matter of policy with her that on trips like this, she never brings her mobile. She likes the feeling of being untethered, being in nowhere land, unreachable. That feels transgressive these days.

Veer left on to ramp for Circular Road. Her whole life is veering just now. Sniffing her armpits to see has she developed the old lady smell yet, that perfumed mix of sweet decay she remembers from aunts of long ago – talcum powder, sherry and eau de something like cologne. Who's she codding? She's trying to avoid thinking about death. Delma's kind of death, in particular. Delma is her best friend. That sounds meagre and inadequate; her life-long companion, that's more like it. *Pace* Jim.

Before Delma went into the nursing home, Jim had begun to get tetchy about the time Christine spent with her. Her visits to Delma's increasingly chaotic house took longer and longer, partly because Delma told her everything twice over. There was always a bottle of wine on the go, even if she called in the morning, and when she tried to leave there were scenes.

Don't go, Delma would say, clutching her sleeve, don't leave me.

Christine had felt torn, afraid of Delma's drowning grip and dreading Jim's low-lying hostility. All he was worried about was that she was spilling the beans to Delma.

About our sex lives, Christine had asked, trying to humour him.

That's what Jim thinks women talk about — even at their age. But it's intimacy he means. He suspects she might share more of herself with Delma than with him. And that's probably true. Or, at least, it was in the past. She kept the details of Delma's decline from him. She didn't know why. To protect Delma? But to protect her from what?

Merge on to the South Link was the next instruction. There was a lot of merging in the Google directions. People say that about the elderly — how they merge into the background, become invisible. Not true of Delma who had become more defined, more definite as she aged. Once she'd given up on colour, her hair underneath turned out to be a majestic and uniform white. She'd acquired a whole new wardrobe. Suddenly she could wear reds and purples because they no longer shouted at her hair. Titian, Delma used to joke, that's the posh name for my shade of carrot. She'd become more flamboyant, buying roomy shift dresses with big pockets and swaddling a pashmina around her neck. A more youthful style than the sober office wardrobe she'd had to wear all her working life. It was a bit mutton dressed as lamb, if you asked Christine, but she said nothing. Now she wonders if this new freedom of expression had been the early signs of Delma's illness taking hold?

Her decline had been so gradual, it was hard to say. It was only when her drinking got out of hand — there'd been some incident with her cleaner – that Delma's niece took charge and moved her into the Mount Helicon Nursing Home.

It had taken Christine months to pluck up the courage to visit. That first time she'd been shocked to see how much weight Delma had lost. Her memory ring was loose on her now skinny middle finger. She used to move the ring from her left hand to her right to remind her of what she might forget – medical appointments, car repairs, the hair salon. Once Delma would have been delighted with her new slender outline, but Christine doesn't know if such things register with her any longer.

Delma had always struggled with her weight and Christine never imagined that in old age *she'd* be the one with the fuller figure – isn't that the euphemism? When she and Delma were younger they were always going on diets. Scarsdale, Atkins. The soup diet, the grapefruit diet. Christine still weighs herself once a week on the bathroom scales. The figures pop up in kilos. She's never got the hang of metric. She memorizes the flashing digits, sometimes even writes them down, promising herself she'll convert them into stones and pounds. But even when she's done the conversion, she doesn't act on it. It's a ritual, something she's observed all her adult life. Self-imposed, punitive. At her age, who cares what weight she is?

She hasn't been back to Mount Helicon since that first visit in November. Jim drove her then and she hadn't taken any notice of the route. When she was the passenger, she switched off her interior compass. It was like being a child again, freed of responsibility. Although not freed of worry, given Jim's buccaneering driving. He still drives with impatient, showy speed like a young blade. That day, he'd dropped her at the foot of the wheelchair ramp leading to the front entrance and swung into the car park to wait.

She'd manoeuvred the large bouquet of flowers wrapped in a cellophane trumpet out of the car with no help from Jim. It was so big in her arms that she must have looked like a garden centre on legs as she made her way up the gentle slope. There were automatic doors that opened with a whoosh and she found herself in the foyer. A bosomy young woman in blossomy scrubs who introduced herself as Sara, had come out from behind the reception desk and offered to take her to Delma's room. They'd travelled down the blush-coloured corridor, passing an open area where a group of residents was gathered, some in wheelchairs, others enveloped by soft chairs. They looked like they were waiting for something to happen.

'We're expecting a fortune teller,' Sara said in explanation.

Really, Christine had thought, couldn't they work out for themselves what the future held.

'Delma, you've got a visitor!' Sara announced as she held the door open to let Christine pass. She was just in time to see Delma make a sour face like a bold child and then immediately readjust it by putting on a wide smile.

It was a big airy room with a large picture window, a view of a distant mountain, snow-veined at the peak. Christine immediately thought of a Swiss sanatorium. Newly thin Delma was propped up on a number of pillows and looking straight at her. She was engulfed by a teal-coloured candlewick dressing gown. Christine remembered it from holidays. Delma wrapped in it, slopping out on to the balcony to light up and inhale the balmy Mediterranean night along with the nicotine. Those holidays had been like small draughts of freedom, away from Jim and the kids. Delma abroad was always so extravagant: buying outsized ceramic bowls that had to be hawked back on the plane, and ordering exotic cocktails with umbrellas, without knowing the ingredients. Despite her colouring, she'd loved the sun, drank it up, while Christine stuck to the shade.

'Jesus!' Delma said, eyeing the flowers, 'Who's dead?'

Christine was taken aback. Delma never used to swear. In the car, she might have called other drivers cretins in her exhalations of scorn but she'd never taken the Lord's name in vain. She'd been quite strait-laced like that.

'It's me, Delma,' she'd said.

'You're dead?' Delma said looking her up and down coolly.

'No, I mean —'

'I know who the hell you are, Chris, I'm not completely gaga.'

She'd placed the flowers on the table tray and sat down beside the bed. For the next twenty minutes they'd had a routine conversation, small talk about Jim and the boys.

Delma had never married. In the early 80s, there'd been a short engagement to Eddie Cloney, a dapper reckless guy who wore three-piece suits and had a weakness for the gee-gees. Not exactly husband material, Delma said. But then, Christine had always felt Delma wasn't exactly wife material. She'd never got the whole story about Eddie and she'd never asked, because it felt like prying and Delma had been very cut-up about it. *See, Jim, female friendship isn't all about blabbing. There are things we don't talk about.*

'And how's my god-daughter?' Delma asked.

Christine's daughter Trudy was in the States. An image of her floated into Christine's head, an old image of her when she was a teenager, her long dark hair swirled up on top of her head, like she is in the framed photo on the piano. Like she was before the two hard-won babies — fertility problems, there's an irony — the ranch house in Cupertino, the tech-wizard American husband with the good teeth.

When she was a teenager, Trudy would disappear instantly when Delma came to visit, or if Christine had insisted she stay, she would roll her eyes and sigh extravagantly at what she considered to be their boring and repetitive conversations. But when Christine and Trudy had gone through their bad patch, it was to Delma that Trudy had turned.

I told her, Delma had said vehemently at the time, that you were my friend first and I wouldn't countenance seeing you put down. Christine remembered flushing with pride at this statement. But when she'd pressed Delma about what Trudy had said about her, Delma had been very firm. She couldn't reveal what had been told to her in confidence.

'Trudy's fine,' Christine said, wanting to add, as far as I know.

Their weekly Skype calls made Christine feel more estranged from Trudy. Sometimes, she longed for the plain old landline. Just voice, no pictures, no performance required. When Trudy and Mike came home, it was the same. It wasn't that she didn't love it, but she was always relieved that American holidays were so short. They usually only stayed a week or two. Christine couldn't bear the intimacy of it all the time – the chaos of two kiddies close in age trapped in a new environment, her daughter's laissez-faire style of mothering, Mike's effervescent optimism. He was a hands-on father and sometimes Christine felt even that was a rebuke to her. Jim had never so much as changed a nappy.

The antics of the American visits mostly passed Jim by. He would whisk Trudy off at some point to get her on her own leaving Christine with Mike and the kids. Let your mother play the granny, he'd say, she loves it. But Christine didn't. She'd never bonded with those children; she was wary of them and they made strange with her. She couldn't get over her resentment that they spoke with American accents. They didn't sound like her – or Trudy. It was as if they didn't belong, as if they were cuckoos in the nest. But she couldn't say that, now could she?

'You know,' Delma announced suddenly. 'I've never really liked Trudy.'

Everything about Christine's solo journey to the nursing home had gone smoothly until she reached the Fingerpost roundabout. In the central island, there was an old-style signpost painted white with the destinations printed in hand-done black lettering and a medieval-sleeved hand with its fingers elegantly pointing at the arrow-shaped tips. But when she looked at the Google directions there was no mention of the Fingerpost. The roundabout had four exits and Google said to veer left. But which left? At least two of these were left. Maybe she was approaching the roundabout from the wrong side? She thought of the Irish joke about directions – *I wouldn't start from here, love*. She drove around the Fingerpost three times, trying each of the exits but was forced to turn back each time since the Google directions didn't match what she was seeing. Well, she thought, that was the beauty of roundabouts; you could keep going around until you got it right. But she was cross with herself. She knew this place, it was only five miles from home as the crow flies, but after she'd driven around it three times she felt like she'd submitted to some ancient superstitious ritual and entered another dimension.

'What?' Christine was sure she must have misheard.

'No,' Delma corrected herself, 'I used to like Trudy, but I don't like how she turned out. I mean your boys ...'

Christine smiled, anticipating Delma indulging in some fond remembrance of Phelim and Tim as children. They'd loved their Auntie Dell; she knew about soccer, played a mean game of cards and pressed folded cash in their palms when Christine wasn't looking.

'Well, let's face it, they were always plodders,' Della ploughed on. 'But Trudy, Trudy had spirit and you stifled it.'

Delma regarded her with those same candid blue eyes Christine had known since they were teenagers. When they were Chris and Del, mending their denims and having their hearts broken. They'd had their spats. Christine recalled a month's silence over a borrowed dress that got ripped at a charity disco, and another feud about a boy one of them fancied and the other one went out with. It was so long ago now that Christine couldn't even remember which way round it was. But she'd never doubted the fact of their friendship. Until now. Then she remembered teaching Delma to drive. Delma had been in her forties before she learned, and, according to one of her many driving tutors, was 'resistant to instruction'. She'd considered it an outrage that she was expected to do various things with her feet, hands, eyes and brain simultaneously. What am I, a juggler, she'd demanded. Christine remembered accompanying her on the test route many times. Delma had carried on a cranky monologue as she bunny-hopped and ground the gears, excoriating the incompetence of the other drivers — look at this, back off buddy, oh no, don't bother to indicate, you know where you're going. It wasn't road rage, exactly, it was more road peeve. Now, she was afraid it was this Delma — Car Delma — who was in the room.

The social brakes were off.

Or was it the gloves?

'I mean the way you behaved about the baby business. Trudy told me that you wouldn't hear of her keeping it ...'

What was Delma doing dragging up ancient history like this?

'It was for her own good, it would have held her back, ruined her life.'

'Nonsense, Christine, *you* couldn't bear it. Sending her off like that.'

She didn't like the way Delma was appropriating her name, like a cold caller. And since when had she become Christine? And she hadn't sent Trudy off anywhere; that made it sound like she'd dispatched her to a Magdalene laundry.

'I told her not to do it,' Delma said. 'If you really want to know.'

Christine didn't.

'I told her she should stand up to you.'

'I thought you were on my side,' Christine said.

'Whatever made you think that?'

So much for, you're my friend first. Christine found herself spluttering. 'Because, because …'

'You could have helped with the baby, Chris, and that way Trudy could have had it all. I mean it was the 90s, not the dark ages.'

No one, Christine thought, could have it all.

'She was a child herself,' Christine said.

'All the more reason for you to be the adult,' Delma snapped.

'So if you felt this strongly, why didn't you ever say anything about it before?'

'It wasn't my place.'

'But it is now?'

Was this the illness talking? Or was this what Delma had felt all along? In the past she'd often been sharpish; now she was a sword unsheathed.

Delma shrugged, eyeing her dubiously.

'It was the best thing, Del, it gave her a second chance,' she said, hearing the appeasing tone in her own voice, even though she was livid.

Delma didn't know what she was talking about. Delma wasn't there when Christine arranged for Trudy to stay with a nice Catholic family in Dublin, where she earned her keep by looking after the woman's children. Delma wasn't the one who got the doctor to certify Trudy's absence from school (ulceritis, a condition to which no blame could attach) so that she'd have a clean record when she went back to do her repeats and no one would be any the wiser. Trudy could never have organized all that on her own. And all without her precious father realizing. She'd told Jim that Trudy had got a transition year placement in Dublin. He'd swallowed that fiction, never questioned it once, because in his eyes, his precious Trudy could do no wrong.

'Look at her now,' Christine said hotly.

'Yeah,' Delma said, 'exactly. She ran away as soon as she could. You taught her to do that. She's a mirror image, settling for less, not to mention the idiot husband —'

'Excuse me …'

She wanted to slap Delma, right across the face, a sharp smack.

'And always so tightly wound up. When they come home, my God, Trudy's on a wire spring all the time. So busy pretending. Just like you — look at you now,' Delma said pointing to Christine's hands which were clenched in fists of rage on her lap. 'You don't know how to let go.'

I have let go, Christine wanted to shout. I've been letting go all my life. Didn't I let Trudy go, off to the States on her own, after the other business, even though all I wanted was to cling on to her. And if I'm not letting go, I'm thinking of how I'll do it when the time comes, with Jim, and you, Delma.

'You've been a terrible mother to her, Chris, and what's more —'

She had to put a stop to Delma's gallop. She inhaled deeply.

'And what exactly would you know about mothering, Delma?'

Fourth time around the Fingerpost, she careened on to the only route left to her, desperately looking for the next turn which should be on the left, after 80 m. Metric again. How far was that? She had no idea. There was no turn at all on the left and a mile had gone up on the clock. She slowed down. The car behind her flashed. She felt herself getting hot under the collar, literally. Long after menopause, she still suffered phantom flushes as if the body was secretly addicted to fire. Her armpits were sticky. Bloody useless directions, she shouted to herself inside the car, spittle flying. She was still fulminating when she came upon another roundabout. The driver behind pulled up level with her as they halted to let traffic go by. He was a young man with a crew cut and she was aware of him watching her sidelong. Crazy old bird, that's what he was thinking as he roared away.

She hugged the inside lane and chugged all the way around to go back to the Fingerpost, picking the first route she'd tried even though she was pretty sure it couldn't be right. Everything about this visit seemed doomed now. And yet she drove on blindly.

There had been a long silence before Delma reacted. 'Duck!' she cried. 'It's Magda!'

'Who?' Christine said half-rising from her chair, and turning towards the door where she expected one of the carers to appear. Meanwhile Delma was sitting up rigid in the bed, flapping her hands about, bowing low then rearing up as if under attack. Then she remembered. Magda was Delma's cleaner who came once a week when she couldn't keep up with the housework. It was Magda who'd alerted Delma's niece that she really wasn't managing. At the time, Christine felt foolish that she hadn't realized how far gone Delma was.

'The crow,' Delma said raising her voice and putting her hands to her ears.

'What crow?' Christine asked though she was scouring the room following Delma's wavering eyes as the bird divebombed about the room. Once in the early days of their marriage, a collared dove had got caught in the kitchen and Christine had nearly lost her mind. It was a summer's afternoon and it flew in the back door. In its panic it had swooped and squawked. She'd flapped a tea towel at it. Jim said, no, stop, you'll only make it worse, but Christine was afraid it might attack her, go for her eyes. That was the trouble with trapped birds — they were terrified and terrifying. Christine had wanted to run out of the house, let the bird have the place, but Jim said — don't do anything, just sit down and ignore it. But how could she ignore it, this feral creature swooping about the kitchen, crashing into the dresser, then the window, and leaving spatters of bird shit all over the floor. It couldn't seem to see the open door through which it had flown. Christine remembered the term bird brain.

'Open the window,' Delma cried.

Even as she stood and reached for the latch, Christine found herself rationalizing the situation — if the window was closed how did the bird get in? — but Delma's terror was such that she didn't question her. She opened the window but when she turned to look at Delma, she could tell from the look on her face that the bird had not left the room. It was still buzzing Delma, it was obviously at her hair. She'd pulled the pillow down over her head and was cowering now, wild-eyed.

'Don't just fucking stand there,' Delma shouted, 'get help!'

Christine hesitated – how would she explain at the nurses' station that she needed assistance to get rid of an imaginary bird?

'You know what it means if you let the effing thing die in here?'

'What?' Christine asked, playing for time.

'Can't you guess?' Delma had said. 'God, I'd forgotten how slow you are on the uptake.'

Delma had never spoken to her like this before and, frankly, she was afraid of her now. She tiptoed towards the door. She didn't want any movement of hers to add to the panic. Just as she reached the door, it opened, and Sara, the carer who'd shown Christine in, appeared with an orange drink in her hand. Christine was frozen in mid-tiptoe and Delma was buried under the bed-clothes, only her hair showing.

'Is it Magda again?' Sara asked matter-of-factly.

She set down the drink on the radiator cover and opened both the top and the side windows, letting in an icy chill. She lifted a blanket from the end of Delma's bed and shook it out, holding it like a curtain in front of her as she moved towards the window. Delma was peering out from under the pillow. Sara narrated her journey as she herded the bird towards escape. 'I'm leading her to the window, Delma, we're nearly there ...'

Delma had unwound herself from behind the pillow.

'Are you sure?'

'Yes, Delma, I'm the expert, remember?'

She went to retrieve the drink. 'Now, Delma, sundowner time!'

Delma's face had lit up, the bird crisis forgotten.

'It's my secret tipple!' Delma said and drank greedily from the beaker. 'Here,' she offered, 'you try it.'

'No,' Christine said, 'no, I'm fine. That's for you.'

'For fuck's sake, Christine, what are you saving yourself for?'

'Now Delma,' Sara said, 'maybe it's too early for your friend.'

Too late, more likely.

'It has vodka,' Delma said.

'Really?' Christine had looked to Sara.

'Oh yes,' Sara said with a minute shake of her head to Christine, 'every patient gets a vodka and orange before dinner.'

When she had left, Delma put the glass down. 'Awful muck! They only wave the vodka bottle at it. And no nibbles.'

'I'd complain to management,' Christine said as if they were talking about bad service in a restaurant.

'Oh don't worry, Chris, I intend to. And if I don't get satisfaction, I'll take my custom elsewhere!'

Christine even managed to smile.

'Remember that awful hotel in Portugal?' Delma said, 'remember, I found a hair on the toilet seat and got us an upgrade?'

This was the Delma she knew.

There's a sharp rap on the car window like the beak of a bird. Christine jumps. She has the heater on and the car has steamed up. She can only see the blurry flesh of the face peering in at her. She wipes a patch in the condensation and sees a man of her own age in a black beanie peering in at her. She releases the window switch. As the glass winds down, she notices the man has a dog at his feet. A small little thing, black, smooching up against his ankle like an amorous cat.

'Is everything alright in there?' he asks. What does he think she's doing, a seventy-year-old woman sitting in her car alone at dusk? He has shaggy eyebrows and rimless glasses and a smirky smile that might once, long ago, have been gamey.

Before she has a chance to deny she needs help, her default position, she says quickly, 'I'm lost.'

She grabs the Google sheet, and jabs at Granary Hill, where she's supposed to turn right.

He takes the page from her and pushes up his glasses to examine it.

'Never heard of it,' he says. 'Where are you trying to get to?'

'The nursing home.'

'Ah well now, I know where that is,' he says and thrusts the useless paper back at her. 'You're almost there. Go back to the junction just here, left on to the main drag there and first left. You can't miss it.'

The dog is whining at the man's trouser leg now. He looks at her bashfully, as if the mutt has thwarted a romantic tryst.

'Thank you,' she says and she feels a surge of gratitude. This man has saved her from her ridiculous panic.

The little dog hares off and Mr Beanie goes after him. Thankfully, he's so distracted that he doesn't look back to see if Christine has followed his directions. He takes a rutted track into a copse of trees that divides this street from the next and is gone.

Still, Christine sits there.

She's probably too late now. They'll be having their tea at Mount Helicon. Why is it that meals are served at nursery hours in these places? Delma will be having her sundowner and won't be in the right frame of mind for a visitor. Better this way, really, Christine thinks. She can make up a story for Jim; he'll never suspect a thing. That part doesn't bother her, but letting Delma down feels like betrayal. She turns the ignition in the car. She'll make her way back to the Fingerpost roundabout. Once there, she'll be in familiar territory and she can pretend that none of this has happened. Next time she'll know exactly how to reach Delma without any confusion.

If there is a next time.

PROPERTY

Here she is, head literally in the clouds. Exactly what her mother warned her about, or against. Now she's living it. A glazed penthouse, seventeen floors up, with a balcony like a knife-edged prow jutting out into thin air. This place is proof of something, though what it is she doesn't know. Success? Maybe, but she still can't call it home. *Carmond* it isn't. An Edwardian red-brick in St Luke's, the auctioneer's bumpf said, on an elegant terrace of officers' housing, lovingly restored by its present owner, with original features, blah blah, blah. *That* was home and Ray had done her out of it.

'It should have a name,' he'd said when they'd mortgaged their lives for a wreck nearly twenty-five years ago. Carmel thought he was joking. Where she came from houses didn't have names. But Ray said it would be like carving their love on a tree. *Carmel loves Raymond*; together they made *Carmond*. Ray was a bit of a fool sometimes. But in time, he was proved right. The wreck grew into its name, came to be the expression of all their homely ambitions. The kitchen extension with a range, the conservatory, the tended lawn, a rockery.

Sometimes as a young mother, she had stood at the old scullery window in *Carmond*, elbow-deep in suds and staring out at the windswept garden (this was the early days when it was littered with kiddy paraphernalia – an upturned slide, flung-down bicycles) and day-dreamed about the kind of existence she has now. An apartment in the city, an entitled sense of leisure. She'd imagined coming home after a day at some ill-defined office job, a decorous career of some sort, and opening a bottle of wine before fixing dinner for one. There was never a lover in these scenarios. Even in her fantasies she couldn't supply a figure who wasn't Ray. A failure of imagination, she supposed. Just as now, she cannot imagine herself into her present situation; a woman in late middle age who has finally become cherished.

Once she had been the linchpin of a busy household though she'd never been cherished for that. It was the natural division of labour as far as Ray was concerned. He was the breadwinner; she did the rest. Her job was to keep the home fires burning, do the school runs, attend the parent-teacher meetings, manage the family budget, read the bedtime stories. Later it included nursing Amy through her breakdown, or propping Ray Junior up when his fiancée left him, or calming Louise when one of the twins was diagnosed on the spectrum. But it's not for any of those reasons that she's living in a top-end apartment with the floor dimensions of a hotel ballroom. This is not Ray's way of extravagantly saying thank you or even telling her she's worth it. She's hiding here. Hiding Ray's wealth in plain sight.

Meanwhile he's in a bed-sit in Reading sitting out his bankruptcy. Living like a building-site Paddy or a layabout student. Except Ray was never a student. He went straight from school into his father's betting shop and never looked back. Built a nationwide chain, he would say proudly. A household name. Now having divested himself, he's the poorest of them and, somehow, it shows. Last time they Zoomed, he was in his stockinged feet and there was a hole in the toe which he lifted up to the screen, wiggling his foot at her as if she could virtually darn it. He raised his empty tumbler like an unasked question. He hasn't completely succumbed to austerity.

Whisky of an evening for a bankrupt? She could, if she wanted to, shake her head at the screen and ask, can you afford it? As he used to once grumble about her buying clothes or getting a Botox treatment. Now, when she could be overdosing on the stuff and no one to question it, her brow is a riven minefield.

In their hey-day Ray was in charge of the finances. Carmel had no idea how rich they were. It was unlucky to ask; if a figure was mentioned, it might all go up in smoke. She only knew there was plenty. Don't you worry, Ray used to say, so she didn't. Wasn't that what people meant when they said they were comfortable? She'd put her hand out and Ray had provided. Under the new dispensation everyone's doing better than him. Amy got the apartment in Nice, Ray Junior was offered the boat but refused it, Louise's twins have an education trust and they're only five. Carmel has the penthouse and a lump sum. At fifty-seven, she's finally a dowried bride.

The trouble is she doesn't know how to live here, in a tower aiming for the sky. She hasn't the energy or the will to fill these vast spaces that refuse to be domesticated. (Why, she wonders, are they called penthouses when you feel the opposite of pent-up in them?) Take the living room, for example, which is a long, lean cavernous space, glass-walled on two sides. On the balcony side, the huge windows are hinged and can be opened. Even so, fresh air seems at a premium up here. Sometimes she feels like a piece of wilted lettuce in a Tupperware box.

Ray had chosen the show-apartment.

'For yourselves, is it?' the garrulous estate agent asked. 'Or is it an investment?' He had a savage crew-cut and looked like a prison inmate let loose in a suit.

Ray had brought her to view the place, though why he bothered she didn't know. He'd already decided to buy it; or rather decided that she would.

'The wife,' Ray said jerking his head towards Carmel. These small betrayals stung more than the dismantling of their life.

'Ah, I see,' the agent said. 'Wife wants, wife gets.'

Because it was the show flat, Carmel had inherited the fittings – heavy curtains which she often draws during the day, turning the middle of the afternoon into night and shutting the views out. It's more restful that way. Ridiculous, but she has the feeling of being overlooked all the time, though she's in the tallest building in the city. *Top of the world, Ma.* (She can just about pick out The Buildings from here.) If she hasn't drawn the curtains during the day, she whips them closed with nightfall. Without them, she can see her own reflection and it troubles her – her double moving about out there unsupported in the dark air. Behind the heavy drapes are filmy full-length muslin nets in various hues from blaze to sickly mustard, depending on the light and the time of day. Sometimes, at sunset, it seems the place is aflame. The interior decorator was intent on injecting warmth into the glacial interior so the large shag rug in the sitting area, the squat, low-lying leather settee, even the one and only solid wall is orange. At the far end of the apartment the sleek cold kitchen retains its steely demeanour.

The open plan is relentless. Just last week Carmel chanced upon a documentary on TV – she watches the History Channel during the day behind the closed curtains – about lighthouse keepers. They lived in threes to stop them turning on one another but still they went a bit mad, apparently, from living in the round. There were no corners, the voiceover said, so there was nowhere they could go where they weren't observable. She knows how the poor sods felt. The windowless main bedroom is the only respite from the persistent transparency, built into the cement core of the construction. Like a burial vault for an ancient queen. She has dreams of being found in

Property

there surrounded by coral amulets and terracotta amphoras, her jewellery in rich piles around her. This from her night course – adult ed art history. Bits of it come back to her at odd times. The ruins of Pompeii, Tutankhamun. Ends of eras and empires. At the time, none of it seemed to apply. Now everything seems weighted with a message specifically aimed at her. Yesterday, for example, she heard a quiz on the radio, the kind where listeners ring in and are grilled while a clock loudly ticks down. *Complete this well-known proverb; people in glasshouses shouldn't throw ... Parties?* was the hapless reply. She'd laughed out loud. Today she thinks, that's me. Except who would she invite here?

She could ask the neighbours, she supposes. Except she doesn't know enough of them to make a party. There's a couple on Floor 8, in their thirties, with chocolate brown mock cane furniture out on the balcony. There's another man in his sixties on Five who parks his bike out there, so that it looks like an exhibit in a museum. Proof of life. Her balcony is bare. She doesn't go out there; every time she does it seems like a cry for help.

When she moved in, she ordered a fig tree to create the illusion of a garden. It was an enormous thing, the weeping variety. She'd never had room for such a specimen in *Carmond* (Oh, but she'd had rambling roses around the door and fragrant bowers of lavender!) But when the man delivered the fig, she thought, no, much more space for it inside, where it could provide shelter from the design cruelty. It serves as a divider now on the marbled catwalk to the kitchen.

Anyway, why is she worried about parties? Nobody comes here. Anyone who managed to breach the plate-glass armoured exterior would have to face the coded lifts. They'd have to be buzzed up. The children come, but intermittently. Well, Amy's in Nice and Louise is terrified on her children's behalf of the balcony and the hard surfaces. (Every sound is magnified here. When Carmel sets a mug on the glass coffee table it makes a ceramic thunk. Putting her keys down sounds like shrapnel.) Ray Junior barely darkens the door. Of all of them, he resents the loss of *Carmond* most and in some obscure way seems to blame Carmel for it, as if she'd done him out of his birth-right. You think I want to be here, she wanted to scream at him, you think this was my idea? Time was when she'd have the kids over for lunch every Sunday; it used to be a tradition at *Carmond*. But it rang hollow here.

The truth is almost everything about her old life has disappeared. The penthouse seems to have swallowed it up. Friends from her *Carmond* existence have fallen away. At first she thought it was the location; then she wondered if it wasn't something to do with the bankruptcy. The whiff of disgrace; a suggestion of moral weakness. Hers. As if she should be sitting on a piece of cardboard on the pavement holding out a paper cup. She supposes she should be grateful – if Ray were a banker, people might be spitting at her in the street. Dee, whom she's known since school, was full of plausible excuses for not visiting. She'd had her own troubles – a round of chemo after breast cancer, but that was over now. She didn't come into town much, Dee said, did her shopping in Mahon. Jacinta, who used to be her next door neighbour in St Luke's, hovered in the lobby a few times but wouldn't come up.

'Feels like City Hall in here,' she joked, 'and I have to pay a parking fine.'

The only person who's actually visited is Margaret. Margaret Bird. And she only came once.

In another life, she was Carmel's cleaning lady. Margaret was her first luxury – get someone in to do, Ray had said after Louise was born, we can afford it. Margaret came recommended, a stout woman who dyed her hair a terrifying black and rouged her cheeks. Her uniform was a nylon navy housecoat which she wore over her street clothes; when she moved she made a sound like grating sand. Although she was only a decade older than Carmel, she'd always seemed as anchoring as a mother. Carmel's mother had died when she was fifteen so she'd come to lean on Margaret for advice. Although she was hired as a cleaner, it wasn't long before Margaret became a child-minder, granny-substitute, counsellor and strict nurse. With four of her own, she had firm ideas about bringing up kids.

Ray Junior was her first cause.

'That child,' she'd intoned pointing to him, 'should be on a puffer.' All of Margaret's diktats began with those words – *that child*. When Carmel resisted – Ray Junior had always been wheezy – Margaret tried again.

'Take him to the specialist,' she'd said. 'There's a grand fella in the Bons who'd look after him.'

Still, Carmel took no notice. He was snuffly, that's all. A month went by. Then Margaret said quietly. 'That child is suffering.'

'He's fine, Margaret,' she'd said. 'Don't worry. He'll grow out of it.'

'I could report you for neglect, you know.'

'I beg your pardon,' Carmel said. The cheek of her!

'You heard me,' Margaret said with a belligerent jut of her lower lip.

Dee told her to fire Margaret. She has no right to speak to you like that, she said. But Carmel didn't sack Margaret. She took Ray Junior to the doctor and, as it turned out, Margaret was right. He was put on an inhaler.

The next battleground was Amy.

'That child should have braces on her teeth,' she told Carmel, 'or she'll have an overbite. It'll ruin her chances.'

This time Carmel ignored Margaret. Unlike Ray Junior's asthma, this was a cosmetic issue; the child wasn't going to keel over and die from prominent teeth. Anyway, Ray was still building the business at the time and they'd just extended the kitchen at *Carmond*. It troubled Carmel now to think that the only reason she didn't take Amy to the orthodontist – apart from the hideous expense – was the satisfaction of defying Margaret. Now she wonders if Amy's failure to thrive, as the psychiatrist put it, didn't stem from that decision. While she was seeing him, Amy told Carmel that the bullying at school had started with the kids calling her Bugs Bunny. But look it, Amy eventually did have her teeth straightened when she was nineteen. (They could afford it then and Ray had gladly paid.) She'd had to wear the dreaded braces for a year-and-a-half. Not that it seemed to help Amy's self-esteem. Because it was too late, Margaret would have told her. If Carmel had asked.

That was the thing with Margaret. Whatever happened, she'd already had experience of it. Or of something worse. Her own family was a nest of social problems. She was a lone parent with a junkie son (Derek), an emigrant – Kev had gone to England – and Sandra who had Downs Syndrome and still lived with Margaret. She was a gloomy, wizened adult (although Carmel thought Downs kids were meant to be cheerful and sunny) who worked in a sheltered workshop making scented candles. Only Terence had fulfilled Margaret's ambitions. He had a trade – he was an electrician with a steady job, he was married with kids and had a purchased house.

A year ago Carmel had let Margaret go. On Ray's urging – one of his ridiculous economies. Talk about shutting the stable door.... It was when he'd told her *Carmond* would have to be sold.

'What's happened?'

'Bitten off more than I can chew.'

'But *Carmond*?'

'Need to liquidate my assets, love,' he said.

'But this is our home,' she'd wailed, 'you can't sell it out from under me.'

'It's part of the plan,' he said. 'I'll give you the proceeds and you'll buy somewhere else that'll be all yours. That way they can't touch it.'

'And what's happening to the shops?'

He didn't answer. He just shook his head.

'And get rid of Margaret,' he added.

Carmel felt she owed Margaret the truth.

'I don't want you to find out about this some other way,' she'd said. 'Or see the house for sale in the paper.' She explained their situation. She used Ray's word but it came out as liquidize, as if they were pulverizing their lives into baby food.

'You're doing a flit?' Margaret said.

'Well, Ray is ...' she remembered saying, hearing already that defensive tone that has crept into almost everything she says these days. The plan was for Ray to go to England, hole up for a year, and then the proceedings would be all over.

'What about all those people?' Carmel noticed Margaret didn't include herself in the ranks of those Ray was making unemployed. 'Leaving them in the lurch, are you?'

She found herself doing Ray's rueful head-shaking. Why should she feel guilty? *She* wasn't the one sacking 160 people. Am I my husband's keeper? she wanted to demand, but she didn't because she was, wasn't she? After thirty years of marriage, she was finally keeping Ray.

'It's not how we would have chosen to do it,' she said helplessly.

Twenty-Twenty Vision

'You're ruining people's lives,' Margaret said. There was something infuriatingly implacable about her, standing there. When Carmel didn't answer, she'd picked up her coat and left the house without saying goodbye. Carmel had to post her the last of her wages – she remembered stuffing a wad of cash into the brown envelope without even counting it because she was so ashamed. Of Ray.

It was a Thursday evening and Carmel had dashed down to the supermarket on the ground floor when she met Margaret again. Now that she was shopping for one, she could do mercy runs to the shop instead of having to make lists and push a huge trolley up and down the aisles piled to the gunwales with groceries. A basket did her now. She'd turned into the frozen foods aisle – dinner-for-one territory – when she'd ploughed into the back of a small woman in a bright red anorak.

'Oh, sorry,' she said.

The woman turned and Carmel was confronted with a pair of dowdy breasts sheathed in a garish blouse. Blue and yellow zig-zags on a white background. It was like walking into a lightning storm. Distracted by the blouse it took Carmel a minute to realize that it was Margaret in mufti.

'Margaret!' she said brightly. It sounded false, but it wasn't. She realized how pleased she was to see a familiar face.

Margaret eyed her, up and down, and nodded but she didn't smile. The cabinets exhaled ice.

'This is a great place for the bargains, isn't it?' Margaret went on as if they were taking up in the middle of an interrupted conversation. 'Not that you have to worry about that, I suppose.'

Carmel let the jibe go.

'How are you keeping, Margaret?' She didn't want to ask had she got other work; that would seem insensitive.

'I come here late on Thursdays for the sell-by-date offers.'

Carmel felt a stab of remorse.

'Where are you these days?' Margaret asked.

'Here,' Carmel said. 'I live upstairs. Would you like to see?'

When Carmel showed her in, Margaret immediately made herself at home. She threw off her anorak and slung it on the burnt orange leather sofa. She padded about in her neon-striped runners and a pair of track pants. Carmel avoided looking at the blouse though the apartment seemed to have neutered its effect. Margaret stared out at the view. She rubbed her hand along the furnishings. She twirled the shade on the standard lamp, the only item Carmel had brought from *Carmond*. She felt the stuff of the curtains.

'Fancy!' Margaret said and Carmel wasn't sure if it was approving.

'Would you like some tea?' Carmel asked.

It was the first time she'd ever played host to Margaret. In *Carmond*, it was Margaret who dictated tea breaks, calling to Carmel over the shouts of the children or the purr of the dust-buster. She made a strong and tarry brew and brought her own Mikado biscuits.

'Do you have one of those George Clooney machines?' Margaret asked casting her eye around the kitchen. It sounded challenging.

' 'Fraid not,' Carmel said. She foostered in the kitchen with the plunger pot. She scoured around in the cavernous kitchen presses for something to serve with the coffee. In the far reaches of one she found a packet of shortbread biscuits well past their prime. She emptied them on to a plate. She was unaccountably nervous.

'Is this where the swimming baths were?' Margaret shouted from the living area. Carmel had learned to swim in the baths, a municipal haven for verrucas. They were a hotbed of life in the raw – toughies from the Buildings, cadets from the barracks with tattoos, regal old biddies (like Rubens models) with sweaty rolls of flesh.

'No,' Carmel said, 'they were on Eglinton Street. The postal sorting office used to be here.'

'The one they moved out to Churchfield, that one?' Margaret asked. Injun territory, Carmel was about to answer. 'My Terence has a lovely house up there.'

Margaret always asserted her claim to her children. Carmel would never say 'my Amy' or 'my Ray'. They were on loan to you, your children, she used to say to Dee, trying to sound philosophical. The words came back to haunt her when Ray had announced they were selling *Carmond*. When she'd baulked, they had ganged up on her. *You've got to for Dad's sake. Poor Dad,* they said as if Carmel had driven him off. She realized then how partisan their affection was. Poor Dad, indeed. Since moving to the tower Carmel finds she has less and less fellow-feeling for Ray. She could, she thinks, quite easily, leave him. He's given her the ammunition, hasn't he? She could walk away, rich. The thought of it made her feel giddy. It was the same sensation as when she stepped out on the balcony for the first time and looked down at the city. Giddy and slightly lethal.

When people gave out about the tower being an eyesore, a folly they said, she wondered why they were so worked up; it was so high you couldn't see the top of it from the street. So it was only people who already had the luxury of a view who had anything to complain about. All the same, it was funny how obliterating it was. Not to the view, but to the memory. This big bruising building had wiped out all that came before it. It was the same when the big road was driven through Douglas. Afterwards Carmel couldn't visualize the little village high street though she'd been there hundreds of times.

'Has he left you, is that it?' Margaret asked as Carmel took the plunger and pushed it down.

'No, no,' she said, 'it's not like that.'

She felt shy in Margaret's presence. In all their years together they'd never had a personal conversation. At least, not personal like this.

'No, Ray will be back,' she said.

Up to this, she hadn't thought about Ray coming back. It would have to be to here, wouldn't it? Where else would he go? The thought of the two of them in this apartment together seemed more outlandish than the present arrangement. Ray had always been a home bird; but that was when *Carmond* was home. You run off with the girls to Florence, he'd said happily when the adult ed tutor arranged a trip to the Uffizi, I'll mind the shop. Ray had never been to a museum as far as Carmel knew. He didn't get what art was all about; he was a man who counted on his fingers. If she'd tried to interest him in Uccello he'd think she was for the birds.

'Are you sure about that?' Margaret said. 'My Kev got divorced once he got to England. He's living with a new one now.'

Carmel thought of her Zoom sessions with Ray. Could there be another woman in his bed-sit, out of frame? A woman who couldn't darn, obviously. No, she shook herself, this was Ray.

'No,' Carmel said firmly, 'this is just for the money.'

Margaret said nothing. Carmel pushed the plate of shortbread at her, but she didn't take one. Maybe she could whiff the staleness off them.

Dusk was gathering and over Margaret's shoulder Carmel could see the sky was putting on a show — a darting sun struggling with long fillets of lilac cloud. But there was no distraction inside. When she and Margaret used to have tea in *Carmond*, there'd never been a quiet moment. Now there was just awkwardness. Maybe it was the wretched penthouse — maybe that was what spoilt everything. It had got in the way with her children; now it was stymying Margaret.

'That fig,' Margaret said pointing to the tree which was shedding its leaves. 'Looks like you've been overwatering it.'

Carmel smiled. For the first time in months she felt anchored. The one constant in her life had been Margaret's chastisements. If it wasn't her child-rearing, it was her plant care. She doubted that Margaret knew much about houseplants, but she couldn't be sure. Outside the enclosure of *Carmond* she didn't know much about Margaret, except what Margaret chose to tell her. After all, even her off-duty wardrobe had been a surprise.

'So,' Margaret said finally when the silence had stretched into unease. 'When would you like me to start?'

'What?'

'Two days a week like before?' Margaret continued.

'Um ... no ...' Carmel began.

'You want me back, don't you?'

'But this place practically cleans itself,' Carmel said. She didn't want to say that cleaning the place kept her sane; it was her only occupation these days. But she wished she hadn't answered so quickly because Margaret looked crestfallen.

'I just thought when you asked me up ...' she said plaintively.

This was like a date gone bad, Carmel thought. She wanted to protest, to say, no I *do* want you back, just not to clean.

(She used to have to go around *Carmond* after Margaret was finished her chores, redoing streaked mirrors and soap-limed windows.) What she wanted was Margaret's companionship. Perhaps that's what she'd been paying her for all along. To be her mother; to be her conscience.

'I'd best be off so ...' Margaret said rising.

'No, no, please,' Carmel said, 'you don't understand.'

Margaret was shrugging on her anorak and zipping it up, eclipsing the lightning blouse.

'It's alright, Ma'm, I do understand.'

Did she just call me Ma'm? Carmel thought. Margaret had never called her that before; she'd never called Carmel anything. Margaret made for the balcony.

'No,' Carmel said, 'this way' and steered Margaret towards the lift. She pressed the button and the doors opened immediately.

'Now you know where I am,' Carmel said as Margaret stepped inside. Even to her own ears, she sounded desperate. 'Do call in – any Thursday evening.'

'Mind yourself now,' Margaret said as the doors shut on her. 'And don't forget, let the fig dry out.'

Carmel went out on to the balcony and waited for Margaret to emerge. Looking down she felt the magnetic pull of solid ground and a pressing desire to let go, to fall. Just as well the balcony was glassed-in. When Margaret appeared at street level she looked like one of those tiny striving figures in an architect's drawing, put in to show scale. She didn't look up. Even if she had, she wouldn't be able to see Carmel. But Carmel waved just the same, half-heartedly though, in case it might be mistaken for something else.

REPOSSESSION

I had gone to bed early – taken a pill, in fact – I have to these days, so I came to, in an open-mouthed panic as if fresh from some nightmare, and there was a woman standing at the end of the bed. And the strange thing is I wasn't surprised. It's our stalker, I thought immediately.

'Who are you?' I asked all the same.

She didn't answer.

'Can't you guess?' she said

She was a woman on the wrong side of fifty with lank brown hair parted in the middle, a plain face, prominent pallid eyes, a carbuncle of some kind over her top lip, a canker, a mole, a wart maybe? She was shrouded in something dark, a cape it looked like, which swamped her, and she was gripping the end of the bed, white-knuckled, as if the frame was all that was keeping her grounded. Not a ghost, then.

I could see my mobile winking on the bedside table.

'Don't,' she said as if she knew what I was thinking.

'Is it money you're after?' I looked at her eyes; they seemed clear so her problem wasn't drugs.

'What good is your money to me?'

'Look, tell me what you want or I'll have to call the police. You shouldn't be here. You're in my house.'

'Actually, Shel,' she said, 'that's just it.'

Shel? Only Brian calls me Shel.

'What do you mean?'

'I mean, it's my house, actually.'

That's when I went to nudge Brian awake. And then I remembered. Brian wasn't there.

*

It was the first time I'd been alone in the new house. That's what we call it because it's new to us but it's actually old, a cut-stone nineteenth-century gatelodge, with diamond-paned windows and curlicued eaves, a Hansel and Gretel house set in a little wooded hollow, beside a sweeping driveway that once led to the Vandeleur Estate. The big house was demolished in the 80s and an estate for commuters built in its place. They're big, double-fronted palaces, classy enough if you like that sort of thing, with a landscaped green in the centre, where the original Vandeleur House stood. It's as if the developers superstitiously left the spot vacant like a portal to the past. Was this where the woman had come from? From some cleavage in time?

Years ago, when I was helping one of the girls with a school project, I'd looked into the history of Vandeleur House. It had its usual catalogue of scandal. A titled family beset by generations of beleaguered marriages, renegade sons, financial ineptitude. The last incumbent of the house was in the 1950s, an ex-British Army major, all handlebar moustache and regimental epaulettes, who in his dotage had impregnated his housekeeper. That was the story, anyway. Not a maid, mind you, but an older woman who should have had more sense. The unfortunate woman gave birth to the baby and then walked out into the sea. Oh yes, didn't I mention that? We face the sea.

Opposite us, across the road, there's a small, shingled beach, spattered with seaweed and shells.

In the Vandeleur story it wasn't clear what had happened to the child – probably shipped off to an orphanage somewhere, farmed out. Major What-What wasn't going to have a little bastard running around the place. Don't you just love these historical tragedies? So bleak, so merciless in their resolution.

It was a fright I can tell you. The house, I mean. There were times when I thought, my God, what have we done? Upstairs, where the previous owners' renovation hadn't reached, they had resorted to metal pails to catch the rain coming through the dodgy roof slates. The kitchen was tragic, although this was the part of the house that had been worked on. Awful country-style cabinets, faux rustic vinyl on the floor. The bedrooms were painted icy colours; the peppermint green of the bathroom would give you a migraine. There was a charming sun lounge at the back rotting quietly away into compost.

The stalker and the skip came together. At first, I thought she was one of those skip scavengers, as I used to be myself in my student days. Couldn't pass one without a rummage. But she wasn't one of those. Too passive, for one. She never budged from her spot under the laburnum tree, where the road forked – one way went towards the Vandeleur Estate houses, the other turned into our property.

'You're out of your mind,' Brian had said when I told him about her.

Stalker, I realized, was the wrong word because it was too active for what this woman had been doing. She'd just been standing there since the start of our occupation. Occupation, that's a funny word. Since we'd started work on the place, I mean. Brian hadn't noticed her. He's not observant like that and, anyway, all his attention was turned inward on what was happening inside the house.

'See,' I said to Brian, 'there she is again.'

I pointed to the shadowy figure sheltering under the yellow spread of the tree. He peered out.

'Okay,' he said doubtfully.

'Go out,' I said, 'ask her what's she doing.'

'Last time I checked, Shel, it's not an offence to stand out on the public road minding your own business.'

'But she's not,' I said.

'Not what?'

'Minding her own business. She's minding ours.'

'Now you're being paranoid, Shel. If you're so het up about her, why don't you go and talk to her?'

But I didn't.

Why?

Because I didn't trust myself, or my own instincts. Maybe she had a reason to stand there looking out to sea? Did she have a secret assignation that had nothing to do with us at all? Or was she homeless and this was part of her regular beat, passing the time before the hostel in town opened up? Had she squatted here while the place was empty? Or maybe it was just sheer coincidence that every so often when I would look out, she just happened to be standing there on that particular spot. Not looking up or in at us; turned away, in fact, from the house. Implacable as a gate post. And then we went away on holidays – to escape the builders – and I forgot all about her.

The pool in Crete was curved like a woman's hip with a floor of turquoise mosaic. There was a little bar with a thatched roof in the middle of the water and a waiter sleek in swimming trunks gliding around with a drinks tray held high. Our apartment, pool-side, was posh-plain, a white box with minimal furniture, marble tiles, chrome finishes. The only excess was the bougainvillea sprawling around the windows. There was a time when Brian and I might have scoffed at the notion of a resort, but we've reached an age where we want some comfort. Why else would we be lolling on a Greek island while the builders took a ball and chain to our pet project at home?

Well, Brian's pet project.

I remember the day Brian came home with the news the house was up for sale. That's something I remember very clearly.

'The gate lodge at Drunkard's Island is for sale,' he said.

'Where?'

'Drunkard's Island – you know, the Vandeleur place. That's what the locals always called it.'

Brian is from here so knows all the lore.

'My mother charred for the last of the Vandeleurs. When I was a boy she'd take me with her during the school holidays.'

He reminisced about the mirrored ballroom of the old house, the big old basement kitchen, the down-at-heel reception rooms with parquet floors that clacked underfoot like loose teeth.

'All the mops and buckets and things were stored in the gatelodge at that time. That's where my mother would go to change into her overalls. She had a key. And sometimes I'd just kick about there while she walked up the driveway to do her slaving. It's funny but it makes me feel connected to the place, somehow,' he said.

It seemed a pretty meagre connection to me.

Repossession

I'd never met Brian's mother; she had died before we got together. But she was a big presence in his life, so big that I was glad not to have had to deal with her. A gritty independent woman who had raised Brian alone after his father vamoosed to England to make some money on the buildings and never came back. Brian has a photo of her on his desk as a young woman, with her starched hat like a working girl's tiara, her nurse's cape and those shiny lace-up shoes they all seemed to have worn, standing by her bicycle. She was one of those practically beautiful women, as in she wasn't a beauty, but she was vibrant and pert, with dark hair and a brave smile. And that passes for beauty when you look back at it. She delivered babies, that's what Brian had told me when I'd asked what she did. The image of a down-trodden char on her hands and knees didn't fit with my image of his mother at all.

'I thought your mother was a nurse,' I said.

'Well, she was,' he said, 'but this was after.'

'After what?'

'After she gave up being a midwife.'

'You don't just *give up* a good job like nursing for nothing,' I said.

'She lost a baby, that's all,' Brian said eventually. 'Not her fault, the baby would have died even if it'd been born in the hospital. But mud sticks ...'

I felt unaccountably put out.

'You never told me,' I said.

'Of course, I did, Shel. You've just forgotten.'

But you don't forget things like that, do you?

I didn't go to the auction. Call it sticking my head in the sand.

'They won't be there if that's what you're afraid of,' Brian said, meaning the previous owners.

He'd been campaigning for weeks, wearing me down.

'It's the kind of place we always dreamed of, Shel. And what's to stop us? Girls all gone. And what's more it's a bank sale so it'll be a steal.'

'You think so?'

'Look, some couple got in over their heads and couldn't make the repayments.'

'So someone's been evicted from the place?'

'Oh Shel, do you think any other potential buyer is thinking that way? Anyway, it's a repossession, not the same thing.'

'Still and all.'

'We're doing no harm here, Shel.'

'I know but –'

'But nothing … we don't owe these people anything. They're as faceless as the banks.'

It wasn't Brian's arguments that won me over. It was seeing the place. It's hard to explain it because it was in such a parlous state – the dark dingy rooms, the smell of damp. But as I walked through it, I knew I was in love. I felt my heart expanding with that same mix of dread and surrender I remember from my youth. And it was so good to feel that again, to know I could, that I said yes, with my heart in my mouth.

'I knew you'd come round,' Brian said and his eyes were shining.

It was a second chance for us. Another second chance, I suppose. We'd made compromises all along the way. Got married in a hurry because Sue was on the way. The house we brought our girls up in, 9 Fallowfield, wasn't what we wanted either. We'd have chosen a red-bricked Victorian if we'd had our way, but there was no way we could afford that. So we just knuckled down. It was a new estate then with rubbled open spaces, a once-in-a-blue-moon bus service and a single shop operating out of a caravan. Makeshift, in other words, but not as bad as those ghost estates left after the crash with gaping manholes and unfinished electrics.

By the time we left, the Fallowfield estate had matured. Blowsy gardens, wooden decks, two cars on the driveways. A huge shopping centre was built a five-minute drive away so it'd become a very desirable location, as the estate agent told us. Funny, it was only when we were selling it, I realized how little it meant to me even after spending a half a lifetime there. The girls were the ones who were sentimental about it. Sue wept over the marks at the end of the stairs where the baby gate had been. Linda sighed about the melamine bed and desk set we had installed in her room. Maura was lovingly condescending about 'the den', which we'd created for the girls when they were teenagers by converting the garage. At great expense, I might add. Now it was a battered-looking tunnel of a room with a jaded sofa and bean bags and the walls still sporting their posters of 90s heart-throbs; a room Brian and I rarely ventured into anymore, a museum to adolescence.

'Now,' Brian had said, 'it's our turn.'

He bid on the lodge and got it for just under a hundred thou. We sold off all the furniture – Brian's mother's sun-striped sideboard, my parents' dining room table. Frightful stuff that we'd never liked. We gave away a lifetime of bad ornaments (gifts from the girls) and fractured dinner services to the charity shop and vowed that at Drunkard's Island we'd start again.

And we did. The house is now painted in cool tones, open-plan kitchen in a full-blown modern extension. We've turned the peppermint bathroom into a dressing room and moved the facilities downstairs for our old age.

'It's so tasteful,' Maura cooed when she saw it finished. She's the middle child – or third, if you count Brian Junior – and the hardest to please. She sounded surprised. Did she think we were going to reproduce 9 Fallowfield? I felt the decades collapsing, as if Brian and I were at the beginning again, except this time without children, just Briney and Shel, pet names, old dreams ...

*

The woman ordered me to get up out of bed and, perhaps shamefully, I did what I was told. Though afterwards I couldn't tell the police why, because she didn't have a weapon. She didn't threaten me in any way. She simply said, 'Please get up and follow me' like a firm matron. When they questioned me on this, it made me sound feeble. But though her tone was gentle, I'd have called her manner gently bullying.

She took me on a tour, starting with the bedroom. 'Here is where I measured my children's heights.' She pointed to a hollow behind the shutters which the painters must have missed. There seemed to be pencil marks on the old plaster like faint Ogham markings. She moved into the dressing room – 'This is where my husband put up shelves on Christmas Eve. They fell down in the night and my daughter thought the noise was Santa Claus coming down the chimney.' She went out into the landing, turning on the lights as she went so the house was ablaze. She pointed to the now carpeted stairs – 'Nick and I sanded and varnished this one hot summer night wearing only our swimming togs, breathing in the fumes and getting high on them.' She laughed fondly.

Down we went. In the tiled hallway she paused and said – 'My youngest had his first epileptic fit right on this spot.' She pointed to the shadow of a door on the wall I'd never noticed. 'We blocked this up to stop the children chasing between the front parlour and the dining room.' How quaint the designation of the rooms, I thought. All gone now.

In the kitchen, she stopped in front of the Belfast sink, the only legacy item we'd kept. 'Here's where Nick told me it was all over.'

'And here,' she said, back in the hall, pointing to the glass panels on the front door, which we'd also kept. 'Here is where the bank plastered the repossession notice.'

Then she opened the door and manacling me by the arm, she pushed me out. Seeing it was raining, she fished one of Brian's rain ponchos from the hall stand and handed it to me – a silly, yellow wizardy thing – and then she closed the door on me.

Outside, I felt foolish and rejected. I should have called Brian, or the police, but I had no phone. I stood there, chilly and barefoot. I needed something for my feet. I made my way around the side of the house to the back porch where I knew there were spare Wellingtons. As I did, the woman inside followed my progress, scurrying from one window to the next, drawing the curtains in the lounge area, pulling down the blinds in the kitchen, quenching the warm lozenges of light. When I got to the shelter of the porch, I heard the lock turning in the back door. The only boots I could find were Brian's, miles too big, but they were better than nothing. I put my feet in and felt their clammy roominess. I began walking, awkwardly, draped in the rain poncho, to the end of the driveway determined not to look back. I wanted to appear as if I was just taking a walk, and that everything was normal. But the rain had turned to a downpour and when I reached the road, I had to take shelter under the laburnum tree. It had shed its blossoms now and its straw-coloured pods were scattered all over the ground. I bent to pick one up remembering those dire warnings from childhood – everything about this tree is poisonous. And that's the last thing I remember.

They found me – Brian and the search party – lying on the foreshore hidden behind rocks, ensnared in bladder-wrack, still in my nightie and wearing his boots. They reckoned I'd been there for nearly twenty-four hours.

'What possessed you to go wandering about in the middle of the night like that?' Brian asked testily when I came out of sedation in the hospital.

'Let's not press her just now,' one of the attending nurses said.

I knew what he suspected. A return of my old problem. I allowed him to think that. It was easier than trying to tell him what had really happened. I thought maybe it would be easier to explain to the police, but they had their own ideas. No sign of a break-in, no forced lock or smashed window, they said to Brian. If there was an intruder in the house, they said, then Mrs Clerkin invited her in. Mrs Clerkin, that's me. Sounded odd. I didn't recognize myself.

Once, shortly after we moved into the house I woke early in the morning and had the strangest sensation of not knowing who I was, as if I didn't recognize the inside of myself. You've no idea what an odd feeling it was, like a kind of unmooring, a slippage. I had to get up quietly and tiptoe around the house to find a mirror. I found one leaning against the wall in the spare bedroom. Once I saw my face, I knew of course. It wasn't like being lost, I knew where I was, I just needed my reflection. I didn't say anything to Brian; I mean, it sounds stupid, doesn't it? I put it down to the move, being cut adrift from the familiar.

'It's the previous occupant of the house,' I told the plain-clothes detective who came to interview me in the hospital. 'She told me who she was.'

'I know the previous owners,' the detective said. 'Sad case.'

'The repossession, you mean,' Brian said.

'No, I mean the wife dying like that.'

'The wife died?' Brian said. He looked chastened.

'Suicide,' the detective said and looked embarrassed. 'After the sale. The times that are in it, I'm afraid. They lost everything.'

Brian looked at me. So much for doing no harm.

'So, you see,' the detective said looking straight at me, 'it couldn't have been Mrs Sewell you met.'

'Was her husband's name, Nick? She said her husband's name was —'

The nurse shushed me and asked Brian and the detective to leave and give me some rest. As the door suctioned close, I heard him ask:

'Generally speaking, is everything okay with Mrs Clerkin?'

I didn't hear Brian's reply.

When he came back in, I decided to have it out with him.

'I can't go back there,' I told him.

'Don't be ridiculous,' he said, 'you just got a fright, that's all.'

'No, Brian, she's still there. Don't you get it?'

'Come on, now, Shel …'

'I can't be on my own there anymore.'

'But I'll be there,' he protested.

'Not always,' I said, 'you can't guarantee that.'

'Well, if I'm away, we'll get one of the girls to stay.' I recognized that tone. His mountains-out-of-molehills voice.

'I'm not going to be baby-sat by my own children. Anyway, they have their own lives to lead. Isn't that why we moved? Free as birds, you said, empty-nesters.'

'And that's how it's going to be,' Brian insisted.

He took my hand and clenched it in his.

'I'm not going to leave you, Shel,' he said. 'In sickness and in health, remember?'

But that's not what I'm afraid of.

I've never doubted Brian, not for a moment, but there are things about me he just doesn't understand, things I've never been able to tell him. Like when we lost Brian Junior. Never took to him, can a mother say that about her own baby? Well, not out loud, she can't. And now, it's the same. I can't tell Brian … it's not the house, it's her, Mrs Sewell, the ghost, the dead woman, the stalker, whatever you want to call her.

It isn't the house she's taken possession of, it's me.

MORTIFICATION

I

When she heard it, Freddie was clearing up after lunch and she had an empty coffee cup and a crumbed plate in her hand. It was on a phone-in radio programme that she'd been only half-listening to. A woman's voice was explaining about the problem of expressing victimhood. If you don't have the words you can't formulate the experience, the woman was saying. She was an academic doing some kind of research so she had all the jargon.

'So, put simply,' the radio host said, 'what you're talking about here is bullying, is that right?'

'Yes,' the academic said, 'bullying.'

The word stood out.

Suddenly Freddie understood the phrase 'light-bulb moment'. The word became fixed in her mind, like other significant memories. When she'd lost her virginity or when her father told her he was dying. She sat down as if she'd heard bad news and felt a sinking sense of doomy knowledge.

Is that what it was, she thought to herself? Is that what happened to me?

She listened to the rest of the programme in a daze. Loads of women phoned in to relate their experiences. That should have been a comfort. But, unlike her, they'd known what it was while it was happening. It'd taken her over forty years to recognize that she'd been bullied. It made her feel so stupid, as if she'd found soft porn in those outer reaches of the TV channels with the high numbers and watched the heaving flesh waiting for the sex scene to be over.

II

She didn't tell anyone – well, who would she tell? Brendan? Explains a lot, he might say, and nod his head to imply thoughtful empathy. At fifty-five, after a life in IT, he's decided to switch careers. Or diversify as he calls it. He's training to be a shrink. She loves him, of course she does, but the thought of her big-boned, lumbering, affable husband listening to people's problems with his fingers steepled makes her want to snort with laughter. As if he was running a help desk, only this time to fix humans. Is this the kind of thing Brendan's clients were telling him? Tales of victimhood.

Down through the years, she'd heard dozens of people talk about bullying at dinners and parties – boys grown into men glorying in recounting how they were belted by Christian Brothers for being late or missing homework, or merely being alive. Or beaten up by their peers because they wore glasses or spoke with a lisp or were the teacher's favourite. And women arguing that girls were worse because they ganged up in spiteful covens to undermine, mock and exclude the lesser mortals, the girls with braces, the girls who smelled funny. Freddie had never seen herself in any of it. She'd even read *Cat's Eye*, for God's sake, and even then she hadn't twigged. Because she thought she was simply being picked on.

III

Bel and Eva groomed her. That's what it'd be called now. They pretended to like her, sidling up to her at break time and inviting her opinion on the Bay City Rollers or the Eurovision. They had a superior game of German Jumps on the go. Freddie was no good at it, although given her clumsiness you'd think getting her feet tied up in intricate knots would come naturally. But it was Bel and Eva asking so you didn't say no. See, she thought she was being smart – she knew they'd pick on her if she didn't comply. But by being asked in, she had lost any allies she might have had, girls who might have been genuine friends. They pulled away because they sensed betrayal. She'd gone over to the dark side, sold her soul to gain entrance to the golden circle.

Once inside, you were deemed to have been granted the great favour of Bel and Eva's company, and then the demands started coming. Little errands – run to the tuck shop and get … Loans of money – I've forgotten my bus fare, and then you'd see your sixpence being eaten in the form of an ice cream or a chocolate bar. And still she knew they sniggered behind her back at her frizzy hair and her girth.

Then they moved on to homework. Did you do the comprehension question in English, have you translated your Latin? And because she was now, technically, a friend, she couldn't refuse. The only subject they couldn't pick on her about was art, which was impossible to plagiarize. Was that why she chose it as a career? Because it was the one thing she couldn't be bullied out of.

IV

Throughout her teenage years she'd lived with the sick feeling that went with being picked on – a turnover in her deepest innards and too much spittle in her mouth. Bel and Eva were like a gun-metal sky hanging over her head, but in her stomach they were vitriol. Then one Monday morning when Eva sidled up to her and said simply – Have you got your German homework? she suddenly saw red. Why? She doesn't know. And why then? – she doesn't know that either. The rage came directly from her tormented gut, by-passing her brain altogether. She looked Eva straight in the face and told her to fuck off. Something about that obscenity – a word she had never used before – made Eva take a step back, as if she'd smacked her. She remembered Eva's very pale eyes under a glossy fringe widening in shock.

Theirs was a school that was intent on breeding young ladies and this was such an outrage that Eva reported her for using bad language, even though this risked her and Bel's behaviour being unmasked. But in their value system, Freddie's sin was the more grave.

Mother Berchmans had a smooth, untroubled face which she cocked to one side like a friendly question.

The question was why.

But Freddie didn't shop Bel and Eva – it didn't even occur to her. She had four more years of secondary school to get through.

'I lost my temper,' she said.

'But why, Winnifred?' said the face like an ad for Palmolive.

'I'm having my monthlies.'

'But where did you hear such language?'

And she couldn't say – You haven't met my father.

'On the tele,' she said.

'One of the foreign stations, I presume?'

She'd got 500 lines and had to do clean-up after domestic science for a month. But Bel and Eva never came near her again. One curt fuck off was all it took.

It might have stopped them, but Freddie has experienced that sick feeling many times since and she has never again retaliated, so, in fact, it changed nothing. It just drove her courage underground.

V

At fifteen, she went to extra art classes with Miss Gunn in a dingy little studio at the top of a house on Charlotte Street. She used to feel sick before the class and get sick after. Dread and relief, a familiar cycle.

Everything about Freddie seemed to provoke Miss Gunn: her timidity with colour, her size, her determination to keep her head down, not to draw attention to herself.

'Speak up,' Miss Gunn would say when Freddie was forced into answering a question. Questions from Miss Gunn were like gauntlets thrown down.

Once, during the break, Miss Gunn halted in mid-conversation with the others, who were all much older than Freddie, and turned to her.

'You eat like a cow,' she said.

Freddie was battling with a toffee.

'Disgusting,' she spat. 'Anyway, look at the size of you, you should be staying away from sweets.'

There was a ripple of laughter though Miss Gunn was overweight and slovenly and had greasy hair.

Freddie swallowed the gnawed mess in one go.

Miss Gunn's thin spindly mother, who helped out in the studio, saw the episode and tried to make it up to her. She and Freddie were rinsing out the watercolour brushes in the studio's Spartan kitchen. They had to stoop double over the sink because the eaves were so low.

'You mustn't mind her,' her mother whispered, 'she gets frustrated, takes it out on people; feels her work has never been recognized.'

Freddie Daly knows what that's like. Now.

At art college she did her thesis on 'Ailsa Gunn; a painter eclipsed'.

VI

Her final portfolio was a series of miniature crucifixions, but with female figures on her crosses. No nails – she couldn't bear the violence; sometimes she had to look away from too graphic depictions of the crucifixion that showed torn and ragged limbs, the rust-red blood. She preferred quieter renditions. Dali's bloodless 'Salvator Mundi', for example, the entire world viewed from Christ's point of view high on the cross looking down. Above it all, not mired in it. For her portfolio she decided she'd do a complete cycle depicting women's torments. The scourging at the pillar was done with the flex of an iron, the crowning with thorns was a beauty pageant tiara. Veronica was burdened with a pile of Christ's soiled laundry – a series of tea towels with other women's faces on them. Simon of Cyrene helped a beleaguered mother with a double buggy. I'll be the next Judy Chicago, she thought.

When she left college she survived for a bit on small residencies and drew the dole. The long anti-social hours in the studio made her feel justified in her choice of life's work but she never found her artistic theme. Maybe she hadn't given it enough time. On her own, her imagination flourished and for the first time she had no dread, no fear of what others might say, because there were no others.

But she needed money. She started guiding at the National Gallery and found she was good at it. She did kiddies' groups and adult enthusiasts and she liked how she was left to her own devices. People said she talked about art in a way that was comprehensible, made them 'see' more. She was particularly kind to fat children and lone men, of whom Brendan was one.

VII

After the radio programme she looked up Bel Figgis and Eva Mulhone on Facebook. Bel owned a restaurant. She'd been featured in interviews in the Sunday supplements. She ran one of those chi-chi places with one name, 'Soup' or 'Spoon' or somesuch. But it had gone belly-up in the crash. Eva was a champion for disabled rights. She'd had one of those births that had gone wrong and her eldest boy had been catastrophically affected. There were pictures of her outside the courthouse when her case against the hospital was settled. No sign of a husband. Couldn't hack it, Freddie had heard on the grapevine. But neither of these life experiences could be seen as punishment, could they?

VIII

When Brendan came in from seeing clients he parked himself in front of the television. Freddie was in the kitchen making dinner. She was still a bit aghast about the radio programme. It was as if a portal had opened up in her head, through which the evidence poured like sugar through a sieve. Everything was of a piece when she used the bullying filter. That time when she was teaching in secondary school and there was a student – Kathryn Dunville – who'd reported her. The girl had a hare lip and Freddie knew she shouldn't think it, but it was like her whole personality had been knitted up around her flawed mouth. Everything that came out of it was crooked.

Miss Daly had bullied her, she'd claimed, had humiliated her in front of others.

'I corrected her,' Freddie said, 'she was wrong'.

'We don't use the word wrong,' the principal said, 'that's not a word in our vocabulary.'

I am the teacher, Freddie wanted to say, isn't it my job to put students on the right path, not to allow them to labour under misapprehensions?

'She's targeting me,' Kathryn Dunville said, 'she's never liked me, she's never given me a chance. She called my paintings crap.'

Well, that was a downright lie.

But Freddie found herself unable to fight back. And she wasn't able to see clearly enough to say – Can't you *see*? It's the other way round.

In the end she left the school with the cloud of an official enquiry hanging over her, which is still rumbling on even though it's years ago and Kathryn Dunville is now a thirty-year-old woman.

When she went to call Brendan for dinner, he was scrolling on his phone while in the background a documentary about St Peter played out unwatched. Freddie found herself arrested by it, watching silently from the door. She's not religious, mind. Gave that up years ago, painfully, and the separation hurt so much she couldn't afford to get involved again, even if it was only for the comfort of communal worship. Some famous actor with a moustache was tramping around Rome and Jerusalem trying to fill in the blanks about Jesus's most trusted disciple.

St Peter, apparently, didn't quite 'get' the whole Messiah thing, and he was forever going off the rails. He chopped off the ear of the servant to the high priest Caiaphas in the Garden of Gethsemane – who did he think he was, Van Gogh? – in a bid to halt Jesus's arrest, nearly throwing God's highly planned scenario out of kilter. Then later, he denied he knew Jesus in front of everyone and only stopped when the cock crowed three times. Just as Jesus had predicted.

Like her, St Peter was a slow learner.

And like Peter, she was apt to betray people.

IX

Standing in the doorway, a memory of Johnny Fedrgioni assaulted her. Out of nowhere. They'd had a thing at college, an innocent kind of courtship. He was the son of Italian parents who ran a chip-shop. Rangy and warm-skinned and brown-eyed. He had a mop of curly black hair and a puckish smile. Her heart seized just remembering him as he was – the graceful heedless beauty of the young. But she just didn't believe him when he declared his love. She couldn't envisage them together because she saw him as part of that golden circle she had already ruled herself out of.

Years passed and they met again. Or rather, they didn't meet. It was at the funeral of a friend of theirs from that era, Jem Lovett, who hadn't made it past forty. The church was packed. Jem was the first of their contemporaries to go. The funeral-goers milled around the hearse in the churchyard, loath to let Jem go because they'd have to face up to their own mortality. There was a lot of laughter, enforced gaiety, a *we're all fine* vibe, while Jem's wife shook hands and his children sobbed. Freddie saw Johnny in the distance. At first, she couldn't quite believe it was him. He was enormously fat, a belly on him like a meal sack, a double chin, a dishevelled air, shirt buttons straining, tie askew. Is that my Johnny? she thought. No, it couldn't be! She could see he had seen her, but as he made his way laboriously through the crowd towards her, she pretended not to see him. Rather than face this wreck of a man, she ducked around by the side of the church and left. What she felt was shame. As if his appearance had emanated from how poorly she had treated him. She'd rather betray their love then than be seen with a fat man now.

X

Still waters run deep, was how Brendan described her. Mars in the twelfth house, the astrologer at Pam's hen party said. There's great power in it, she'd said, there's steel, but it's often about suppression.

'Suppression of what?' Freddie had asked the woman, who had platinum hair and wore a garish smock.

'Rage.'

XI

The evidence just kept on piling up. The art shop boss who told her she just wasn't up to the job, wasn't ever going to make the grade at selling. His repeated assertions were self-fulfilling. Her returns got worse and worse, until she had to leave. In the adult world it's called exerting pressure. This is what we like to do to one another – torment and dominate. Exactly like bullying children. You couldn't challenge it, not then. It was what the whole system encouraged. It got results. Freddie's policy had been to stay silent and let it happen. If she'd fought back, she'd have been mistaken for shrill, or neurotic.

XII

Her last job was at the New Masters Gallery which had seen Brendan through his counselling course. Her boss, Billy Stone, was in his thirties, a man who presented a boyish bonhomie to the world. His self-deprecation was legendary – if he'd been an old-fashioned woman, he'd have batted his eyelashes and made a moué with his lips. What am I like, he'd say to cover missed openings and bad hangings. And then he'd go on to give the impression that he was surrounded by fools, which meant Freddie. He effected a civilized tolerance towards her, as if he'd given a second chance to a friend of his mother's. But behind her back he referred to her as if she was disabled in some way, someone whom he'd been lumbered with, although she did all the programming and took on the weekend work when he was swanning off to conferences and making media appearances. She was the one who'd trained as an artist; he was a mere manager. But he treated her like a skivvy and what was worse, she'd acted like one.

In the end, even Brendan said, leave that job. He's always made allowances for her. Her rackety mothering of Pam, the long period being out of sorts as she weathered all the indignities of the female experience, the murderous pre-menstrual tension, the gunshot wound periods and then on into the mood-storms and incontinences of menopause. He put it down to her artistic nature, though she was no longer a practising artist. That had, somehow, fallen by the wayside.

That wasn't Brendan's fault; she'd done that all on her own. But standing behind him now in the TV room, the back of his head visible over the chair, she's suddenly furious. The kindliness in him she'd always been grateful for, is mummified now with a top coat of waxed professional concern. It makes her want to chop his ear off.

'Dinner's ready,' she says.

XIII

Blessed are the meek, isn't that what they say? And that's what she is. Meek. If only she still believed, she'd have the comfort of knowing she'd get her reward in heaven. And what is she to do with this new knowledge? She's gained nothing from it. The opposite in fact – she's been robbed, her memories all repurposed into a depressing, repeating loop. It reminds her of listening to the Gospels in church when she was a kid, where so many things seemed only to happen to satisfy the prophets of old.

The day after the radio programme, Pam arrives with news from the battlefront of contemporary mothering. Freddie has always been slightly afraid of her daughter because of her forthrightness, her sense of certainty.

'Tilly's been bullied,' Pam says matter-of-factly. Tilly is Freddie's twelve-year-old granddaughter.

There it is again,

'What?' She tries to keep the alarm out of her voice.

'Her best friend bad-mouthed her to someone else on TikTok. Now there's a whole thread going. Luckily Tilly had the presence of mind to take a screen grab of the first message and show it me.'

'You have to do something.' Freddie's voice comes out panicky. Is this history repeating itself? Is meekness genetic? Has it skipped a generation?

'Don't worry, I'm dealing with it,' Pam says.

'You need to go down to that school and have them stamp it out,' Freddie says.

'No, Mam, they can't control it, this stuff's all online now.'

'So what did you do?'

'I got on to the mother immediately. I mean, it's alright to have a row with someone, even on social media. But you can't do what she did with a third party. For everyone to see. That's bullying.'

It's as if the scales have fallen from Freddie's eyes and now it's everywhere.

'It's simple netiquette,' Pam says. 'What am I saying? It's common decency, isn't that right? You taught us that.'

Freddie considers her fiercely capable daughter with her brusque, no-nonsense mothering and is chastened. Even twelve-year-old Tilly knows more about self-protection than she does.

'Alright, Mum?' Pam says looking at her oddly.

I'm proud of you, Freddie wants to say, but doesn't. Because what she means is that she's proud her daughter is nothing like her. But she wonders, silently, if Pam is right. Is keeping Tilly's problem between the parents another way of brushing it under the carpet?

XIV

That night after Brendan has gone to bed, she fishes out some old pieces of white cardboard she used for storing frames and lays them out on the kitchen table. She finds her brushes and some paint in the spare room where she's stowed them, but it's so long since she's used them, the paint is encrusted and the brushes have spread. Markers will do, she decides, but even with them, the task takes hours because Freddie is a perfectionist and she wants the letters to be evenly spaced. She measures everything before she starts and then she has to decide what to say. Also there are two sides to do. She labours through the night, something she hasn't done since she was a student. It feels good, despite the petrolly fumes of the markers. At 4 am she's finished and goes to the garage where she finds two lengths of untreated wood, off-cuts from one of Brendan's DIY misadventures. She hammers them into a cross and staples the two-sided placard on to it.

Afraid that sleep will smother her resolve, she doesn't bother going to bed. Fuelling up on coffee she slips out of the house at 7:30, puts the placard in the boot, and drives to Tilly's school. It's a good forty minutes away and there's rush-hour traffic to contend with but she wants to be in situ when the students arrive. She parks in the teacher's area (well, she was a teacher once) which is not yet full and rescues the placard from the boot. She makes her way to the main entrance and waits. The place is deserted but by 8:30 there's a stream of kids trekking up the two or three shallow steps to the swing doors. The parents are mostly outside on the street with car doors open disgorging their cargo. Freddie stands by one of the concrete urns planted with straggling flowers that have gone to seed. Most of the kids just pass by her and don't even see the placard, which she's leaning on like a crutch. A woman of her age is mostly invisible to them.

But she has come here *not* to be that.

It's now or never, Freddie, she tells herself and hoists the placard up. The moment itself is mortifying but once the awkward transition is over and the placard is aloft, she finds a kind of defiant calm. She looks up at her handiwork, a blood red message stapled to a cross: TILLY MANNING'S GRANNY WAS ALSO BULLIED.

HEARTBURN

Greta Diehl was disappointed, Bernard could tell. Not surprising. Even though they'd been pen pals for three years, he'd been careful to send Greta only one photo, and that was of his older brother, Gerard. Gerard was the good-looking one; wasted on the seminary his mother said. Greta had sent several pictures of herself so he knew who he was looking for as he stood with stinging palms on the platform at Hamburg Hauptbahnhof, his suitcase splayed by his side.

He'd grown to hate it. There had been three changes of trains on the journey from Ostend and it had thwarted him at every transfer. On the last leg, he'd struck up a conversation with a young Englishman called Philip who'd pointed to his own luggage in the rack overhead, a small attaché case, in tanned leather, polished with venom, with capped corners and thick ornate stitching.

'If it doesn't fit in there, it doesn't come,' he said. 'That's the whole point of travel, don't you think?'

Bernard didn't know what the point of travel was. He was seventeen and this was his first trip to Europe. He had just finished secondary school and would shortly start a clerking job in the county council. The trip to see Greta would form the interlude between these two stages in his life.

'You get to shed your possessions,' Philip said when Bernard failed to respond. 'That's the point: you become your most essential self.'

Bernard's case, crammed with clothes for every season and too cumbersome to be lifted on to the rack, colonised the aisle of the carriage and was in everybody's way.

The air in the station was gritty. Destinations were called on the booming public address system and trains huffed and puffed importantly, seemingly impatient with loiterers like him. He was wondering if he should have worn a large card strung around his neck with his name on it like a war orphan when he felt his sleeve being tugged. He turned and there was Greta and her dismay. He recognized her dark bouncy hair, but she had different glasses. They made her look much more secretarial than the school shots she'd sent him. Or was it the clothes? In the photos she was wearing a uniform of some sort, but now she had a flouncy kind of dress with flowers all over it and a black jacket. And she was tall. Way taller than him.

'Really?' she asked. 'It is you?'

He stuck out his hand and she shook it manfully.

'You are more fat,' she said.

Charitably, Bernard put this down to her English, though he knew that being fat seemed to license other people to be very pass-remarkable, as his mother would put it. Greta's mother came up beside them, small, sad-eyed, her high-built blonde hair shrouded in a gauzy scarf.

'This,' Greta said, 'is Mutti.'

Mutti said something very fast in German that sounded like a question and ended with his name.

Burn heart.

For the first weekend, Greta marched him into the centre of town. She took him to the small museum. One room was full of dour altarpieces and painted wooden statues of monks; the other was devoted to religious torture. There was a tram ride to a large park with a lake but when they got there, there wasn't much to do. Bernard had surreptitiously brought his togs with him but once he saw the murky waters he kept quiet about them. He wasn't prepared to disrobe in front of Greta and she clearly had no plans for swimming. Instead they watched a group of muscly young men dive from a little jetty and cavort athletically in the water. Then they got back on the tram and went directly home. The perfunctory aimlessness of this trip filled Bernard with dread about what other activities Greta had lined up. But come Monday, she resumed what he presumed was her normal life, which didn't include him. She had a complicated schedule of choir practice, tennis matches and study groups (she was a year younger than Bernard and still at the *gymnasium*) to which Bernard was pointedly not invited. She disappeared early in the morning and was gone for the day, leaving him alone with her mother.

He tooled around the apartment with its stained floors and heavy dark furniture, feeling like a trespasser. His room was bare; a single bed and a hospital-style locker, more of the stained floorboards and a full wall of wardrobe with sliding doors which, when he opened them, was as gloomy as a vault. It was packed full of tweedy clothes he was convinced belonged to the dead. That's what they smelled of, these slack-shouldered ranks. He slid the door closed. He felt it wrong to put his own clothes in there. He could hear his mother's voice warning him to unpack his good shirt immediately to shake out the creases. She had visions of him going to concert halls because she believed all Germans were interested in classical music and didn't Greta tell him she was in a choir? Well, Mam, he thought, I won't be needing my good shirt. So he kept his clothes intact in the big suitcase — that way he wouldn't have to struggle to get the lid closed as he had when leaving home. In truth he wanted to pack himself away out of this unhappy household.

The kitchen with its bright white cabinets was the only non-brown room. This was Mutti's territory. Any time he came into the room she would be sitting at the red Formica table, smoking languidly, yet she cooked three full meals a day and the house looked clean as far as Bernard could judge. He'd brought one book to read — Nevil Shute's *On the Beach* — and he'd finished it by Tuesday morning. The only relief from the tedium was the food, which was meaty. There were stews and breaded chops, pies and sausage. He liked the sausage, in particular, which came in several guises, but he ate everything and Mutti seemed to enjoy feeding him. He said '*sehr gut*' after everything and she was always pleased to see his polished plate.

On Wednesday afternoon, he couldn't stick the brown flat any longer and determined to go out. He didn't know if he should ask permission. At home he and Gerard would have to account for their movements, before and after. He knocked at the kitchen door and said in English, 'Frau Diehl, I'm going out now,' and pointed to the front door. Mutti just nodded. She pointed to her tiny wristwatch and he raised six fingers.

It was inevitable, Olivia said to him years later. Olivia was the only person he'd ever told. But Bernard had seen nothing inevitable about it.

The Diehls lived in an apartment block on an austere, respectable street with grassy patches out front and leafy trees. He started walking towards where he thought the centre was, but it led into docklands with enormous monolithic factories and grim sidings where trains seemed to have been shunted and left to die. Greta's father worked in the docks as a nightwatchman, if Bernard understood correctly. He was a ghostly presence in the flat. Seen at the breakfast table in blue overalls, bleary-eyed, with his hangdog face and bulbous eyes, he wolfed his food and eyed Bernard incuriously. Frau Diehl serviced him like a sullen waitress, planting the heaped plate down in front of him without a word. Then he would shuffle off to bed.

The town centre proved elusive so he found a pub, Der Insel Teufel. Devil's Island, Bernard thought, just perfect. It was in a red-bricked, flat-iron type building jutting like a prow on to a street, one side of which was a quay, with tracks scored into the cobbles. It looked over a basin of water to another quay, where a number of ships were docked. Behind them were rows of brick warehouses, and behind them a row of cranes, their muscled necks frozen and their idle hooks like inverted question marks. The place seemed deserted. Was Wednesday half-day at the docks, he wondered.

It was equally quiet inside the pub. A couple of old men played dominoes noisily at the tables but Bernard sat at the bar and ordered a beer. He was expecting to be challenged but wasn't. The barman, with a dead cigarette between his lips, produced a big blonde beer in a large tankard with a handle and smiled at him as he set it down. Then he slapped his towel over his shoulder and went somewhere out the back – to restart his cigarette, Bernard supposed. He was grateful for the lack of curiosity. His German wasn't up to conversation. Here he felt blessedly ignored, and let's face it, manly.

He'd spent very little money since he arrived so he ordered two more tankards of beer. Live dangerously, he told himself. He knew he would have to fabricate a version of this trip for his mother who had helped him with the ferry fare. He couldn't disappoint her by saying that the highlight of his week away was getting drunk in a pub on his own.

Night was falling as he stepped outside. It was a fresh evening and he was glad of the wind as he walked home. It would sober him up. He'd missed dinner and he worried how he was going to explain his absence. He hadn't been given a key to the apartment – in that, it was just like home – so he had to ring the bell when he got back. When Mutti opened the door, she looked different. First of all she had shed her apron and was wearing a blouse in a peachy colour with a ruffled neck and a porridge-coloured skirt that was just above her knee. And instead of her usual house slippers she had a pair of patent sling-backs with a kitten heel. In her hand she held a thimble glass which she sipped from as she greeted him with a wide smile. There was no remonstration about dinner. He followed her into the dark sitting room where the television, housed in a mahogany cabinet with doors, was on at murmuring level. She offered him a glass of what she was drinking – it was honey-coloured and awfully sweet. He drank slowly, relieved that it wasn't another beer. He didn't feel manly now; he felt bloated and sluggish. There was news first, followed by some kind of documentary about the war. Mutti said nothing but seemed to be watching intently as the screen illuminated the dark room with vivid explosions.

'*Krieg*,' she said looking at him directly for the first time. She made it sound like a lament.

'*Ja*,' he said and nodded his head assertively.

More Krieg followed – marching columns of hard-hatted troops, close-ups of the ribbed tyres of tanks, epaulettes and raised salutes. He stole a sidelong glance at her.

She shook her head sorrowfully. He found himself smiling though it felt like the wrong response.

He wondered why she was all dolled up. Was she expecting a visitor? He knew that in his state, he wouldn't be able to handle two monosyllabic conversations at once, so he tossed back the stuff in the glass – it tasted sticky, like glue – and extravagantly made to rise. In response, she stretched out her hand on the shiny brown leatherette of the sofa and covered his with it. She shook her head and pursed her lips and kept her hand on his quite firmly. They sat like that for several minutes. He felt his hand blushing in her tender prison. Then with great resolve, she stood up, and going over to the TV she switched it off.

Damn! Whatever chance he had with the TV between them as a source of conversation, he'd be useless on his own. She went to another cabinet in the room which opened on top and hid a record player. Why did the Germans coffin everything like this? She picked up an LP and slid the record out placing it on the turntable. Liftng the needle very carefully – was she drunk, Bernard wondered, then chastised himself; who was he to point the finger – she set it down on the vinyl. A bombastic brass section declared its intentions. Beaming at him, she brought the cover over for his inspection. James Last, *Games that Lovers Play*. Bernard recognized the title track immediately. He smiled at her accommodatingly.

'*Möchten Sie tanzen?*' she queried and for a minute Bernard got a glimpse of what she might have been like when she was young. Winsome, fey, appealing. For the first time in this house he felt emboldened. There was a lot of stuff he was crap at, but he *was* able to dance.

'Nothing happened,' he told Olivia, when she winkled the story out of him thirty years later. She was inordinately pleased to discover what she called a Mrs Robinson episode in his past. Olivia was always convinced he was withholding on her. He'd never gone as far as telling her he was a virgin. She wouldn't believe him, he was sure. It wasn't a credible thing to be in this day and age. He was a fat, middle-aged man living with his brother – a defrocked priest, although Gerard insisted he'd left the priesthood of his own volition – in the house they'd grown up in. That was enough of a social handicap to bear; it told most people all they wanted to know. Declaring the extent of his sexual innocence would have been a burden. For Olivia, that is.

'Nothing happened,' he repeated as Olivia wiggled her eyebrows at him like a smutty comedian.

He didn't describe the nesting sensation of Mutti in his arms, the animal closeness of another body, the trustingness of her. Not a bit like Auntie Min who'd taught him, who was vibrant and lip-sticked and smoked a cigarette as she swung around the sitting room in green silk, while imperiously pushing and pulling him about the place, like some jousting bully. There was initially some awkwardness with Mutti, which hand went where, etc. Because of his age, she expected him only capable of that modern shuffle business, arms at waist level, gripping your partner's love handles. But he didn't want that because he was afraid of how his own body might react to such frictive proximity. So he placed a hand firmly in the small of her back and took the lead.

Mutti was quite solid in his arms; he discovered comforting little rolls of flesh under her armpits that felt like baby fat and when he looked down – he was a good foot taller than her – he could see fair down on her cheeks. Mutti (even in his head, he couldn't keep calling her Frau Diehl) complied, surrendered. She knew most of the steps too, although he could tell it was a while since she'd danced. When she'd forget or stumble she'd look up and smile but otherwise their bodies did the talking. Even as Bernard shimmied and jived with Mutti, he knew her loneliness was more intense than his, but it chimed with what he felt was his deep unloveability. After a while he forgot he was dancing with his pen pal's mother and he believed she forgot that he was the soft pouchy boy her daughter had brought home. That was the joy of it. They forgot themselves.

He recognized several other tracks – 'A Man and A Woman', 'Fly me to the Moon', 'What Now My Love' – from Hospital Requests, which his mother liked to listen to, though she didn't care much for James Last. James Blast, more like, she said.

Mutti was turning the record for a second time when they heard Greta's key in the door. She dropped the needle noisily on the vinyl and tamped down her hair then wordlessly she went to her end of the sofa, he to his. She patted her cheeks with her palms while he tried to regulate his breathing. When Greta peered around the door, they were sitting as stiffly together as when they'd started. The lush strings of 'Lara's Theme' filled the room.

'Oh Mutti,' Greta said in English for his benefit, 'Bernard is not liking this altmodisch music.'

Bernard found himself bristling; what did Greta know about him? Nothing ... His letters to her in his stilted German allowed only the tedious cataloguing of activities – much of them invented – and he found himself tongue-tied in her presence, all his paltry learning deserting him. She crossed the room and pulled the needle roughly off the record. Behind her back, Mutti looked at him, shrugged ruefully and smiled.

Greta turned the TV back on.

'*Ein Platz an der Sonne*,' a hectic TV voice declared with matching words on screen. A flashing starburst showed a large sum in Deutschmarks.

'This,' Greta explained patiently, 'is our game of chance.'

A lottery, Bernard had already guessed.

Unsurprisingly, Greta never made the planned return visit to Ireland.

'It's a wonder Mutti didn't show up on your doorstep instead,' Olivia said.

It was one of the few times Bernard was disappointed in her. For Olivia, intimacy was always a joking matter, something to be belittled, perhaps because she'd never really mastered it. Nothing short of full-scale penetration would have counted as something happening, whereas this experience belonged to the realm of the unrequited. You can love someone, he longed to say, without ever having sex with them. From what he could gather, most people used sex to work off hostile energy. But he didn't say any of that because he knew how threatened Olivia was by unspoken longing. His, in particular.

Bernard's underground feeling for Olivia had long been the sandpapery grit in their friendship. Olivia recognized it, he knew, and feared the power of its pathos.

'Didn't Greta notice anything?' Olivia asked.

'No, she was too wrapped up in herself. '

'And wasn't it awkward afterwards?' she asked. 'With Mutti?'

'No,' he said, 'it wasn't. We just went back to being who we had been.'

But Olivia didn't believe him.

'Are you sure she didn't tiptoe into your monkish room in a pink négligée and have her wicked way with you? Go on, you can tell me.'

It was on the tip of his tongue to lie, to satisfy Olivia's appetite for what she called the dirt. But he demurred, faithful to the memory of Mutti. As they spoke, it occurred to him that she must be long dead now.

'She gave me a packed lunch for the return journey with a note inside.'

'With kisses at the bottom?'

'Really, Oliv, no ... She wished me a safe journey and signed her name – Agnetha.'

'Aw,' Olivia said but it was sardonic.

He couldn't tell Olivia that for decades he had drawn amorous solace remembering the half hour that he danced with Mutti. That it sustained him when nothing like it was on offer to him; no one would ever declare love, full-blown, unconditional, lustful love for him. Neither did he tell her that he still had the note. The paper was fragile now after so many years of folding and unfolding but still bore the fat, greasy watermark of what had been mustard smeared on the sausage sandwiches. Sometimes, even still he reads its message which, at this remove, seemed both urgent and valedictory.

Gute Reise, Agnetha.

NOTES ON BIOLOGY

Sally's mother discovers the word behind an icon on her daughter's tablet labelled Biology Notes. When she was Sally's age she used to keep her secrets in a locked diary wearing the key on a chain around her neck, even in bed. You'll have to take my virginity first, she used to declare. It turned out in the end that she was more easily broken into than the fat five-year diary.

I'm in THE DREADS, Sally has written. Are the capital letters like the ironic quote marks her daugther uses in conversation to scratch the air?

Sally's mother tries the word out but can make no sense of it. Is it a code for something? Depression? Anxiety? Is it drugs? Or, worse, is it withdrawal?

She's immediately catapulted back to when she was eighteen. She was already out in the world, working in a dry cleaner's, having nothing better in mind. After two years she'd saved enough money to go inter-railing in Europe for a month, leaving a boyfriend behind. When she got to Florence, she'd gone rambling in the market place near the Duomo one day and struck up a conversation with a stall-holder – or rather he had with her – after she'd toyed with a golden purse, shaped like a clam shell. (She still has it. She keeps it as a memento though it's too girly to wear. She thinks Sally might like it, some day. Not now, though; it doesn't fit with her present aesthetic, a kind of grunge meets athleisure.) The stallholder was a fat luscious man with impossibly green eyes. As he wrapped the purse in a netted pouch bag and drew the strings together, he gestured to her to draw closer.

'Would you like five minutes of madness?' he'd whispered in perfect English.

'Pardon?'

'Five minutes of madness,' he repeated. He smiled at her. Avuncular, like he was offering a treat to a child.

'What do you mean? What kind of madness?'

'Ah no, Signorina,' he replied wagging his finger. 'You must say yes first.'

'Is it sex,' she asked, 'or drugs?'

'No, no,' he said. 'I cannot tell you. That is the deal. But I promise it is an experience you will never forget.'

The reckless part of her was tempted. But she was a lone girl in Florence contemplating going off with a stranger. A lone girl who was already six weeks pregnant, but, of course, she didn't realize that. The stallholder was probably in league with a gang who would rob her or rape her or take her passport. And yet she hesitated. He saw that.

'Signorina?' he queried with a gamey tilt of his head.

She shook her head as she backed away. He pouted theatrically, then grabbed her hand and grazed his lips on her knuckles. How cheesy, she thought, but she'd almost changed her mind, her hormones aflame. (Different hormones, as it turned out.) Afterwards, she felt a swell of disappointment – in herself. What a coward she was! She returned the next day in search of him, determined to say yes this time, but she couldn't find him or his stall. After three days in Florence she had to move on.

She hadn't thought about the episode in years and yet here she was, decades later, with the same questions, the same impatient demands as when she was eighteen — is it sex, is it drugs, is it danger? Tell me!

Except now it's about her daughter.

She's snooping on Sally for no good reason. Because there's really nothing *obviously* wrong. Sally is not gloomy or anxious or acting out. She's a teenager who wears crotch-hugging Lycra, loses her phone, keeps her bedroom like a pig sty. In other words, perfectly normal.

As far as Sally's mother can tell.

As far as any mother can tell, that is. But then, look at Denise Barton. She didn't have an inkling that anything was amiss when her Conor hanged himself from a beam in the garage. It came out of a clear blue sky, she kept on saying on the day of the funeral. Sally's mother remembered the phrase, maybe because the day of Conor's funeral — a day of high summer — the church gutters streamed, the pewter sky wept, and everyone's shoes were marked with frothy-white, high-tide marks.

At the cemetery she had caught Sally's eye as she stood in a huddle beside Denise, and Conor's sister Jen. She couldn't say exactly what it was, but there was something contemptuous in her daughter's gaze, something hardening between them. Sally's mother had vowed then — *this* is not going to happen to me. Sally is her life's work, the reason she stopped being flaky Grace Penrose. Sally is her only real achievement; she *has* to turn out right.

Conor had been Sally's playmate. Sally's mother remembers him sprawled on the living room floor, tongue between his teeth, building Lego towers, while Sally pouted because he was ignoring her. When she was eight, Sally had announced she was going to marry Conor Barton.

Why? Sally's mother asked, trying hard to keep a straight face.

Because, Sally explained, he lives across the road.

Sally's mother and Denise Barton had a good laugh about this marriage of convenience. Won't it be great, they'd joked, we won't have the bother of getting to know new in-laws. There's only one fly in the ointment, Denise had said, I'm not sure that Conor has been told he's the chosen one.

At thirteen, Conor was sent away to boarding school (family tradition – Conor's father insisted) so he and Sally didn't see as much of one another, but they'd stayed in touch; he'd even asked her to his debs dance in September.

Wouldn't it be nice, she'd mused in front of Sally, if a romance developed between you two in the end?

Sally looked at her as if she was deranged.

Enough of the MUSHY stuff, Mum, she'd said.

It's September now, months now since the funeral and Sally has said nothing about Conor, nothing about how she's feeling. If Sally's mother so much as mentions Conor's name, Sally clams up.

I'm over it, she insists, but Sally's mother doesn't believe her.

She looks up grief advice websites, which urge patience and understanding. Make empathic statements – *I know you must be feeling* (fill in the blank) – but don't interrogate. Mostly they say, wait. But Sally's mother can't wait. She simply *has* to find out what's going on with her daughter. Which is why she's broken into Sally's tablet, having figured out her password. It's not hard; she's her mother, after all.

She scours Sally's 'notes' for an explanation of the dreads, but there is nothing, just the bald fact of them. Unlike her own teenage diary, which had been an adrenaline rush of voracious crushes, vengeful escape scenarios, and pregnancy scares. (The funny thing is the pregnancy scare that turned into Sally wasn't in her diary at all.)

The dreads: she repeats it again and again. It sounds squalid, like a Rastafarian's hair. She had a friend once who had venerated Bob Marley and grown his hair into locks to emulate his hero. He'd hold mad dope parties starting precisely at 4:20 pm on Marley's anniversary – 20 April. What made her think of him? She reads on. There is worse. Sally has been in the dreads since Conor's funeral – he had it too, she writes, as if it's some kind of infection they pass from one to another like venereal disease.

But what is it? Despair? A feeling of emptiness? The kind of feeling that drives Sally's mother out running every night, pounding the pavements so her heartbeat is loud as a drum in her chest, so that she can be sure her heart is in the right place.

She turns to Sally's grandmother.

'What do I do? What is she afraid of?'

Nana is sixty-nine and knows a thing or two about dread, the common-or-garden variety. Two years ago she found a lump in her neck. She's got the all-clear, prognosis good, but all the chemical blasting in the world can't exterminate the dread of the next lump. Or the dread of the next piece of bad news. The friend with a dicky heart who suddenly can't go up the stairs without stopping for air half-way up, or the brother-in-law who's fallen prey to some lingering nervous disease that will close up his throat in the end. The remembered dread of a violent man. Or the present dread of looking at the world that no longer seems to include her – people mesmerized by the screens in their palms, and no one talking to anyone anymore. The fear of all the things she can't fathom and the fear of no longer being here to try. Oh yes, Sally's grandmother knows about dread.

'Has she spoken to *you*?' Sally's mother asks urgently.

'Oh Gracie, she's gone beyond confiding in her old Nana. It's probably boyfriend trouble.'

'There *is* no boyfriend ...' Sally's mother says.

'There's always a boyfriend,' Sally's grandmother says, 'you should know that.'

Sally's mother grimaces.

'She's just lost her little friend,' Nana says.

'But it's not just Conor, there's something else.'

'She's not pregnant, is she?' Sally's grandmother couldn't face that again. Gracie nearly three months gone before she realized and then refusing to name the father. (Probably because she'd slept with more than one fella when she was haring about Europe.) She's often scrutinized Sally for genetic cues. Her sallow skin, those brown eyes? Definitely Mediterranean, she'd say.

'No,' Sally's mother says sighing.

And before Sally's grandmother can respond, her daughter launches into a salvo: 'There's no shortage of things it could be. Suicidal thoughts, slut-shaming, the housing crisis, migrants, climate change, Trump, nuclear war ...'

Sally's grandmother recalls civil defence leaflets dropping though the letter box when she was a kid. Lurid cartoons of burnt faces and families cowering behind torn-down doors set against the wall like an indoor lean-to, eating baked beans out of the tin. Get ready to meet your maker, *her* mother used to say, the Bay of Pigs, the mushroom cloud. *That* was dread. It was the Rooskies then ...

'It's the Rooskies now,' Sally's mother says.

Nana realizes she has spoken aloud.

'And what did you say to her?'

'Nothing, what can I say? She'll know I've gone through her tablet, she'll never trust me again.'

'Just tell her everything's going to be alright.'

Like you did, Sally's mother thinks sourly. When she'd got pregnant with Sally. Nana had acted like she was grief-stricken, but it was new life, wasn't it? What was there to mourn? Then she turned relentless. Take the boat, and when Grace had said, never, Nana had softened and said – what about adoption? Give it up, she kept on saying, give it up or it'll ruin your life. Destroy the evidence is what Sally's mother heard.

'Is everything going to be alright?' she asks her mother now.

Sally's grandmother looks at her daughter and wonders – did I make her like this? So timid, so helpless? Where is the fearless girl Gracie used to be? Now she's out pounding the pavements in the name of health, when it's just another excuse to stick the earplugs in and run away. We couldn't do that, she thinks fiercely. We had to hold our nerve, stick with things.

'Oh for God's sake, lie then,' she says.

She thinks of all the lies she's told. Big and small. The biggest one to her husband, Denis, that old bastard.

'I don't know what to do.'

'Then do nothing,' Sally's grandmother hisses.

But Sally's mother can't do nothing.

Sally always knows when they're fighting, not that there's shouting and screaming, like a NORMAL family. If you interrupt one of their feuds, there's this scratchy silence, as if they've pulled the scab off a wound and then have to quickly put the crusty cap back on. You have to give them a chance to settle, to wipe an eye and clear a throat and LIE – *no, nothing wrong, you're imagining things,* that'll be Sally's mother. And Nana will say – *we're just chewing the fat.* Whatever THAT means. She loves her Nana, but she can be a PAIN, trying to boss Sally's Mum about as if she isn't a GROWN ADULT. But then Sally's Mum encourages it, acts like a little girl, all curled up and flinching as if Nana is going to – what, HIT her? When Sally was small, Nana used to threaten her with the wooden spoon, though she never used it. Never did your mother any harm, she would say, wagging it at Sally. Is that why her Mum never answers back? And another thing, she can't stand the way her Mum is always enquiring about how Sally FEELS, like a detective with a crush. And now there's all this Conor business, it's like GRIEF PORN with her, big doe eyes and pawing her arm as if she wants to get inside Sally's head and Sally wants to scream KEEP OUT. It's a TOTAL MESS in there ...

For days Sally's mother rehearses how she's going to introduce the topic. Each time she contemplates it, she can feel what she thinks of as her conscience rising as a lump in her throat. Go on, go, she urges herself, remembering all the recklessness of her youth – the one-night stands, the casual drug-taking, the relationship that had produced Sally, all of them marked by a bravado she has, somehow, lost. Then she just comes out with it.

'What are the dreads?'

It's like plunging from a high diving board into a cold pool, anticipating the shock of impact and not knowing if you'll survive it.

They're eating pizza and Sally halts mid-bite with strings of cheese trailing from her mouth.

'What did you say?' she says.

Before she can repeat it she sees on Sally's face the dawning realization of how she's come by the information. Sally screams and rages at her. How COULD you spy on me like that? Doesn't a person's PRIVACY mean anything to you? I will NEVER forgive you. That was the worst.

She even raises a hand to strike her and Sally's mother would have welcomed it, to tell the truth; she's not afraid of fists. Living with a violent father taught her that. She'd often stepped in between him and Nana. But talking to Sally, *really* talking to her, has induced real terror.

'What are they? Tell me!'

Sally packs her bag and goes to Nana's. She stays away for three nights until Nana's hot water rules got too much for her. Her long years as a widow have made Nana a slave to the immersion heater – only so much hot water to go around and when it's gone, it's gone. Sally's mother knows the refrain. *When I was growing up, we had a bath once a week and we shared the water, Missy. And **my** mother only had an outside lav and a tin bath in front of the fire. That was during the time of the Emergency.*

When she comes back, Sally's mother thinks it's all over.

'Couldn't stand the shower ban?' she asks.

'At least Nana isn't a spy,' Sally says and then seals her lips for three weeks, won't answer even the most banal question.

Sally's mother marvels at her iron-willed silence – she could have joined an enclosed order! No blandishments would shift her and Sally's mother thinks – well, it's peace and quiet, isn't this what every mother of a teenager longs for?

Then one evening there's a report on the TV in the kitchen about the amount of plastics in the ocean and how they're killing the wildlife.

'We've made such a mess of the world,' she ventures.

Sally throws her eyes to heaven.

'Oh, MUM!'

And that's all it takes, the ruin of the world, to get them talking about the dreads.

'It's just …' Sally starts, 'it's what it's like to be a teenager now. And YOU can never know what that's like.'

'But Conor had them, is that why he …'

'Don't Mum, don't GO there …'

'I just don't want you –'

'MUM,' Sally says.

'But is it why …?'

Sally pushes the kitchen chair back. It scrapes noisily on the floor.

'YOU only want to know that to make sure it won't happen to me.'

'No, it's just I don't want it to happen to you because I never bothered to ask.'

'No, Mum, you're looking for GUARANTEES that I can't give you.'

'I worry –'

'That's your JOB.'

'But –'

'You have your secrets, don't you?'

Sally's mother finds herself blushing. She feels hot-faced, caught out.

Paulie Meacham is her secret. Glorious dope head. Last she'd heard he was living in Morocco, probably with the same worldly possessions he'd had when she knew him: an army surplus rucksack and a motor bike. It wouldn't surprise her. Why does she always presume people's natural drift is downwards? Africa he'd once said to her, last place on earth that hasn't been contaminated by tourism. Maybe he's sold out and is running a golf resort in Agadir? But she really can't see it. Paulie loved idleness, it was his main charm. He was a spendthrift with time. That was his seduction. Not the drugs or his ill-kempt good looks. His heavy blonde hair, his speckled chin, his crinkly well-meaning eyes. No, it was the fact that he lived so lightly, had nothing bearing down on him. No parents to please or duties to take on. No notion of expectation. He was playing at life. He was called a drop-out, though it seemed to the teenage Grace that he was the opposite – fully immersed in life, living it for its own sake, each day unspooling into lazy drinking and even lazier smoking, listening to music, walking the streets at 4 am, sleeping till noon, while she punched a clock at the dry-cleaner's.

The months she spent with Paulie Meacham seemed golden, afternoons in empty pubs, riding pillion to the sea on midweek afternoons, making love on a picnic rug in a burrow in the sand dunes, seagrass whistling in their ears. It was winter – of course, Paulie was an off-season man – then back on the bike to his place, a tiny nest of a bed-sit, on the return of a big old house that he kept surprisingly clean. A strange mix of Spartan and cosy. What he lived on, how he survived, she had no idea. The dole, she supposed, casual work here and there, humping for bands, probably dealing. She never asked. I'm a simple man, he used to say. And he was a man, she thought, his own man at twenty-six. Looking back on it she thought theirs was not really like love at all; it was like its aftermath, a tried and fond companionship. Not really romantic, but heartfelt. She could still feel it, here in her breastbone.

In the end, though, she'd finished with him, otherwise she'd have drowned in his gorgeous aimlessness. For the break-up she'd manufactured a newly discovered sense of ambition, a dirty word for Paulie.

College? he'd queried. It's all a con. Two-bit diplomas not worth the paper they're written on. And all to trap you in the glorious rat race.

She knew about Sally then, or at least the pregnancy but she wouldn't, couldn't do that to Paulie, pin him down, and, anyway, it might, conceivably, have been that Greek bloke in the hostel in Paris or the fella on the Holyhead ferry.

And college wasn't just a line for Paulie. After Sally was born, she did go to college, with her mother's help, so, retrospectively, she'd made a truth out of a lie.

It's not just ONE feeling, one thing, the dreads are a wave, but bigger, a TSUNAMI, one of those GINORMOUS curling tubes that hovers overhead and you're like a TINY little surfer about to be SWALLOWED up and if you enter it and it curls around you, you'd be afraid you wouldn't get out in time, before it CRASHES on top of you, but sometimes you think it'd be a good thing if it did, you might BREAK the surface that way and burst into something cleaner, purer, at the other side, but if it did crash, you'd be destroyed, SMASHED into little pieces, vomited up on the shore, but there is no shore only the curling inside of the wave and NO light at the end of the tunnel, it's like it sucks you in but it wants to spit you out, it wants you and wants to EXPEL you and you feel the same way, you want to it to crash so you won't feel the WAITING, WAITING for the splashy axe to fall but the dreads have so filled you up that you can't imagine not having them either, without them what would be left of ... YOU?

Once a year Nana visits the cemetery. Not on the anniversary, mind. She doesn't believe in that stuff. Dressing the grave, whoever heard of such nonsense! There's no dressing up naked death. Most people imagine it's Denis's grave she visits. Why would she do that? That old bastard never gave her a moment's happiness. It's Gracie's father she attends to. If Denis had known about it, he'd have killed her. Literally killed her. That's been her biggest dread.

She speaks to Maurice, even though he's gone twenty years now, during that terrible summer when Gracie went travelling and came back ... well, enough said. She finds herself still explaining, reiterating why she wouldn't leave Denis for him. Because she tells him, it would have ruined him. He was a good man whose children looked up to him. No one looked up to Denis Penrose, she says, and my life was already ruined by then. Gracie was her revenge, a way of clawing something precious from the shit.

When she remembers the feelings that produced Gracie, it still makes her blush, or is it glow? If she knew, Gracie would laugh the idea off. Love-child, she'd say disbelievingly, as if unbridled passion were confined to her generation. We knew passion too, she wants to say to Gracie, but then she'd have to explain herself to her daughter and there's too much water under the bridge for that now.

She brings Maurice the news. Our Gracie, she tells him, so unlike either of us — where did she come from? Worried sick over Sally, when there's no need. When Sally is keeping her own counsel and holding her own. When she's done, she visits Conor's grave. It's too early for a headstone so the plot is a mess of raw turned earth. There's the remains of a bouquet of dead flowers lying on the clods, a lattice of spindly headless stems. Only the cellophane trumpet survives, flapping in the wind like the shiver of a secret.

SEIZE THE DAY

When Dr Dundon delivered the verdict on Dom, Rosalie was aghast, because everything had seemed to be going so well. He was a spiffy oncologist with tapered wings of white at his temples, a healthy bronzed complexion thanks to some Mediterranean resort, and cufflinks. His office on the fifth floor had a picture window that looked out on to a golf course. Maybe that's why Rosalie always thought he had just come off the tee, breezy, wind-blown.

'It's carpe diem, Mr Comer, ' he said.

'Fish of the day, you mean,' Dom said and the pair of them laughed. Dom wheezily, Dundon with a false guffaw. So, Rosalie thought, this is how it's going to be, two old boys trading classical code.

Afterwards, she and Dom walked out into the car park into a day of blithe high summer. Fast-moving clouds pedalled across a blue sky, fuchsia dropped its bleeding lanterns on the car roof, everything around them seemed intent on destination. Dom halted by the passenger door. He'd already given up driving, didn't trust himself. He looked over the red roof at her.

'I wonder,' he said musingly as if he were on his own, 'if I did the right thing marrying you.'

It was a slap in the face, particularly from Dom who had never in all their years together been consciously cruel. But, shocking as it was, Rosalie felt she deserved it.

When she and Dom were first married, she used to ask herself that self-same question. Had she made a terrible mistake? Had she been seduced by Dom's persuasive camaraderie and his ability to wear his burdens lightly, one of which came to include her? When her doubts overcame her discretion she would ask Dom directly, for which now she felt only remorse. He would laugh it off, or crush her to him in a bruising hug as if he could squeeze those thoughts out of her. He'd always been a believer in the recuperative powers of sex, whereas she, when sad, found his touch only made her feel bleaker.

Now, in some strange reversal of their positions, Dom was grappling with the kind of doubts that had blighted her all along.

Her first thought, meanly, was – At last!

In the months to come, marrying her wasn't the only thing Dom wondered about. Should he have emigrated to Boston? His brother Philip had a construction company there and he'd offered to sponsor Dom when Ireland was going through the hard-pressed 80s. Should he have followed his original vocation and gone for the priesthood like his mother had wanted? Rosalie could imagine Dom as the pastor of a flock. She could see the ladies of the parish bringing casseroles to the presbytery door and Dom flirting mildly with them. Should they have tried for another child? (Even though it was Dom who'd ruled that out. Don't want to lose you again, he'd said, as if Rosalie had been absent during those early years with Caroline, whereas she had been uselessly, painfully present.)

Oh yes, and should he have declared his love for Cora Moran?

Cora was the reason she and Dom were together. They had met at a teaching college party. Cora was a classmate of his and she'd brought Rosalie along after befriending her in the student cafeteria. Even though she wasn't a student, Rosalie ate there to get away from the straight-laced older set in Admin. She had a job on the switch. The closest she'd got to college was saying 'Hello, St Catherine's', and plugging people into one another.

Cora was willowy with russet shoulder-length hair and a face that was just short of beautiful. She was one of those intense democratic kind of girls who was guilty about her opportunities and was always trying to compensate for them. She took Rosalie on as one of her projects.

'Cora!' Dom had said that night coming up to them in the kitchen, 'Introduce me! Who's this?'

Rosalie got an impression of bushy beard and bearish warmth as Dom nudged in close. No one had ever said *who's this* in that tone about her before. It was a pick-up line; she knew that much. But out of Dom's mouth it rang sincere. More than sincere. It was like being seen afresh. Seen. He offered her a lift home on the back of his scooter. They put-putted through the rain-slicked streets, he chattering constantly though most of his words were stolen by the wind.

After they got together, Dom had told her he'd always had a bit of a thing for Cora. Rosalie had presumed their relationship was fond, matey, like honorary room-mates and she'd discounted Dom's confession as one of those inconsequential confidences with no danger attached that new couples share. She'd certainly never suspected any subterfuge. They had lost touch with Cora anyway. After getting married, she and Dom had moved to the suburbs while Cora had got hitched to some musician and continued with a student life in the city. Cora's marriage hadn't lasted but by then their lives and hers seemed to have irretrievably forked. Not only had she and Dom not seen Cora, but her name hadn't been mentioned in decades.

But with Dom's declaration, Rosalie realized that Cora had been with them all along.

'I'm going to write to her,' he said shortly after Dr Dundon's verdict.

'Really?' Rosalie asked trying to sound only mildly interested. 'Are you sure you want to dredge all that old stuff up again? Wasn't it just a crush?'

'Oh no. It was much more than that.'

The old Dom would have considered such an admission as bad form.

'Anyway, it's time I put my affairs in order.'

She looked up, thinking that he was being ironic. That this was the old jokey Dom. The one who had cackled at the oncologist's name. (What a handle for a cancer specialist – Dr Done-Done!) Who had given his tumour a name – Vladimir – and made light of it in company. But after that day in the car park, Dom had became deadly serious. There was no more joking.

'Time to make my peace,' he said softly.

But to Rosalie it sounded like a war cry. When he was finished with his ancient love life, who would he turn to next?

Caroline, that's who. With his new taste for honesty, would he tell Caroline how her mother had to be persuaded and cajoled into staying when she was still a baby? Or divulge that looking after an infant had terrified and terrorized her, an infant who would only relent when in her father's arms? Or repeat Rosalie's conviction that she was not up to mothering? When Rosalie remembered this, she felt her own scorn rising for that whining young woman who had been her.

It was Dom who had saved her. Saved her from her worst self when she had been at the point of giving up and running away. It was what he did; he chivvied people along and he was good at it.

'This too will pass,' he used to say every time he had to unburden Rosalie of the angry bundle that was Caroline, all peeved red face and flailing fists. He'd silently wipe away the tears glistening on her cheeks and take over the night feed, sending Rosalie back to bed.

Caroline had been put on the bottle after a few days of failed breastfeeding. Rosalie remembered how greedily rough she had been, scrabbling at her nipple, sucking and sucking and coming up empty. She's a poor feeder, the post-natal nurse said. That was the simple explanation. But Rosalie believed otherwise. She felt she was poisoning Caroline, that her milk was tainted with malevolent sadness. Sadness about what she didn't know. She was a new mother, with a good man by her side who would never harm her, and yet in the midst of all that wholesome newness, she felt old and grief-stricken.

'How's Dad?' Caroline asked when she made her weekly call.

Skype reduced her to a dreamy, drugged-up image in slow motion. For Rosalie Cairns, Australia, was a low unmade bed, a set of Ikea shelves and a small cell-like window high up in the wall. Hanging from the window catch there was often a large black wet suit like a menacing, beached mammal. It was a permanent reminder that Caroline was not alone in the box-room. Sometimes, a haunch in shorts would cross unremarked behind her on the screen. Greg, Rosalie presumed, though she'd never seen his face.

'Bright and breezy, I suppose.' Caroline smiled, willing Rosalie to agree. Takes after her father, Rosalie thought, I've turned them both into believers in small talk.

'Should I be thinking of coming?' Caroline asked leaning into the screen as if they were sharing a secret. Greg must be about. But that couldn't be it. Any time before when Greg was in the room, Caroline acted like he wasn't there. Rosalie realized with a soft shock that Caroline was trying to get closer to her.

Dom had absolutely forbidden her to tell Caroline he only had months. In that alone, his denial held. Let her have her ignorant happiness while she can, he said, you'll know when the time is right.

'No,' she said decisively to Caroline. 'No need for that. He's just going through a rough patch.'

When the hospice nurses suggested the morphine pump, Rosalie imagined all the puns the old Dom would have come up with. *Pump it up, Sista! Going to the well for morphine.* The hospice nurse instructed Dom on how to use it.

'Just press the red button whenever you need a hit.'

'I've been hit already, love,' he said.

Rosalie had to curb the instinct to chastize, to warn against self-pity.

The pain relief was a double-edged sword. The morphine gave him terrible dreams. When he was awake and making sense he would say that he was constantly underwater in these dreams. There were sharks making for him, their jaws working, serrated teeth bared, eyes like bloodied gashes. The room was a tank he was condemned to patrol pursued by them. He was the fish-food, already in dandruff flakes. He showed no distress while having these dreams but when he awoke, they seemed to haunt him. Ordinary things would startle him. The shiver of the blinds, or the swirl of the net curtains in the breeze from the open window, would spook him as if he'd been momentarily yanked back into the nightmare, as if the sharks were still there beneath the skin of the room and were more real to him than anything else – her, Caroline. Even Cora.

It took several weeks for Cora to reply to Dom's letter. As well it might, Rosalie thought. Imagine getting a declaration of love from a dying man three decades too late. When she did reply, it was to Rosalie.

Dear Rosalie, it read, *I understand that Dominic is gravely ill. He has asked me to visit but I want to make sure that this would be suitable for you. I'm so sorry that we should have to meet again in such circumstances. Kind regards, Cora Temperley.*

Rosalie's first thought was that Cora had found a much nicer name. Then when she read between the lines, she realized that Cora wasn't really asking her permission to visit. She spoke as if their meeting 'in such circumstances' was a foregone conclusion.

By then, Dom was in bed full-time and there were two nurses, Marion and Orla looking after him. He'd wanted to die at home and Rosalie had turned the sitting room into a sick-room and hired a bed for downstairs. This was the part Rosalie had been dreading. The final furlong. Something about death had always made her giddy. Not laugh-out loud giddy, but flighty, like an excitable horse shying to be out of the stalls, wanting the race to be over as soon as the klaxon had been sounded. Dom had never understood this about her. He'd never lost anyone close; both of his parents were still living. Unlike Rosalie whose mother died when she was twelve. She remembered the parting as a kind of maternal crash course, her mother issuing instructions from a hospital bed, some of it useful, most of it not – her recipes for Christmas mincemeat, how to clean the kitchen floor, what to do when her and Emer's periods came.

'You know your father,' she rasped. She was suspended in a kind of sling over the bed, her shrivelled breasts sagging limply under her nightie, her lips blistered. 'He'll be useless.'

She was right. Rosalie's father floundered. Even with two daughters who could cook and clean and knew where the tampons were. She and Emer had been there at the end, sleep-deprived and rapt, counting her mother's breaths until they stopped, while he was, of course, out of the room. Afterwards, they had had to clear out their mother's wardrobe and dressing table because he couldn't bear to part with her things. Auntie Mona told them to do it while he was out of the house, so six months after the funeral, they stuffed her mother's dresses and coats into large black refuse sacks and humped them over to the St Vincent de Paul shop in the next town. Not the local one, Mona warned, you don't want to see the neighbours swanning around in your mother's cast-offs.

When they opened the drawer of the bedside locker on her mother's side, Emer discovered an opened, half-smoked packet of Major. Coffin nails her mother used to call them as she gaily lit up. Rosalie remembered Emer sitting out on the steps by the back door and smoking her way through seven of them, one after the other.

'They're stale,' she said, making a sour face every time she inhaled. But she kept on smoking, lighting one from the fag end of the other in a grim relay. She offered one to Rosalie.

'Here,' she said, 'have a drag.'

But Rosalie didn't dare to. She was afraid, even then, of the contagion of death.

Cora arrived on a Saturday afternoon at precisely the pre-arranged time. When Rosalie opened the front door, Cora's composure deserted her immediately. Tears came before she opened her mouth. Rosalie steered her into the study off the hallway and shut the door so that Dom wouldn't hear the sounds of grief. It felt a suitably neutral place to receive Cora – Dom's computer, which had lain idle for weeks now, stared back at them. In its black reflection Rosalie could see the two of them, wife and ... what, she didn't know, what exactly was Cora?

She looked much the same as she had at those college parties thirty years ago. Her long hair was still rusty red, her skin pale; her figure intact. If she was thickening around the belly she'd hidden it well in a silk shirt the colour of green olives. Her age showed only in her face. Deep lines were scored in the papery skin around her mouth and eyes.

'I was in love with him too,' she said snuffling noisily.

Those were her first words. Oh God, Rosalie thought, here's another one who has dispensed with the niceties. 'I just never thought ...'

She smiled at Rosalie sardonically. 'What a waste!'

Everything shifted. A woman in her home declaring her love for her husband by proxy. As if Rosalie's life with Dom had been second best, some faint-hearted imitation. She was so angry she could barely speak. Eventually, she managed to say, 'Why don't I bring you to him?'

Cora followed her meekly. They crossed the hallway and went down the corridor to the sickroom. When they got to the door, Rosalie halted and placed a restraining hand on Cora's forearm.

'Don't be alarmed by his appearance. He's lost a lot of weight. And he tires quickly.' Then she opened the door and practically shoved Cora inside.

Let her have him now. See how she likes it.

Cora emerged two hours later. Two hours! Rosalie had paced from the kitchen to the breakfast room and back like a nervous matchmaker, sat in the nook under the framed David Hamilton poster, finding herself suddenly steeped in the time of her youth. Everyone of their age had a Hamilton; it was standard 1970s bed-sit fare. There was a whole series of posters, soft-focus photographs, usually of scantily dressed young women cavorting out in the countryside, in barns, or draped suggestively on bicycles. They were popular with girls because of the filmy, floaty clothes and appreciated by boys for their arty, thinly veiled lesbianism. Their Hamilton featured a lone girl in flowing garments and a floppy hat swinging from the low-hanging branch of a tree by her arms in a sun-dappled, flower-drenched meadow. Dom had insisted they keep it because it had been tacked to the walls of several flats Rosalie had lived in during their courtship. To save it from getting battered, he'd got it framed and in the intervening decades it had acquired vintage chic. (Except with Caroline. She had hooted with laughter when she discovered it had belonged to Rosalie. Really Mum? It's sort of chocolate boxy, isn't it? This was at a time when Caroline had posters of booted and snarling heavy metal bands pasted all over her bedroom walls and was angling for a tattoo.)

The sound of the sickroom door opening and closing roused Rosalie. She got up and went out into the hall. She wanted to head Cora off, didn't want to be put into the position of being her comforter or sharing reminiscences.

'Oh Rosalie,' Cora lamented. Her eyes were red and she fiddled nervously with her hair.

'It's so sad.'

Who is it sad for, Rosalie wanted to shout.

'I just wish I'd known.'

Rosalie couldn't help hearing blame in this. She helped Cora into her coat; her mane of hair fell over the fur collar like she was some feral émigré from a Russian novel. Rosalie didn't want to hear any more; she wanted rid of Cora.

'May I come again?' she asked on the doorstep.

She came several more times, always ringing beforehand to check if it was alright with Rosalie. After the first time, it became an unspoken agreement between that they wouldn't talk. Rosalie couldn't very well ask her how it was going between the pair of them, and Cora must have known from Rosalie's coolness the first time that she wouldn't welcome confidences. After her visits, Rosalie would tiptoe into the sickroom and Dom would smile at her sheepishly. She had to curb her tongue, had to stop herself asking in a curdled tone – How's love's young dream?

It was Cora who brought the dope. When she thrust the plastic baggie, complete with tobacco pouch and papers into her hand, Rosalie wondered where on earth she had got it. She couldn't imagine Cora in her muted mossy shirts and fur-trimmed jackets, doing a deal on the street.

'Did Dom ...?' Rosalie asked.

She shook her head. 'No, no, this was my idea.'

Rosalie cocked an enquiring eyebrow; were the pair of them ganging up on her now?

'In our time, we did a bit of this,' she said bashfully, 'with Fleetwood Mac's 'Rumours' playing in the background.'

That was the first and only time she reminisced in Rosalie's presence, or played up her prior association with Dom.

'I thought it might help with the pain. I know he has the morphine but this might be gentler. Maybe save him from the nightmares?'

Rosalie was annoyed that Dom had told Cora about them, and more annoyed that Cora had acted on it. She couldn't help feeling rebuked.

'Well, it's very thoughtful,' she said taking the package, 'but I'll have to ask the nurses.'

'Of course,' Cora said.

Rosalie wondered what she and Dom did in the sickroom with no one to witness. Marion, the day nurse always took a cigarette break when Cora arrived, so Rosalie couldn't ask her what she wanted to know.

Did they talk? If so, what about?

Then one day, quite by accident, really, Rosalie found out.

A call came on the house phone for Marion. It was some kind of emergency, the caller said, one of Marion's kids was ill or something. All Rosalie knew about Marion was that she was a young mother and often spent her breaks issuing instructions over her mobile to a child-minder. This might have been the child-minder calling but Rosalie didn't hear the details. Since Dom had got sick she hadn't got space in her head for the minutiae of other people's problems. Something was up, that's all she knew. She headed automatically for the sickroom, and had opened the door when she remembered that Cora was visiting.

That was when she saw what they did. There was Cora, bending over Dom, her shirt unbuttoned, her bare breast in her hand and Dom's face buried in her flesh. She couldn't see his face but the expression on Cora's was unmistakable. It was ecstasy. Rosalie shut the door quickly, then rushed towards the front door. Marion was standing in her usual spot in the garden, among the flower-beds, smoking fiercely.

'It's for you,' she called, her voice sounding thready, with what Marion would probably mistake for grief.

Marion halted in mid-inhale. Did she know what was going on, Rosalie wondered, and why didn't she stop it.

'Call for you on the landline,' Rosalie repeated.

Marion made an exaggeratd grimace.

'Sorry, sorry!' she gushed. 'My mobile went down the loo this morning.'

The next time Cora visited, Rosalie accompanied her to the sickroom.

'Oh let me,' Cora protested, 'you must be exhausted.'

But Rosalie firmly demurred. She pulled up a chair for Cora and took Marion's place on the other side of the bed, telling Marion to take a break. Dom was very out of it that day – delirious, in the grip of the sea-creatures, Rosalie was sure. Neither of them mentioned Cora's last visit. Rosalie wasn't even sure if Cora realized what she had seen, so transported had she been. Cora didn't stay too long – there wasn't much point, really – and when she was leaving she brushed Dom's inert hand with her fingers, no more. Rosalie followed her out. As usual, Cora hovered, as if she had something to say.

But Rosalie was having none of it. She linked Cora down the corridor. The door to the breakfast room was open and Cora halted, her face alight. 'Oh look, you have that poster!'

She stepped in, uninvited.

'That brings me back,' she said. 'I had the exact same one in my bedroom. I used to love it, though it's not politically correct to admit that now. The more undressed ones are considered to be soft porn these days.'

'Dom loved this one, too,' Rosalie said, though she didn't want to be drawn into talk of the old days. 'Maybe he's been mentally undressing her all these years.'

'Oh no,' Cora said, 'quite the opposite. He joked with me one night that the girl's hands had been nailed to the tree. And any time after that, I just couldn't bear to look at it without thinking of that.'

Dom made it easy for her in the end, slipping in and out of consciousness so that what she said to him was reduced to platitudinous lies. *Everything's going to be alright* and *Caroline's on her way*. He tried to hold out for her but Caroline didn't make it in time. Rosalie had spared her the death-bed and protected her from Dom's new honesty.

'Was he happy at the end, Mum?' Caroline asked, meaning the weeks she'd missed by Rosalie's prevarication.

'Yes,' Rosalie told her, 'absolutely. You know your Dad. He'd made his peace.'

And it was nearly the truth. He was happy till the end, and then he wasn't.

Cora didn't come to the funeral. Rosalie was relieved. She'd had visions of dramatic demonstrations – single roses flung on to the coffin – which she'd have to explain to poor Dom's parents, not to speak of Caroline. She probably visits his grave and leaves tokens and has her private time with him now, but Rosalie doesn't know because she hasn't been back since the funeral. Graveyards give her the creeps.

After several weeks, Caroline had to go back to Australia. They parted, dry-eyed.

'I have to go,' Caroline said, 'you understand that, don't you. Mum? My life ... Greg is there.'

Rosalie does understand, really. The uneasiness between them has nothing to do with emigration, the new life elsewhere. It has to do with the unlived life of her infancy that Caroline doesn't know about and Rosalie can't make up for.

'You'll be fine, Mum,' Caroline said patting her on the shoulder at the airport and sounding just like her father.

With Caroline gone, Rosalie finds herself at a loss, wandering the house, standing in the sitting room, with its sickroom hangover, and staring out the bay window at the straggling roses, the pocket-sized front lawn going to clover. She should get busy, she tells herself, setting the sitting room to rights. She's been putting it off ever since the men – or engineers, that's what they're called, bed engineers – came to take Dom's rented bed apart. It was a noisy procedure. They made a tubular gonging sound as if they were dismantling scaffolding inside the house.

She steps into the dining room. Most of the sitting room furniture was moved in here to make way for Dom's bed. Armchairs jostle against one another, the sofa looks bullied. The table has been pushed against the far wall to make way and the chairs upended on top of it, so that the room looks like an auction sale or an out-of-season restaurant. Rosalie can't quite imagine either room ever being itself again.

She starts by moving the sofa. It's hard work pushing and shoving a sofa on your own. She should wait for help – though exactly whom would she ask? – but this is Rosalie's way. To push on. She is glad of the exertion, the heaving and pushing, like childbirth without the pain. When she has manoeuvred the sofa into position, she notices something stuck down between one of the cushions and the arm. When she investigates, she finds it's Cora's dope stash. She is about to throw it out, then she thinks better of it. Instead, she brings it out to the breakfast room, boils the kettle and makes tea. She's only ever watched other people do this, though she remembers boys in her youth who could roll single-handed, or could steer cars with their elbows while they skinned up. But she needs both hands to crumble the spidery green leaves covered with flower dust, add the moist tobacco and kiss the papers together into an inept single skin joint. She smokes it, then rolls a second one, sitting in the breakfast nook with the hippie paraphernalia around her. She inhales and gazes at the Hamilton poster and, after a while, she swears she can see the marks on the swinging girl's hands where the nails must have been.

LOST PROPERTY

Carmel Dromey stands with a knot of people at the gates of Lichfield Cottage. Through the bars she can see the long low house with its church-shaped dormer windows and gingerbready eaves, which the *Examiner* called the Strawberry Hill gothic style. Carmel is a hungry reader of property supplements and she has often passed this house and lusted after it. It reminds her of ... but no, she's not going there. The viewing is set for eleven, but there is no sign of the auctioneer. He arrives ten minutes late, just as the group has begun getting restive, tired of smiling at one another reassuringly as if they were queue comrades at a bus stop.

'Apologies, folks,' Richie Barker (according to his lanyard) says breezily as he walks among them with a sheaf of brochures under his armpit. He's electively bald but with a blue five o'clock shadow where the regrowth is starting, so he's like a baby man. He's dressed in a tight navy suit and a white shirt. But his skewed knitted tie and trainers give off a dress-down-Friday vibe. He pushes open the elaborate double gates of Lichfield and ushers the group into the gravelled driveway. Behind him, Carmel gets the impression of a tended leafy garden.

'Well, folks,' Richie says, 'as you know we have a charming historic property here. Once home of George Boole, world-famous mathematician and father of computer science.

Founder of Boolean mathematics.' Richie pauses. 'You know, the and/or option you use for internet searches?'

Carmel does know. She has measured out her middle age in night classes. On Renaissance art and Greek myths and poetry. Her most recent foray into adult ed has been 'Historic Corkonians'. (When she saw the course advertised, she'd read it as Cork Onions. 'Know your Cork Onions', they should call it, she'd thought.) George Boole was on the syllabus. It's the first class she's taken since being made a widow. She likes that designation – makes her sound statuesque.

*

It's three years since she lost Ray. Ray, once beloved, who plunged the family into bankruptcy in 2017 when his chain of betting shops went belly-up. He'd had to go off to England for a year, leaving Carmel on her own to face the music. He'd forced the sale of her beloved house – oh yes, it felt like hers, all hers, even though it was called 'Carmond', their names jammed together in forced congress. Ray had sunk the proceeds of the sale into a penthouse apartment in the Elysian Tower in Carmel's name. She'd lived there in solitary splendour while he weathered his year of financial exile in a bed-sit in Reading. And she was still stuck up there five years later.

'How bad,' her friend Jacinta had said to her. 'I wouldn't mind being given a fancy apartment for my very own.'

But Carmel didn't see the penthouse like that. It was simply where Ray had installed her.

Nothing was right about the place. The coffee table had knife-edges, the steel cold kitchen was full of traps – such as the toothed waste disposal unit. The occluded handles of the cabinets seemed designed to thwart Louise's twins, suggesting entry, then denying it. Harry could be persuaded to watch Paw

Patrol on his iPad but the floor-to-ceiling plate-glass windows in the cavernous living room distressed Megan, who was one of those kids who wouldn't look you in the eye. She'd howled and howled the first time she'd seen the vertiginous view. Even with the curtains drawn, the child was mesmerically drawn to the awful drop. Just knowing it was there was enough to set off a tantrum. Louise would have to carry her off, a furious ball of rage. Carmel could hear her shrieks echoing down the elevator shaft, all seventeen floors of it, and found it chimed with a desolate protest of her own.

Ray Junior did his visiting duties standing up. He paced up and down as if he was waiting to be brought into a boardroom to be fired. Carmel could feel his disapproval. I didn't choose this, she wanted to say to him, none of this is my fault. But Ray Junior's disenchantment seemed so savagely intransigent that it silenced her. After his brief visits, he would trek down to the underground garage at the Elysian, and start Ray's Audi, another useless thing in her name.

Carmel had never learned to drive. It terrified her. Her father had been a forklift operator. Once when her mother was ill, he'd taken her to work with him. He'd done tricks with the forks, spearing a tower of empty pallets and raising them up and down on the mast. Then he put her sitting in the cab. Through the windscreen she could see the prongs protruding like a pair of medieval battering rams. Every time she imagined driving, that was what she saw.

After Louise was born, Ray had urged her to take lessons.

'I'll buy you a little run-around,' he'd said.

Her school pal Dee said she'd take her on practice runs in the Tesco car park after-hours.

'Look, girl, if I can drive, any fecking eejit can.'

But Carmel had baulked. She couldn't justify her fear of driving to herself, so how could she to anyone else?

When Ray Junior emerged from underground he would throw the car keys into the glass bowl on the kitchen island with the clatter of gunfire.

'You know what that car really needs,' he'd mutter darkly.

'What?' Carmel asked.

'The fuck driven out of it.'

But Ray Junior wouldn't oblige. He on principle. If he didn't approve of the grandeur of Carmel's accommodations, he was contemptuously ashamed of his father.

Only Amy, in France, was intrigued by Carmel's new situation. All she wanted was for Carmel to steer her through the penthouse on the laptop so that she could take it all in.

*

Richie leads them into the hallway where he sets down a clipboard on a delicate-legged, half-moon table and asks them to sign in. To frighten off the rubber-neckers, Carmel suspects, those only here for a good snoop. Not like her.

'The Booles moved to "Lichfield" because it was close to Blackrock train station, and Professor Boole could take the train directly to college,' Richie is saying. 'The station is long gone but the prospective owner will have access to the lovely Leeside greenway, a terrific amenity.'

'I suppose you know,' Carmel says as she stoops to sign her name, 'that Boole's wife was very clever too. She was a self-taught mathematician.'

'Is that so,' Richie says. He swirls the clipboard around and stares at her signature.

'Dromey? Are you anything to do with the betting shop crowd?'

*

Lost Property

There was no escape from it. For the year Ray was away on his bankruptcy penance, Carmel had kept her sights low and her head lower. When she went out, she felt she should wear a black, fine mesh veil with tiny rosettes on it like a Mafia widow, though at that stage it was 'Carmond' she was in mourning for, not Ray. She thought it best to give up the night classes even though she was half-way through 'The Victorian Poets'. But she couldn't be sure who might show. The last thing she needed was one of Ray's former employees with time on their hands and a grudge.

Alone in the tower and without the crutch of further education, Carmel had had plenty of time to wonder how things had got to this pass. Had she missed something in the run-up to the collapse of the Dromey empire? Had Ray sent up flares about his financial distress? But no, that wasn't his style. He'd never been one to bring work home. Let me take care of the money, he used to say. So she did. He was the breadwinner. When she wanted something, he'd unfold a wad of cash and hand it over. She was a home-maker, that was her end of the bargain.

Ray had inherited the betting shops from his father so Carmel had always presumed business came naturally to him. Until the night when he declared 'Carmond' would have to go.

'I've had sleepless nights over this,' he'd said, reaching out and squeezing her hand as they sat in the sitting room with the TV sound turned off. 'I'm a wreck.'

When he said it, she saw the bruised shadows under his eyes but up until then she hadn't noticed anything amiss.

'I'm doing this for all of us,' he'd said pleadingly as he cleared a patch in the middle of her dahlias in the front garden for the auctioneer's placard and drove the post home. That night, the wrought iron front gate was stolen from the house. An opportunistic theft, Ray said, they saw the sign. It upset Carmel that her beloved house had been flogged off looking like a child missing its front tooth. But the worst part of the whole business was that Ray had treated 'Carmond' as a strippable asset and in the process made her feel like an over-the-hill pole-dancer. In one fell swoop he had dismantled the meaning of their life together.

She and Ray had been together since her teens. She'd quit school at fifteen to look after her father and brothers after her mother died. But as the boys got older she'd got a part-time job during school hours on the till at Dromey's. The money came in handy given her father's precarious employment, particularly after the accident. But it wasn't just that. She didn't want to become a maiden aunt, the kind of woman who grew old and whiskery playing mother to children who weren't her own and tending an aging father who'd turn her into a spinster.

'Your poor mother was a saint,' her father used to lament.

And I won't be a martyr, Carmel would vow silently.

Ray had interviewed her for the job. Within a year she was going out with him. He'd made all the running. He'd pacified his father who thought anyone born in the Buildings must be a slapper or a gold-digger. He'd seen off her father's resistance to a Pres boy sniffing around her by insisting on paying for the wedding reception at the Imperial. He'd arranged everything; well, he *was* the boss's son. Carmel had distrusted Ray's certainty about her, about them. But she'd surrendered to it, happy to be swept up in an upward movement out of the Buildings. No one had ever fought for her before. That must mean something, she'd thought.

It wasn't that they'd grown apart over the years. Ray had expended all his romantic energy in the early years on winning her, and having won her, providing for her. He showed his love in his financial constancy not with displays of affection. So when she'd come in from a class agog with her latest discoveries – the mysteries of Pompei, the splendours of Rome – he'd look up from his recliner and say, 'It's alright, Carm, I don't need a blow-by-blow.' It wasn't cruelty; it was a kind of heedlessness. Despite all their years together, he'd never properly understood that the night courses were her badges of honour, her empire.

The longer she lived alone in the Elysian, the more Carmel suspected that her marriage might not survive the break. But after his year of purdah, Ray came back and where else was he going to go? There were two of them then, rattling around in the glass palace. Ray no longer had work to go to so he was under her feet all day. It annoyed her that he kept on admiring all the things she found disorienting about the penthouse – the lofty, disabling views, the merciless appurtenances. Oh this is nifty, he would say tricking with the wall-mounted can opener, or trying out the waste disposal unit. He delighted in swinging from the hanging rattan chair which had had to be unhooked from a beam in the ceiling every time the children came. A basket case, she thought sourly. If he felt bad about the bankruptcy, it didn't show. He seemed unscathed by the experience. He adapted to the lifestyle of an unemployed man with the same appetite that he had run the business. He rose late and watched television in the afternoon with the drapes drawn. Sports channels, of course, his former occupation now a full-time hobby. Horse-racing, European football, mixed martial arts. It was like the Coliseum in the echoey living room, the air filled with the sounds of male combat.

She'd thought that once Ray was back, normal service would resume.

'Can we get it back?' she asked him.

'Get what back?'

'Carmond'.'

'Have you understood nothing?' he said.

'It was the only place I felt myself.' She knew she sounded whiney but it was true.

'Oh please,' Ray said, 'look around you. Most people would kill for this.'

It was then she directed him towards the second bedroom. She would never pardon him for allowing her to live in a fool's paradise.

Lockdown had been a blessing at first. Suddenly everyone was living like her and Ray – under siege. Masked and gloved, she went to Aldi in the basement once a week to do the shop. Ray had taken up running in Reading. He did a loop around Centre Park Road under cover of dark. Sheathed in black Lycra, he looked like a portly cat burglar. They spoke to the kids over Zoom. Louise lined the twins up in front of the screen and made them wave. Even Megan accidentally caught Carmel's eye once or twice and didn't flinch. Amy had started giving Carmel French lessons online in preparation for the time when she and Ray would be able to visit. They seemed to be approaching a kind of normality, or as normal as things could be living in an eyrie in a time of plague with a broken husband who'd failed her.

But then Ray upped and died.

Well, no, there was nothing up about it because he'd been downed by Covid, like an aircraft shot out of the sky. In all her years nursing her kids, Carmel had never seen anything like it. It was like watching someone drown in clogged mud. She could see his outstretched hands waving like a swimmer in difficulties but she could do nothing to help. The ambulance men who came to take him away were shrouded in plastic head to toe with masks, shower caps on their heads, pampootees on their feet like police pathologists from a TV show visiting a crime scene.

'Don't leave me,' Ray had said to her as the doors of the ambulance were slammed shut.

She succumbed to a stifling passivity after Ray was taken away. She didn't, couldn't fight for him. She blamed the Covid restrictions which meant she couldn't visit him in hospital and when she phoned the ward, no one answered. Three days after he was admitted, she had to say goodbye on the mobile phone before he was intubated. She looked into his eyes and saw an alien terror behind his mask. She had to do all the talking because he couldn't. She told him she loved him. What else was she going to say with a nurse in blue gloves holding the phone at his end eavesdropping on every word?

It wasn't a lie. She had loved him, but it just wasn't in her to forgive him. Even after he was gone. There was an impoverished funeral in an empty church with just the family. Amy watched remotely. Carmel knew Ray had bought a grave plot but she didn't want to have a permanent monument to him. Wasn't she living in that? She opted for cremation. When the urn came, she tipped the ashes down the waste disposal unit.

*

The visitors scatter through the house once Richie has finished his spiel. Carmel is in the main bedroom alone, luxuriating in the summery light which bathes the entire house in a benign graciousness, when Richie, on his rounds, catches up with her. By then she has successfully imagined herself into Lichfield. Into the lovely living room with the French windows, the Persian runner and the grand piano, the rustic kitchen with the Aga and the country pine table; or being abed here in the mornings, adrift on the soft white bed linen, the bowing branches of wisteria crowding at the window. She sees her reflection in the gold-framed mirror over the mantelpiece and she doesn't look out of place. Then a thought strikes her.

'I wonder if this is the room he died in?' she says to Richie.

He looks at her askance.

'Boole, I mean.'

'Oh,' Richie says and tries to jolly his way out of it. 'I'm afraid that's not the kind of info we have on our specs.'

'You know there were those who said Mrs Boole was responsible for her husband's demise.'

'You don't say.'

'The professor got soaked in a downpour after walking to the campus. He delivered a full day's lectures in wet clothes. When he came down with a cough and a cold, Mrs Boole called in a doctor who was a believer in hydrotherapy.'

'Hydro – ?' A twin crease, like a ghostly coin slot, appears on Richie's brow.

'It's the principle of treating the illness with the cause,' Carmel explains. She's warming to her subject. 'So it was the doctor who suggested Boole be wrapped in wet bed sheets as a cure, not Mrs Boole.'

'Poor sod!' Richie mutters.

'Oh come on,' she appeals to him. 'Boole was a brilliant mathematician studying logic. Why did nobody ever question *his* logic? Teaching in damp robes all day. Sure any fool knows that's asking for trouble.'

'Maybe his wife secretly wanted rid of him,' Richie says.

He's been streaming too many true crime serials, Carmel thinks.

'Oh no,' she says. 'It was a very happy marriage – they had five children.'

'So did my olds but that proves nothing,' Richie says glumly. For a moment she sees him not as a shiny-headed young Turk, but as an overlooked child of warring parents, and she feels a stab of pity for him.

'So,' he says and there's an odd hostile glint in his eye. 'You're *not* related to that Dromey guy then?'

The truce is over.

She takes a deep breath.

'Yes, I am,' she says evenly. 'But that chapter is closed.'

'For some, maybe,' Richie says. 'My father worked for Dromey's all his life and they threw him out on the street with nothing.' There's a little crack in his voice.

'It broke him,' Richie says. 'Broke him and killed him.'

An image of her own father flashes into Carmel's head. A weak man giving off drink fumes who'd killed a workmate by impaling him on one of the blades of the forklift. It was an accident, he kept on saying, but Carmel remembered the tricks he'd done for her in the warehouse, like a pilot doing loop-the-loops at an air spectacular.

'I mean, literally killed him,' Richie insists.

Dead air seems to reverberate around the words as if he'd shouted them. 'I'm sorry.' It's out before Carmel can stop it.

She looks around to see if anyone else has heard. But she and Richie are alone, stranded in the odd intimacy of strangers in an unfamiliar bedroom.

'I'm sorry,' she repeats while inside her head the old chorus gets louder – *it's not my fault*. 'My husband,' she begins but it's as if Richie has heard her inner voice.

'Nothing to do with you, that's what you're going to tell me, I suppose,' Richie says, 'you're just the wife.'

The widow, she wants to say, but then she thinks of Ray's lonely death. She thinks of his ashes travelling in clouds down the waste chute and the lie she told the children, that the funeral home had lost them. A huge sob swells up in her throat. She tries to swallow it back down while rummaging in her bag for a tissue. She can't be the one weeping here; she knows that much.

'I'm sorry,' she says for the third time.

Richie changes tack.

'And where would you be moving from, Mrs Dromey?'

'I'm in the Elysian,' she says, relieved at the change of mood. 'For the moment.'

'Well for some,' Richie says in a light testy way.

'Look,' she begins, but one of the other viewers comes into the room and asks: 'Is there an ensuite?'

Richie gathers himself and puts on his work expression.

'Let me show you, Sir.'

Carmel is left alone. A shower is turned on in the ensuite and she can hear Richie crooning about the plumbing. A sweat of shadow peels over the room as the sun goes behind cloud. Goosepimples rise on her arms. It's as if the dead have gathered in the room – Boole, her father, Richie's father. And Ray. Always Ray. She feels oddly spent. Her apology has dissipated the rage of years. Now what? She crushes the auctioneer's

Lost Property

bumpf in her hand, feeling her own monstrosity in these genteel surroundings. But she lingers in Lichfield all the same, clinging to the last remnants of her property libido.

She's the last to leave, Richie clicking the bolts shut on the gates behind her. There'll be no moving on for her. She thinks of 'The Lady of Shalott' from her poetry course. *The mirror crack'd.* That's her. She'll end her days as a prisoner in the tower. There will be no escape.

KISS OF LIFE

Choking, like deception, is silent. That's why I sat for several moments watching my friend Jane make urgent eyes at me across the table before I realized, my God, she's choking. I expected coughing, gasping, thrashing, loud distress. I'm an asthmatic; this I know. Instead, there was just Jane's stricken expression as she reached across the table and thumped my hand. She was trying to reach the water jug.

'Jane, what is it?' I asked.

Foolishly, as it turned out, since she couldn't speak.

I grabbed the jug and filled her glass. She drank greedily using the hand that was not scrabbling at her throat. The water made her splutter and something about that sound galvanized me into action. I leapt up and scurried round. I thumped her on her back, feeling odd to be so violent, but she nodded vigorously – do it again, she was saying – and so I did. Harder, she seemed to say. But there was something sadistic about clouting her like this, on command, with my closed fist. At my own dinner table. It seemed wrong. Like punishment. As if she was inviting punishment. With her eyes, she urged me to hit her again.

That's when Derek, my Derek, made his move. He's become heavy-set in middle-age but he moved swiftly from the head of the table for this. He made for Jane, upending the empty chair beside her. Ferg who'd been sitting beside me was the only one not ministering to her. He was gaping at us, not understanding what was happening. Meanwhile, Derek elbowed me out of the way and lifted Jane to standing. He twirled her around, as if he was jiving with her, then grabbed her from behind in a mauling kind of bear hug. He began stabbing her in the chest with his clenched fists. I'd never felt so unnecessary in all my life. I was mesmerized by how rhythmic and practised Derek seemed. Suddenly Jane emitted a throaty gargle and the gristly piece of lamb shot out of her mouth and across the table to land in Ferg's plate, sitting there like a grubby lie.

After it was over, when Jane's half-coughing, half-sobbing subsided, we carried on as before. Jane insisted on it. I'm fine, she kept on saying, really, my throat doesn't even hurt. But it was a strange night. The bully of death, having arm-wrestled its way into the company, would not go away. Imagine, I kept on thinking, imagine if Jane had died. All I could think of was Cluedo. Marie Fenwick with the lamb tagine in the dining room. And then I thought of that Roald Dahl story about the wife who does her husband in with a frozen leg of lamb and is cooking the evidence in the oven when the police arrive.

At the time it seemed wrong to dwell on it and equally wrong not to talk about it.

'Good job you knew the Heimlich Manoeuvre,' Ferg said to Derek.

'I have to know these things for work,' Derek said. He's a counsellor in a young offenders' centre. 'That's the first time I've had to use it.'

'Just like Dr Heimlich himself,' Ferg said and I thought, here we go; Ferg counts himself an expert on most things based on half-digested Facebook posts. 'Read it online a while back. He invented the manoeuvre in the 70s but never had cause to use it till a woman in the nursing home he's living in choked on a sausage beside him ...'

'And did he save her?' I asked.

But I can't remember what Ferg answered.

I had other things on my mind; the thought that Jane could have died for one. The evening stuttered on. At ten, Derek suggested we call it a night.

'Ferg, I think you should take Jane home.'

'Really, Derek, I'm fine. Don't let this spoil the party,' Jane said.

What party, I thought, it was more like a wake.

'Ferg,' Derek said warningly. He can be a tender bully.

Reluctantly Ferg rose from the table. He's a wiry man, heroin-thin and although he's tall, it's like he never grew the body of a man. He knocked back his wine and shrugged his jacket on. Meanwhile Derek tenderly placed Jane's cardigan across her shoulders as if she were an invalid, and gingerly steered her through the hall and outside. As soon as we got out into the night air, Ferg lit up. We watched as Derek opened the passenger door of the car for Jane and helped her in. We all waited while Ferg finished his cigarette. Then Derek and I retreated to the doorstep and stood together waving them off.

Thank God, I thought, that's over.

Except it wasn't.

Derek stalked into the dining room where there was still half a bottle of red left on the table. Only Ferg had had the appetite for drink after the episode.

'Are you alright?' Derek asked peering at me. Shouldn't I have been asking him that, I thought. After all, he'd just saved my best friend's life.

Kiss of Life

'Yes, yes,' I remember saying absently as I began to clear up.

I'd put a white linen cloth on the table and lit candles which now seemed funereal. We've known Ferg and Jane forever; we've been a foursome for twenty years or more. Jane and I met when the kids were in the same nursery school. The men have less in common, but the friendship between Jane and myself used to be enough to fuel the association. So once every couple of months we'd meet for a drink or to go to the theatre or, in this instance, have dinner together. I knew they'd been going through a rough patch of late. Ferg was about to be let go from the bank. With a package, granted, but it was enforced retirement all the same and Jane confided that she dreaded having him at home all day.

'You know what he's like,' she'd said to me, 'so angry all the time and not just with the world.'

'You don't mean ...'

'And with Rachel gone, there's no one to deflect him.'

Which, I thought, is exactly why Rachel has flown the coop.

I looked at the tablecloth and saw there were red wine stains all over it, and in Jane's place, the smeared brown remains of the incident, as if a child had been sitting in the spot and had daubed the food on the cloth rather than eating it.

Derek was rummaging in the sideboard.

'Are *you* alright?' I asked.

'I need a drink,' he said. 'A *real* drink.'

He fished out a bottle of ten-year-old whisky that he'd got as a Christmas gift at work. (I've always thought it ironic that the parents of the drug-addled give him alcohol as proof of their gratitude.) He twisted the top off the bottle and drank from the neck. In all our years together I'd never seen him do that.

'You're in shock,' I said and tried laying a calming hand on his forearm but he batted me off.

'Jesus, Marie, she might have died,' he said.

As if I hadn't grasped the gravity of the situation.

'You're in shock,' I repeated but I didn't try to touch him again.

The following Saturday, a week after the choking episode, I went to see Jane. I was worried about her. I'd tried ringing and left several messages but she hadn't called back. I'd texted but she didn't respond to those either. When she came to the door she didn't look herself. Jane is a neat person. Hair in a pert bob, neat, tame clothes. That morning she looked different. I mean she wasn't slopping around in her pyjamas but there was something careless about her attire. Something not put together about it.

'You look terrible,' I said.

I thought it must be the after-effects of the choking. I mean, she might have died. That thought can't have escaped her. I was sorry then I hadn't brought flowers or something to make it up to her. Not that she blamed me or anything. She kept on saying that night, it's just a mishap, nobody's fault.

'Are you alright?' I asked.

'It's Ferg,' she said and oddly I found my stomach doing a lurch. I was frightened, somehow. I couldn't help feeling this implicated me. Well, of course, it implicated me; I'm her best friend.

Was, *was* her best friend.

'What's happened?' I asked feeling the panic rise.

'You'd better come in,' she said.

We went into the kitchen and I sat on one of the stools at the island. Jane made coffee and broke open a packet of biscuits and while she did I could convince myself that nothing had changed between us. How often had we sat here over the years, having heart-to-hearts that would last for hours. Worries about the kids, money troubles, Ferg. And it wasn't just talk. We helped one another out. Jane tutored my Kevin in French. I advised her on her garden; I'm quite green-fingered, as it happens.

I'd always thought of Jane as a calm person, a soothing presence. But when she brought the pot to the counter and then – viciously – pushed the plunger down, I thought, no, something *has* changed.

She poured the coffee sloppily into two cups.

'He's threatening to leave me,' she said simply.

'What?'

'You heard.'

That blew away my first certitude about Jane – I had always thought she'd be the one to leave Ferg. Look, I've always thought Jane's too good for him. The night of the episode, he was droning on about the refugee crisis, calling for quotas and wire fences and border closures. He was so taken up with his argument that he was the last one to notice what was happening. As usual, he was making too much noise and Jane, not enough. That's how their marriage has been, if you ask me.

'But why?'

'Oh Marie,' Jane said and if she weren't my friend I'd have thought her tone condescending. 'Why do you think?'

'There's someone else,' I said finally coming to my senses.

'*Exactement!*' Jane said – she's a part-time French teacher.

'Who is it? Someone he works with?'

'No Marie, it's me, there's someone else for me,' she said.

You could have knocked me down with a feather. I thought we shared everything. No, correction, I thought she shared everything with me. You see, I've always had a very dull life. I sit at home all day and write and there's not much drama in that, so I suppose I had lived vicariously on the ups and downs of Jane's marriage and Ferg's bad behaviour.

'Who is it?' I asked.

'Nobody you know,' she said.

'Come on, Jane, you can tell me ...'

'No,' she said, 'I can't, it wouldn't be fair.'

'But if I don't know the person what odds?'

'Don't turn this into a gossip thing,' she pleaded. 'And you're not to write about it, do you hear?'

I was hurt by that. I've never used my friends in my fiction. Couldn't imagine it. I write romantic fiction on commission for Second Union – it's a niche market, formula stuff for the over forties. The novels follow a familiar trajectory. Long lost loves recovered, obstacles to happiness in the form of living or dead wives, or tarty mistresses, or bolshy step-children, a crisis and then all is right in the end. Okay, so I'm not educating the masses like Jane, or saving the downtrodden of the earth like Derek is. He calls it writing by numbers. But it's more than that. Sure, you're given the plot outline, but you have to put flesh on the bones, breathe life into your characters, imagine your way into their minds so that each love story has its own individual flavour, and is different in its atmosphere and details. So, it's not without its skills. But it has nothing to do with real life. I know that.

Yet here was my dear friend, who had nearly died and who was now facing a marriage break-up after twenty-five years, and she was treating me as if I couldn't be trusted. It stung, I can tell you.

'Look, Marie, it's not even an affair. Nothing has really happened.'

'Then what's the problem?'

She left a silence that grew and thrummed.

'I've had feelings for this person for quite some time and fool that I was, I told Ferg about it. I thought it was just a silly crush – I know, at my age! – and that if I owned up to it, it would wear off.'

She snorted derisively.

I couldn't believe it. This was like a conversation we might have had in our twenties, bemoaning the helplessness of passion. But now? My God, we're practically pensioners! And Jane, of all people! Groomed and self-contained Jane. Undone.

'And it didn't?'

'Well, no, but something has happened in the last week. On the other side. A change in this other person's circumstances. He's married but wants out and now it seems there's a chance ...'

She stopped there.

'When I said this to Ferg, he flew into one of his rages –'

'He didn't ...?'

'No, Marie, nothing like that. I know you've never thought highly of Ferg –'

'Oh that's unfair –' I began but she raised her hand to silence me.

'He's never lifted a hand to me. He just issued me with an ultimatum. Shit or get off the pot.'

That was Ferg talking, I was sure.

'He said I'd have to decide.'

'And have you?'

She looked at me miserably and shook her head.

'What are you going to do?'

'I don't know.'

'Can you depend on this other person?'

Jane's eyes filled up. 'Oh yes,' she said.

I knew then it was serious. Apart from the choking episode, I'd never seen Jane cry.

I thought of phoning Derek with the news, but something stopped me. I waited for him to come home. As soon as he got in the door, before he even had a chance to take off his coat, I blurted it out.

'You'll never guess ...'

'What?'

'Ferg and Jane,' I started.

'What about them?' he said sharply.

'They're splitting up. Or at least threatening to, and Jane has someone on the go!'

'What do you mean, on the go?'

Derek often treats conversations like they were counselling sessions – an occupational hazard. He wants specifics, exactitude in the descriptions of emotions. I told him what Jane had told me.

'Who is it?' Derek asked.

You see, I said to myself, that's the first question everyone asks.

'Well, that's just it, she wouldn't say, said it wasn't anyone I knew.'

I had, of course, run through possible candidates in my mind – there were Jane's teaching colleagues, and she goes to the gym so there are people there I wouldn't know either, and she has her French book club, but I think they're mostly women.

'I suppose,' Derek said, 'that's her prerogative.'

Something about this word annoyed me. It seemed like office jargon, a word for the politically correct. It was a word you would use to deflect, to dissemble. And that's what alerted me, and once I thought it, I couldn't unthink it. Like the thought that Jane might have died, I just couldn't shake it off.

Say, I reasoned, trying to steady myself, say if Derek is the person for whom Jane has feelings. Could that be?

I'd never thought about Jane in the context of Derek. She was *my* friend, after all. But I couldn't remember any special bond between the two of them. In fact, it was more often the three of us ranged against Ferg. Ferg, who wanted to ban immigration and re-introduce smoking in pubs, who thought marijuana should be legalized and that there should be a driving test for having children.

'You'd never have passed,' I remember Derek saying jocosely to him.

Poor Ferg, always the villain.

But when I looked back on it, I noticed that though I had spent long sessions commiserating with Jane about Ferg's shortcomings, I'd never heard her say a bad word about Derek.

If Jane hadn't been involved, this would have been exactly the thing I would have confided in her about because I could predict her answer. She'd say, don't be a fool, Marie, Derek's a treasure, he'd never betray you.

But now, even imagining her advice was like a provocation.

I could have asked Derek straight out, I suppose. But I was afraid. I knew how he'd treat it. He'd say, wearing his professional face, what's this *really* all about, Marie? And then there'd be a rehearsal of all those other times when I'd imagined myself into what he would call a state – when I suspected the next door neighbour was running a cannabis grow house, how I thought Ferg was cheating on Jane with the nursery school teacher, or when I broke off contact with Derek's sister, June, because I thought her boyfriend was a paedophile.

But I was right about that, in a way, wasn't I?

Twenty-Twenty Vision

So I said nothing to Derek.

But I did examine the circumstances of our marriage to see if I could detect any change of late. Something that might prompt Derek to consider leaving me. But there hadn't been any rows, or even differences of opinion. There had been no other tell-tale signs either – unexplained absences, longer hours at the office, the sort of device I use in fiction to signal an affair. Everything on the surface was just as it had been. Apart from the night of the Heimlich Manoeuvre, that is.

The night Jane nearly died.

It's surprisingly easy to shake off a friend, I've found, even a friend of long standing like Jane. It's a kind of a dance, where you shimmy up close using all the old dance moves, but you actually don't connect. You don't answer the doorbell and when challenged you say you were out in the back garden and didn't hear it. You break regular appointments at the last minute with excuses about sick dogs and unexpected weekend trips. (It helps that your twins are both away in college and come home at short notice with large bundles of laundry and new girlfriends.) You leave the book club, saying you simply don't have the time for reading.

Then the lockdown comes along and hey presto, everyone is shunning their friends. With your asthma, you can't afford the risk of infection so visits are out. You screen calls. You play phone tag. Voicemail replaces actual conversations, then text messages. Then silence.

Jane never challenged me on it, not once. Was I not worth fighting for? Obviously not. She simply let our friendship die.

Kiss of Life

Why would she do that if she weren't guilty of something? Derek hasn't asked why either, beyond saying we don't see much of Jane and Ferg these days. Has he not realized how deliberate a process it's been?

Or maybe he has realized what I know ...

Maybe they both have?

Either way, their silence speaks volumes.

If I see Jane on the street, I wave gaily like a good neighbour and pass on. She and Ferg are still together, as far as I know. Maybe the affair fizzled out. Maybe she and Derek decided to be sensible in the end.

Once in a while I wonder could I have been mistaken? But I don't dwell on that.

I don't blame Jane, really I don't. I mean nothing happened, did it? Isn't that what she said? And I can see the attraction of Derek after a lifetime with prickly Ferg. Derek is an admirable human being, caring, loyal. But he's mine, and I can't have my best friend having feelings for him, even unrequited ones.

Unrequited. I turn the word over in my mind. Well, I'm a writer. How do you know if the love call has been answered? Consummation; there's another word. What are the signs? Had I nipped something in the bud or was I already too late? Lately, I find myself returning to the night of the Heimlich Manoeuvre. I find the scene unfurling before me in oiled slow motion, but each time a little bit differently. Now I see Derek rising from the table, some pained look on his face I've never seen before, and in an oddly balletic, slow motion movement, gliding around the end of the table. Then he takes Jane in his arms and bending over her as if he were going to dip her low in a movie clinch, he kisses her full on the lips.

SURVIVORS

They made an odd couple, strangers in mid-life, undressing surreptitiously in the bathroom. The holiday together had been Triona's idea. Post-lockdown, it would be a victory lap for her after finishing treatment, and she could be a travelling companion for her newly widowed brother. When Triona saw him in his pyjamas she realized how thin Colm had become; how he'd developed a little stoop, as if his grief was a slackened sack on his back. She, on the other hand, had fattened up after the treatment. Every pound gained was a fist raised against death, but she couldn't gloat about it with Colm because, in the same lottery, Penny had lost.

Colm was her baby brother, the quiet one, the conformist; she, the rule-breaker. The one who smashed curfew, who smoked dope in the bathroom, who smuggled drink into the house while Colm covered for her. He had married, had kids; she'd had affairs. But none of that made any difference now. They were two adults chastened by life. Or was it death? He didn't confide about how he was coping and she didn't want to keep on asking as if she were a nurse wielding a clipboard. They could just *be*, couldn't they? Revert to the children they'd once been where they rubbed along together and took one another for granted.

She wasn't prepared for the terrible yearning that came off him, a tentacle of grief she was afraid might wrap itself around her. It seemed more solid and present than he was. He acted like he wasn't quite with her, like a cousin once removed on the family tree. He started most sentences addressing her by his dead wife's name before he remembered.

'Penny?'

Sorry, he'd say bashfully, as if caught out in a foolish declaration of love. And she would demur, saying it didn't matter, though after a while it began to irritate her, as if she was invisible to him, or a stand-in of some sort.

They had planned to do a trip to Santa Margherita on the last day of the holiday. They took the metro to the central railway station. On the subway platform, there was a pale, heavily pregnant young woman with Madonna eyes, slumped against a pillar. She looked ready to pop, her bump only half-covered by a stretched jersey top. Triona thought of Francesca, Colm's daughter, who was due in three weeks. His first grandchild. This, she told herself, could be Francesca lying here and yet, after the first shock of it, she shrugged at the young woman, as if she was helpless, as if there was nothing she could do. Then, unexpectedly, she was furious. Really, she wanted to shout out, I'm a cancer survivor.

All through the holiday, Triona had handed out coin to all and sundry, though Colm reprimanded her for it.

'All it does is make you feel better,' he'd said.

'And what's wrong with wanting to feel better?' Triona had asked.

He'd looked at her as if she'd slapped him. Mourning had made him imperious as if he'd been elevated to a higher plane by his loss, but now he winced and his face crumpled. It wasn't crying; it was failing to cry.

'Did you see her?' she'd asked Colm when they boarded the train.

'See who?'

It was as if Colm saw nothing from the waist down. He looked up – at spires, at the sky.

She felt something like spite overtake her. A feeling she hadn't felt since she was a little girl. Okay, she thought, let's try it your way, Colm. For the rest of the day she turned everyone away. The Moroccan who tried to sell her a lighter, the double amputee on a little trolley who'd approached with a single rose, the blind old woman in a shawl with a card around her neck that read *Auitami*.

It took effort, though Colm didn't seem to notice the change in her behaviour. She had to harden her heart to do it, but the more she hardened it, the more emboldened she felt and the harder it became to climb down. After a day of adamantine refusal, she lay in bed with the lights out and Colm a foot away, and felt doubly trapped. The guilt held at bay for the day flooded in and she realized guiltily, that her guilt was just another luxury she could afford. She couldn't bear it. Couldn't bear herself.

There was a terrible storm during the night. The wind howled and the giant canopies of the umbrella pines brushed and scraped against the window of their room. Shutters swung open, then banged shut. Their hotel was built on a cliff over a railway line and when the trains – which seemed to run all night – thundered through, it felt like they were sitting on a volcano that was about to explode beneath them. Colm slept soundly.

At 3 am, Triona woke with a jolt to a loud knocking on the door. She got out of bed and tiptoed to the door.

Was someone in trouble out there? Or was it some other kind of emergency, a fire, a bomb scare? Or was it just the wind? The door rattled and shook. She put her hand on the knob.

Don't, that's what Colm would say. Don't leave yourself open.

She opened it.

The pregnant girl from the station was there in a slick black raincoat with the hood up. The tips of her hair were pendulant with drops. She moved in a damp wave past Triona and stationed herself in the narrow aisle between their twin beds.

Triona hurried after her to Colm's bedside. She tried to nudge him awake but he was dead to the world.

'Colm!'

She shook him. The pregnant girl watched.

'Colm!'

She shook him again. Nothing. Jesus, was he dead?

'Help me,' Triona said weakly to the pregnant girl.

But the girl clamped her hands over her bump and turned her face away.

Suddenly, Colm reared up in the bed, Lazarus-like.

'Penny?'

He looked directly at Triona.

'She's here,' Triona said meaning the girl. She felt, obscurely, that this was her fault, that she had invited need into their room by denying it earlier. She looked across the bed towards the girl, but she had disappeared. She and Colm were entirely alone. Had they been dreaming in unison?

'There's no one here, Triona,' he said disconsolately.

Meanwhile, the door kept on swinging open then crashing minutely to, the metal tongue yearning to find the mortice but failing every time. They lay there listening to it, neither of them willing to get up and make it stop.

HUSBANDRY

When Cora answered the door, she was taken aback, not by the fact that it was Fran, but that she was here, now, in the middle of lockdown. It was 9:30 on a Tuesday night. She'd been listening to the radio as she made a late dinner. It was a nature programme and there were two botanical experts on, both men, arguing about ivy. No, no, no, the more impassioned one said, ivy has no ecological value, it damages trees basically choking them to death and it weakens bio-diversity turning a tree-rich environment into a mono-habitat. That was rubbish, the other one said. The idea that ivy physically chokes the tree was science fiction. The trees on which ivy grows are not damaged by it; the ivy merely masks signs of already existing fungus and decay. And the so-called strangle marks that ivy leaves on the bark? Well, that is to apply human morphology to trees, he scoffed. It was at that point in the discussion the doorbell went.

Fran was well outside her 5k limit. Just being here was already a transgression. The most natural human impulses had been made illicit by this pandemic – welcome, support, love. But Cora didn't think twice about inviting her in. They've been friends for nearly thirty years, since they were young teachers together and Cora's place has always been Fran's refuge.

In the early days of her marriage Fran would frequently turn up like this, having driven through the night, Melanie in her arms, the boys in overcoats over their pyjamas.

Husbandry

'I'm leaving him,' she would say by way of greeting.

Cora would pull out the sofa bed for the boys and put Fran and the baby in the spare room. Emboldened by her flight, Fran would stay a night or two and then be gone, leaving a note on the kitchen table. Or else Bill would arrive in person. There is something sour about Bill, a belligerent downturn of the mouth that Cora has always disliked, but it seems a petty thing to base a character assessment on. When he would come, as he always did, Cora would make herself scarce for the impassioned negotiations that invariably followed. At some stage, Fran would capitulate and there would be a feverish packing of soft toys and a shame-faced departure with the confused children in tow.

This time, Fran says nothing; she weeps.

Cora shows her into the kitchen. It's a white room – the units, the table, the walls; surgical, you could almost say.

'The thing that's so hard about it is there was no warning,' Fran wails. 'I thought after all these years our troubles were over.'

What she means is that her old doubts about Bill seemed to have receded as the children grew. Or maybe she just got used to living with them? For whatever reason, and against all the odds, Fran has become a contented empty-nester. Or had. She dabs her flushed face with a sodden tissue. Betrayal is a messy business and mortifying when you're fifty-two and your husband has just left you. In the middle of a pandemic. Which, of course, is probably why it happened in the first place. It's a long time since Fran and Bill spent any significant amount of time alone together.

If Cora were to be blunt with Fran, she would say – your whole marriage has been a warning, a warning against commitment to the wrong man, against getting pregnant, before or after wedlock. But she doesn't say this, because she only has a short-lived, childless marriage to draw on, so long ago now that even her closest friends, like Fran, have forgotten about it.

Paradoxically, poor Fran's protests remind her of her own experience. As a young untried couple, she and Neil had been perfectly happy, or so she thought, so that when the break came, it was a total shock. To her. Neil did the honourable thing and spared her the usual subterfuges. He told her before he went off with his new wife, or the woman who would become his new wife. He didn't skulk around behind her back; she wasn't made a fool of, wasn't the last to know. Men often think that being physical with someone is the real benchmark of betrayal. But the betrayal begins with the intention, doesn't it?

Neil met his new wife at a folk club he ran on Saturday nights in a pub called The Fiddler's Elbow. He was a musician himself — classical guitar — and they'd clicked immediately. That's how he explained it to Cora. She has always wondered about that phrase, as if sexual attraction were some kind of trick with castanets. She also heard the implied insult; the clicking business was obviously something Neil considered hadn't happened between them. He and Yvonne (much and all as Cora hated it, she eventually had to give the now no longer new wife a name) tried to ignore it, he'd said. But it was no good ... they just couldn't. This helplessness was a trait she'd never noticed in Neil before. Cora knew Yvonne, knew her to see, that is; what she hadn't known was to view Yvonne as a rival. Once Neil had said Yvonne was the object of his newly declared affection, Cora realized that she'd been wrong about there being no warnings. There had been a warning. Just one. Not about Yvonne, but about someone else, a long time before.

*

Husbandry

'You're going to love her,' Neil had said.

His enthusiasms worried Cora because she herself was one of them. She was twenty-two but with Neil she felt decades older. It was in the early days of their courtship.

'Annie's American,' he said, 'and wait till you see where she lives. It's really cool.' Cool was enjoying its first round of popularity then. (Cora is waiting for groovy and hip to come back into favour.) It was a late summer's day in 1978 and they were rattling down Leinster Road in Neil's brother's VW. There had just been a downpour but it was over now and the sun was glittering fiercely. The drenched trees were in full leaf.

Cora felt her heart contract. She was afraid, not of meeting some random woman Neil had enthused about, but for herself. New people confounded her, particularly those she was importuned to love. She found comfort in private contempt. *Annie!* Her name sounded faux cutesy; for Cora, it was an old lady's moniker, belonging to a simple-minded aunt with a lame leg. (This was before the musical had caught on.)

In Neil's company she felt laced-up like a Victorian woman in a too-tight corset; she wondered what he was doing with her. He was still like a student – though he worked a few days a week in a record shop in town. But compared to her, he was a free spirit. She was a supply teacher desperate to be pensionable. Neil would have derided such aspirations so she knew enough to keep them to herself. And yet, after two dates, he had declared himself in love with her. He said it on the front steps leading to her flat on Charleston Road. Moon, railings and Neil looking up at her – she was on a higher step than him. How could he know so soon, she wondered, and she immediately distrusted him, it. He had wanted to come up that night but she said no, her place was too small. But, really, she didn't want her first received declaration of love to be muddied by any physical expression of it.

It was also true. Her place *was* too small and she was ashamed of it. Her bedsit was an L-shaped hutch on the second floor. A single bed, a two-ring cooker in the corner, a leafed table and two folding chairs that had to be stowed away for her to get into bed. There was a tall Georgian window lording it over her and looking down on to a paved yard below that housed the bins. The window saved the flat from utter squalor because it allowed the light in. But the light showed up the makeshift dinginess of the place with her clothes in piles on the floor, the ones she couldn't fit into the chest of drawers you had to squeeze by in the long side of the L that led from the flat's front door.

This is how people lived then, she tries to explain to her pupils, in hovels designed only for sleeping and for people with only a couple of changes of clothes. The twenty-first century convent schoolgirls do not believe her, think it's an old wives' tale; that is when they express any interest in Cora's personal anecdotes with which she tries to leaven her classes. Though, of course, her stories don't include anything about her marriage to Neil Temperley. She's tempted sometimes to go there, if only because she suspects they see her as a dried-up old maiden, a deeply unmarriageable woman who's all past tense. But discretion prevents her. Neil has subsequently made a name for himself doing cross-over classical recordings with his new wife. With Yvonne, that is. And he enjoys a kind of local fame as a chat show guest, enough to make Cora wary of drawing attention to her connection with him, in case it might be seen as her trying to claim his portion of the sun.

Most of Cora's students think of her merely as Ms Temperley, not realizing that the name is the only thing she has held on to from her first, her only marriage. Her own name was Moran, too close to moron for her liking. She was glad to ditch it, and thankful that Neil had left her with a surname worthy of a character in a Jane Austen novel.

That summer's day, long before Neil had left her with only his euphonious surname, he swung the car flamboyantly into the kerb and parked outside Annie's place. He pushed open the rusty-looking gate and they found themselves in a secret garden amid drifts of white and purple-headed anemones. There were brambles that had gone feral, fat untended hedges, grass at meadow-length bisected by a gravel path. It was one of those villa-type houses with steps up to the front door and another set leading into the basement. This was where Neil headed. Dipping his head under the stone arch, he pressed the bell and then rapped on the glass panels of the door.

'Forgot,' he said, 'bell doesn't work.'

So, Cora thought, he's familiar with the vagaries of the place.

Because she was hanging back, the first Cora saw of Annie Lahart was her brown arms reaching out to clasp Neil around the shoulders.

'Neil!' she said and crushed her cheek against his chest. Then she looked up.

'Oh,' she said and swung her mane of long dark hair over her shoulder. 'You must be Cora!'

She was diminutive, coming up only to Cora's shoulder, but she had a generous figure, not fat but ample, womanly. She had a broad open face, her skin was berry-coloured and there was a sprinkling of freckles across her cheeks. When she smiled, it was toothsome and white; a merry, minty grin. She was wearing an oversized pair of shorts – over heavy-looking thighs, Cora noted – a white singlet and a man's denim shirt. She was barefoot.

'Come in, come in,' she said and they followed her down a dim hallway with dark wood wainscoting and chequered red and black tiles on the floor.

'See these,' Neil said touching the walls and pointing to the floor, 'all original!'

Annie opened a scarred door at the end of the corridor and they stepped into a large basement kitchen. A huge refectory table with a gap down the middle where the planks had parted stood in front of them, surrounded by four or five mismatched chairs, some in bright primary colours, others reduced to plain wood except for the odd fleck of stubborn paint.

Annie busied herself filling a kettle at the Belfast sink at the far dim end of the room. Neil walked around the table, hands thrust into his pockets, like a surveyor valuing the place.

'Well,' he said magisterially to Cora, 'what do you think?'

It reminded Cora of home, her grandmother's house in Coolnacallee, that is, with the cold lino floors and the damp-speckled walls, the house where she'd grown up with her mother. There had been no men in Cora's childhood. Her grandfather had died when she was a baby; even if he hadn't, there'd been some rift between him and Granny and he'd been dispatched to live in what was called 'the old house'.

Grandad had been raised there. He was one of six brothers and sisters, but they'd all taken the emigrant's route across the way to England, or further afield to America and Australia. He'd inherited the old place being the eldest son. He must have done well because when he and Granny had got married, he'd had the new house built. This was where Cora had grown up, among accoutrements that seemed to her relics of a bygone age – a chaise longue and a large horned gramophone in the parlour. Old-fashioned they may have been but they were not decorative props. Cora's granny had a stash of 78s which she listened to on the old record player. It had a rigid needle

Husbandry

that looked as if it was scoring the records as it played. As for the chaise longue, this was reserved for visitors, who weren't encouraged to stay too long. You had to sit stiffly upright on it and it was hard and uncomfortable.

Meanwhile, Grandad had died alone in the old house, in a bare room with lime-washed floorboards and paint-blistered window casements. Cora often visited it, testing herself against its ghostliness. All there was in the room was an iron bedstead, a striped ticking mattress and a pair of atrophied boots still under the bed. In the winter it was perishing there and she wondered how Grandad had withstood the cold; the tin fireplace had been bricked up. She had felt sorry for him, though it was a strange sensation, to feel sorry for someone she hadn't known. Both Granny and her mother were tight-lipped about what had caused the estrangement and by the time Cora was old enough to ask, she was more interested in her own missing father.

'He was local,' her mother told her when Cora broached the question. 'We had a bit of a romance and then he went off to England and I never saw him again. Probably dead by now, given the way he carried on.'

'What was his name?'

'Daly,' she said, 'Ned Daly.'

'Does he know about me?' Cora asked.

Her mother shook her head ruefully.

'He didn't want to know,' she said. 'Why else do you think he left?'

That was the sum total of Cora's knowledge about him. She knew by her mother's tone that the subject would not be revisited.

Cora associated all the silences in her life with the two houses, the old and the newer one, both old now. When she left home, she vowed she would live in a new, modern semi-detached house with no dank corners where the residues of other people's lives could linger.

'It's just *so* authentic,' Annie was saying, waving her arms about in the kitchen like an air hostess. Her voice had a crystal quality, sharp and clear.

The word authentic made Cora sick; people like Annie – and Neil, too – looking for authenticity as if it could only exist in the past.

'It's the real deal, alright,' Neil said rubbing his hand along the bleached table top. 'Annie got this place for buttons. Tell her, Annie.'

'There's an old lady upstairs. A bit crazy,' Annie said screwing her index finger into her temple.

She wet the tea in the pot.

'I talked her into letting the basement to me – she never came down here, anyway. Only the cats did. Here, let me show you,' she said. She led Cora back out into the hallway and pointed to the stairway going up into the rest of the house. The bannister rail was rough and dry to the touch with deep furrows worked into it.

'From cat's claws.' Annie said. 'Reckon those guys might scratch your eyes out, given half a chance.'

A warm baking smell wafted into the hallway.

'Oh gee, I forgot …' Annie said and dipped back into the kitchen.

There was a large cream-coloured range and, wouldn't you know it, Annie opened the door and drew out a freshly baked loaf of currant bread which she placed on a wire tray on the table to cool. Then she fetched cups and plates, all Willow pattern, from the large green dresser.

'If my folks could see this,' Annie said in a wondering tone as she put a crochet cosy on the teapot. 'Real tea!'

What other kind was there, Cora wondered.

'When I got here, I didn't know you had to scald the pot. Neil gave me lessons.'

Neil guffawed and Annie joined him with her tinkling laugh. Cora looked at the pair of them. Neil with his collarless shirt and tweed waistcoat, a halo of dark, bubbly hair – halfway to an Afro, he said – and wispy beard, and Annie, standing beside him, holding the pot by its handle and spout. Like an up-to-date version of that famous painting – the old farm couple, the man with a pitchfork and the grandfather glasses, the woman with the bun and the cameo brooch.

'It's like a museum, isn't it?' Neil asked Cora. Excited.

'And all for a peppercorn rent!' Annie added.

Cora had never heard the term. Peppercorn.

'In the States you'd have to go the boonies to find somewhere like this!' Annie said. 'I'm from Cleveland.' And then she added 'Ohio?' helpfully.

Cora imagined a generous clapboard home bathed in a sitcom light. Annie wrinkled her pert nose and made a sour face. 'Where the river went on fire?'

She seemed to think Cora should know about this.

'So she came to dear old dirty Dublin, instead!' Neil said.

The three of them sat at the table, Neil and Annie on one side, Cora on the other. Annie carved the still hot currant cake and passed it out on the Willow plates, then poured for all of them. She got up and fetched the milk from a cold press with a netted door sitting on the wooden draining board.

'No mod cons, isn't it brilliant?' Neil persisted.

Cora thought of where Neil came from. A comfortable Tudor-look house in Blackrock, gardens front and back, his own room and the loan of his brother's car. And he'd swap it for this? She'd never invited him to her grandmother's house. It was in the wilds of Kerry. Luckily, Neil didn't 'do' the country. That's what Cora thought this was all about then. Location.

'How did you two meet?' she asked.

'I'm a groupie,' Annie said and laughed. 'I heard about the folk club and turned up one night … I play myself, a little …' she said.

'Now she's being modest,' Neil added.

'I'm still learning but it's why I came here. For the traditional music,' Annie explained.

'The diddly-aye stuff,' Neil said loftily to Cora, by way of explanation, as if she were the foreigner in need of having the obvious clarified.

'My grandparents emigrated from here in the 1920s – we did the whole Irish thing. Irish dancing, the ringlets and the costumes, so I thought I should come and find the source of it all … I just love it here. Neil … people have been very kind and so hospitable. I don't know how I'd have survived otherwise.'

Cora watched as if it were a tennis match. Back and forth. Neil and Annie putting on a performance for her benefit. She saw the easiness between them; something she and Neil didn't yet enjoy. She blamed herself. She was secretive, she knew. There were things she wasn't ready to share until she was sure of him. And there were passions she couldn't share with him; she didn't play an instrument, she wasn't interested in folk music and she didn't understand all the reverence that Neil paid to it. At home she could have rambled into a pub any evening of the week and found old men with caps playing the button accordion or the fiddle. The music had always seemed to her a dead end. The songs they sang full of impotent melancholy complaint; the manic cheerfulness of the jigs and reels like a comic rush to oblivion.

Neil didn't seem to mind that she didn't care about such things.

Husbandry

'I love the way you're so true to yourself,' he'd said, 'quiet ... but determined.' And he'd grinned at her as if it was a loveable failing.

Looking at him chattering on to Annie about Pete Seeger, she realized he didn't need her for that kind of conversation; there would always be others. And she'd always felt reassured by that. What a fool she'd been!

'Oh but you play so well, Neil, you shouldn't dream of giving it up, should he, Cora?'

'There's no one wants to hear my kind of music,' he said.

'Well,' Annie said, punching him playfully on the arm. 'I do!'

As Cora now knows, flattery is the sincerest form of flirtation.

She pushed back her chair and wandered to the back door. It was flung open to reveal another jungle out back, dreeping fuchsia, flames of Montbretia, more bushes and brambles.

'What's out here?' she asked. But neither Neil nor Annie answered; Annie was busy showing him the new violin she'd bought. She'd lifted it out of the case which all this time had lain on the table like a shiny little black coffin.

'Give us a tune,' Neil wheedled.

Annie was hunched over the bow, tuning up, as Cora stepped outside. She brushed against the arcing stalk of a rose bush and a little shower of droplets fell on her hair. There was a little muddy track, the width of a human foot, which wound around the bushes and brambles and she followed it. Soon she had lost sight of the house altogether. She could hear Annie's playing, but distantly, haltingly, and she was pretty sure that neither of them had even noticed she was gone. Let them be a couple, she thought savagely, let them have fast furious sex on the kitchen table. It was a measure of her innocence then that she thought everyone was having it off with one another at the slightest provocation – everyone, but her.

At the end of the garden in a trampled down spot there was an old green swing. She sat on it and swung back and forth gently and was happy in her solitude; that was the lesson she should have learned then. That was what Neil saw in her – not a quaint self-possessed shyness, but a cool lack of necessity in her feelings for him.

Annie lasted one winter in the vintage kitchen. As Cora could have told her. There was no heat source besides the range and keeping those old models fed requires heavy labour and commitment. Within a year, she had retreated back to Ohio, armed with a whole new repertoire of jigs and reels. She wrote to Neil care of the folk club – Cora had seen the letters with her return address pinned to the cork noticeboard in the back room of The Fiddler's Elbow; then she resorted to postcards, and finally communication petered out altogether.

At the time, Cora felt she had seen Annie off, though she didn't quite know how. She had done nothing but stick around. But she can see now what Neil was telling her all those years ago. This girl likes me, admires me more than you do; I could have her any time I like. That day Cora had felt threatened by something she thought had already happened. Whereas Neil was issuing a warning – *this* is how I want to be loved.

*

She opens a bottle of wine for herself and Fran. Unlike previous times, there are no children to be fed and pacified or beds to be made up. It's just the two of them facing one another across the table in Cora's kitchenette.

'Why didn't Bill leave?' Cora asks. 'I mean he has somewhere to go to.' She nearly says someone.

'I couldn't bear to be with him a moment longer,' Fran says. Her jowls quiver. There's a rubble of tissues in her fist. 'And he can't go to her because she's moved back in with her parents in Drogheda for the duration.'

'Who is she?'

'She's our dental hygienist. Someone we paid to make his teeth whiter.'

So younger, Cora thinks, Much younger.

'How – '

'Did it come to light, you mean?' 'He blurted it out. We were sitting just like this after dinner and suddenly he said I can't do this anymore and he burst into tears. If he hadn't had to stay at home day in day out he'd probably never have told me.'

'And would you prefer that? To be living a lie?'

'Oh Cora, we've always been living a lie. What do you think all my midnight flits were about? Anyway, I wasn't given a choice, was I?'

She runs a hand through her hair. She's had it streaked ash blonde and it's usually cut quite short but like everyone else's, it's grown straggly with neglect.

'Only this time I'm guessing he won't be hotfooting it after me. Not when he has a thirty-year old in cold storage.'

'It won't last,' Cora says confidently and replenishes Fran's glass. 'These things never do.'

'Why do you say that?'

Cora shrugs. Because it's what you say.

'Because she's thirty?' Fran says. 'What age were you when you met Dominic Comer?'

The dead arose. Dominic Comer. Another husband; someone else's.

'Your feelings didn't lack staying power because of your age.'

Cora didn't think her feelings for him had been so obvious.

'This is ancient history, Fran. Anyway, this isn't about me.'

There's a tense little hiatus.

Fran laughs grimly. 'I suppose it's payback time with Bill. I mean I did keep on crying wolf.'

And I aided and abetted you, Cora thinks as she pours herself another glass; it's going to be a long night.

'Did you know?' Fran asks almost cheerily and Cora dreads what's coming next. 'Ivy is female – it said so on the radio.'

'Oh were you listening to that too?'

'Yes,' Fran says. 'I was trying to take my mind off things.'

'Well,' Cora says, glad of the change of subject. 'I was surprised that even when the ivy's scored deep into the tree bark, it can grow around the obstruction, so it doesn't mean the tree's dead.'

'Are you trying to tell me something, Cora?'

'No, it's just that it doesn't have to be the end, that's all.'

They sit for a while in comradely silence.

'I identified with the tractor,' Fran says finally. 'Useful and abandoned.'

'I missed that.'

'One of those experts said that even a tractor rotting in a field provides biodiversity.' She raises her glass.

'To husbands! Who'd have 'em?'

Cora would have one, but she clinks glasses and says nothing.

TWENTY-TWENTY VISION

Who gave their abortion a name? Wasn't that the whole point of termination? You weren't disposing of a person but a cluster of cells. But Adrienne had christened her cluster Róisín, having already decided it was a girl. Every year on 19 July, the date Adrienne reckoned might have been Róisín's birthday, she marked it with a private ceremony of relief and penance. Relief for the freedom that not having Róisín had given her, and atonement for the lie she'd told to get it. She knew Patrick would never have willingly agreed to her decision; for him, Róisín would have been a baby, a daughter.

At the time, lying seemed the only way out. Now, with the benefit of hindsight, Adrienne realized that wasn't so. There are always several ways out.

Patrick wasn't violent or abusive, but he was not the man with whom she'd walked down the aisle. He'd been wild during their courtship; he drank and smoked everything. He liked to act on impulse. Weekends away in Paris on the spur of the moment, midnight swims in the freezing Atlantic, impromptu parties after the pub. Once he married, though, he'd turned into Husband Material. She thought of those words of St Paul – when I became a man, I put away childish things.

She had no value for the starter home Patrick had scraped up a mortgage to buy. Or for the stuff they'd filled it with – the faux leather settee, the remodelled kitchen, the sleigh bed.

He wanted the full suburban. When she'd plucked up the courage to check their astrology compatibility, she discovered they should never have met, let alone have hitched their destinies to one another. That's what she told herself — irreconcilable astral differences. But the reason she'd left Patrick did not lie in the stars, but in her chthonic innards, her never-to-be tenanted womb.

Her neighbours couldn't believe she was ditching the best-behaved man on the estate. They thought she was mad; Patrick was attentive, good-looking and solvent. Sure enough, a year after they split up, he'd married Deirdre (Aries with Scorpio rising) who lived four doors down. She was already a single mother with three sons so Patrick had hit the jackpot in the family department. Something he'd always wanted. And he and Deirdre went on to have another son between them. So it wasn't as if Adrienne had deprived him of anything.

At the time she got pregnant, Adrienne was going back and forth to London for her astrology courses so she didn't count herself as one of those girls forced to 'take the boat'. She was going anyway so the journey itself wasn't traumatic. But afterwards, she was sick and desolate. She holed up in a bed-and-breakfast near Euston and tried to gather herself. She didn't believe abortion was murder, but she felt like an ugly assassin who'd taken aim at a perfectly good marriage and torpedoed it.

'I'm too good for you, is that it?' Patrick had said when she announced she was leaving him.

She nodded vehemently. He didn't know how true it was.
'Bullshit!'
'You either accept my reasons or you don't,' she'd said.
'I don't,' Patrick said like a reversed wedding vow.

Twenty-Twenty Vision

In the end she'd told him there was someone else because that's what everyone expects, isn't it? That was twenty-four years ago.

Adrienne had got into astrology through the *I Ching* when she was trying to decide if and how she might leave Patrick. She'd sit cross-legged on the living room floor while he was out at work throwing coins to predict her next move. The *I Ching* never gave her a straight answer, but it had led her to astrology and in it she found something she could understand – and believe in. It was comforting to think that there were big sweeps of movements in the heavens that could monumentalize small lives like hers.

She'd started by throwing astrology parties for her friends, then realized that she could charge. Up to this, Adrienne had never been good on paid jobs. She could do them but she couldn't keep them. She'd had a long succession of part-time positions – sales assistant, hotel receptionist, nurse's aide – anything rather than an office job she would say. Something in her chafed against restriction and railed against ambition. But with astrology, it took only a couple of courses for her to set herself up and become a kind of bohemian businesswoman.

At first, she'd done every cheesy gig she could find. She'd visited old folks' homes and community centres, she'd done carnivals and fêtes, but the Celtic Tiger had opened up the coffee mornings market. Women at home suddenly curious about themselves, who had enough money to pursue their psyches. Gone were the darkened tents and the long gypsy skirts. Adrienne became like a mother-confessor; her most used prop was her box of Man-size Kleenex. She'd done alright until the crash when the bottom fell out of one of her major sources of income – hen parties. The L-plated brides dropped their stargazing sessions and settled for supermarket vodka at home and Adrienne's income had dropped like a stone.

'Look Heavenly!' had saved her. It was an online outfit which paid her a retainer. Now she had a world-wide client base and there was no more schlepping around to women's houses and breaking bad news to them over cheap biscuits and plunger-pot coffee.

She'd moved into the Entrepreneur's Hub on the strength of her new cautious optimism. (Well, she *was* a Taurus with Scorpio rising.)

The Hub was on the fourth floor of a new build in the City Quarter. Keelin, the manager, gave her the tour. He sashayed out from behind the reception desk in the front lobby – an echo chamber of speckled grey tile and glass with stainless steel turnstiles near the entrance – and began walking at a clip. Adrienne struggled to keep up, seeing only the back of his skinny red jeans and skinnier white shirt as he gestured left and right and reeled off monosyllabic information like a bored flight attendant.

'Bathrooms, unisex, here.'

'Green Room, there.' He pointed to a restaurant area. 'Nespresso coffee pods, veggie wraps, breakout area for client meetings.'

He came to a halt at the lifts, which were all glass. She and Keelin scooted up to the fourth floor. They stepped out directly into a vast open-plan space divided into booths and pods. Keelin padded down a central aisle.

'And here's your Hubby Cubby,' he said with a flourishing hand. Adrienne grimaced internally.

Twenty-Twenty Vision

It was a perfectly adequate work cubicle, a kidney shaped desk, well-sprung office chair and a half-height baffled partition that afforded a modicum of privacy.

'It's a hot-desking situation,' Keelin said.

Adrienne thought immediately of sex, though it was hard to imagine any animal passions in a place like this, let alone sexual congress.

'No personal clutter of any kind, no knick-knacks, no plants, no baby photos.' He paused. Have you looked at me, Adrienne thought, but then she *was* old enough to have grandchildren.

'Not even Post-its,' Keelin warned. 'When you go, everything goes with you.'

'Just like life then,' she'd said but Keelin didn't get it. He gave her a strained smile.

'Alrighty?' he chirruped then turned on his heel. Adrienne watched his runway walk until the lift took him away.

When Tara Smart arrived, she'd looked like a waif, a child lost in a storm. She was pale and painfully slender – those little bony wrists – a long curtain of chestnut hair falling over a downcast brow. She wore black jeans teamed with shapeless granny cardigans in mulberry and sludge green. The only lively part of her attire was the clownish striped socks that peeped over the top of her Converse. At least, Adrienne thought, it was another woman in the place. Everyone else in the Hub was male. They were mostly young men who came and went in their tight blue suits and brown shoes with their ties flying and a hum of busyness that acted like armour. There was a small 'alternative' culture in the Hub, meaning, Adrienne realized, older. There was Dreadlock Billy, a music promoter, and Rod Furlong, who made memorial videos for funerals, but she gravitated towards the young element in the Hub.

In the spirit of 'leaning in', Adrienne considered introducing herself to Tara but she hesitated. She remembered that ninny Keelin reminding her pointedly that everyone here was a sole trader, which she read as keep your distance. When he'd said it, Adrienne saw it as 'soul trader' and thought – that's what I am in the midst of all this corporate hush. A soul trader. Foolishly she'd taken solace from that.

She'd eventually bumped into Tara in the Green Room, a glass box on the ground floor facing the street. It was a misnomer since it was, like the rest of the place, grey. The green referred to the food not the décor. There were lime-coloured juices, spinach-filled veggie wraps, green tea, all housed in celestial light-filled cabinets. Tara was sitting alone at one of the tables. Adrienne beetled over, introduced herself and sat down without waiting to be invited. She opened her Tupperware box of home-made beetroot salad, which in these surroundings seemed a garish departure from good taste. Tara was nursing a small takeaway Americano and a yogurt-coated rice cake.

Adrienne spooned the livid salad into her mouth, feeling like a vampire.

'I've seen you in the Hub,' she said. 'It's funny, isn't it, to be working alongside people whom you've no idea what they do.'

Tara said nothing.

'So,' Adrienne gently persisted. 'What is it you do?'

'Oh,' Tara said as if surprised to be asked. 'I'm a freelancer. Social media and PR for non-profits.'

How boasting online was a job, Adrienne didn't understand.

'And you?' Tara asked.

'Astrological counselling,' Adrienne said.

The flicker of a smirk crossed Tara's face. Adrienne found herself bristling.

'I know what you're thinking,' Adrienne said. 'That astrology is some kind of New Age hippie stuff. But my clients are often professional people.'

'Really?' Tara said. 'So what is it you actually do?'

'I compile astrological charts and profiles and follow up with phone counselling, and, of course, I meet clients here.' She gestured with the beetrooty spoon. 'The décor helps, actually.'

'Is that so?' Tara asked.

'Oh yes, people feel like they're visiting a broker.'

'And not a tent in a fairground,' Tara said.

'Exactly,' said Adrienne.

What Adrienne didn't tell Tara was that the business end of astrology had pretty much taken over her existence. She now spent half of her working day writing nagging emails to potential customers who'd signed up for a free reading but now had to be dragooned into buying the personal counselling session by phone or Skype or Zoom, or the Look Heavenly! manual and CDs, or the weekly Tarot readings in their inbox. The script which she was required to follow to the letter was a trajectory of accumulated civil hostility written in the royal we.

> *Ever feel life was passing you by and every choice you make is the wrong one? We know that feeling ...*
>
> *We've got an offer you just can't resist ...*
>
> *We can't believe you'd pass up on this chance to change ...*

It made Adrienne feel like an astral loan shark. She looked around the sleek grey Hub. Despite all her youthful protestations, look where she'd ended up. An office.

'So what brought you to the Hub?' Adrienne asked Tara though it sounded like a cheap chat-up line.

'Desperation,' Tara said. 'I'm living with my boyfriend in a tiny flat, I mean like *hobbit-sized*. The kitchen is in a cupboard, literally. And trying to work there was just impossible. Particularly since Pete, Pete's my boyfriend, is at home all day. I just had to get out of there ...'

Adrienne was surprised at the sudden rush of personal information.

'The broadband is woeful – the best reception is sitting on the loo. Can you believe it? And Pete was driving me mad under my feet all the time ...'

Adrienne thought guiltily of the large open-plan living room in her flat where she lived alone. She'd joined the Hub to make her work seem more business-like, more grown-up.

'So I guess you really need this place.'

'You could say that!' Tara said with real conviction.

Adrienne tried to dissipate the intensity.

'What does Pete do?' she asked.

'Sweet FA,' Tara said. 'He *was* the events manager at The Windsock.' She gestured to the only surviving old building in the neighbourhood visible across the street from the Green Room. It was a three-storey nineteenth-century tavern sitting in a rubbled space, which had suddenly become hip with the new offices going up all around it.

'It's how we met,' Tara said sadly. 'At a Police retro night.'

Adrienne felt the yawning chasm of their ages open up. She'd known The Police first time around and she could never hear 'Every Breath you Take' without thinking of Róisín. It was the song that was playing in the taxi on her way to the clinic in Kentish Town.

'What age are you?' Adrienne asked.

Twenty-Twenty Vision

'I'll be twenty-four in July,' Tara said.
Adrienne felt a soft shock.

She and Tara became friends despite the thirty-year age difference, and their mutual incomprehension at what the other did for a living. Physically, they were the original odd couple, Tara's young slightness set against Adrienne's stout middle-age. Her chopped platinum hair, neon red glasses and Aztec-patterned smocks seemed the equivalent of shouting beside Tara's deep camouflage wardrobe. But their booths were adjacent and they worked similar hours. They ordered lunch in from the noodle shop, they had coffee breaks in the Green Room. They shared life experiences. Adrienne told Tara the ancient story of Patrick in broad brush strokes (though, obviously, not all of it). Tara confided about her mother dying when she was fifteen, the little crush she'd nursed at school for her science teacher. (It was her white coat, her streaked blonde hair, her leopardy eyes, Tara said.)

This must be what it's like for a biological mother meeting her daughter for the first time in adulthood, Adrienne thought. Gently, she pressed Tara for details of her growing-up; she wanted to know everything. Tara was an only child, raised in the suburbs. They'd gone caravanning in France every summer when she was a kid, Tara said. Her father was a bit of a boy scout. His idea of getting away from it all was towing a lumbering, swaying tin house on wheels all around Brittany and Normandy. Her mother always got violently seasick on the ferry and they'd had to put a grounding chain on the back of the car to stop her throwing up on the road. When she was dying, she'd confided in Tara how she'd dreaded those trips.

'She hated the ghastly camp sites and the sing-songs my father organized with people who spoke the same language and ate out of cans,' Tara said. 'She wanted red wine and escargots and Edith Piaf in a little bistro in Paris. And when I asked her why she didn't say anything, she said, because your father loved it and that's what you do for someone you love.'

Tara toyed with her coffee.

'That was my mother,' she said.

Adrienne found herself making maternal audits. She would not have been a sweet mother. She would have been bossy, argumentative, interfering. And definitely not self-sacrificing.

Tara's father had been strict, particularly after her mother's death. He was parent cubed, Tara said. No discos till she was eighteen, definitely no boyfriends. She'd done a TEFL course after college and escaped to Japan for a year in order to make the break from him.

'I love him, of course I do, he's my Dad, but he'd have never let me grow up.'

'And what does he think of Pete?'

'What do you think?'

'No boy is good enough for my daughter?' Adrienne offered.

Tara nodded grimly. Adrienne found herself in silent agreement with Dad. This Pete certainly wasn't good enough for her Tara, if you asked her. But nobody, least of all Tara, was asking her, so she kept her views to herself.

As time went on, she and Tara would pop over to The Windsock for a drink after work. The interior was much as it had been when it had been an old man's pub, but the clientele was now predominantly young and music boomed from it all day long.

'So this is where you met Pete?'

Tara explained that he'd been everyone's favourite bartender. Adrienne thought she could predict the rest. A party boy who'd enjoyed his parties too much. But she was wrong. Three months before, Tara said, Pete had simply walked out of the job. Couldn't take it, he said, all that noise, all that fake enthusiasm. Now he sat in the flat all day, watching porn, Tara was sure.

Leave him, Adrienne wanted to shout, but she silenced her burgeoning tiger mother's instincts.

She'd have to be careful, go gently, build slowly. This wasn't the kind of care she was used to lavishing on her own relationships. After her marriage there'd been a series of enjoyable short-term flings which she remembered now with nostalgic fondness because there were no strings attached. But she'd never really yielded to any of them. The truth was sex had left her tepid; freedom had been her drug of choice. She'd left a perfectly nice man to have it.

Her softly, softly approach with Tara would have worked eventually, Adrienne was sure, if only she hadn't seen her aura. Tara's desk was in her sight-line and suddenly it seemed as if there were two of Tara, the real one blurring at the edges into a darker, ghostly double. A trick of the light, Adrienne thought. All this glass in the Hub and the strange reflections it cast, that's what it was. But she couldn't shake off the image, as if some essence of Tara was leaking into the atmosphere. Adrienne had an image of spinal fluid and lumbar punctures. Get a grip, she told herself.

When she'd got into astrology seriously, Adrienne had heard other practitioners – that's what everybody called themselves now – talking about auras. Some of them saw colours; Adrienne imagined rainbows coming out of people's ears. Others could see people's dead grandmothers or lost lovers. But in all the talk about auras none of them mentioned seeing the shadow figure of the person herself, someone who wasn't a dead relation or an old boyfriend. Adrienne blinked and hoped it would go away. But it didn't. She wondered was it time to pay a visit to Specsavers? For years she'd prided herself in having 20-20 vision and she'd only recently had to get distance glasses which spent most of the time on her head.

She didn't want to be someone who saw visions. That just wasn't her.

Reluctantly, she looked up auras. None of the information referred to seeing someone's silhouette blurring into darkness. Why was Tara's imprint on the world becoming indistinct? Was she flirting with some kind of despair that only Adrienne could see? What did it mean? She wasn't contemplating suicide, was she? She wanted it to go away, but Adrienne knew sooner or later she would have to tell Tara.

'You can see my what?'

They were having lunch together in the Green Room with their takeaways from the Wok-In.

'Your aura, except yours seem to be draining away your power.'

Tara actually blanched. Jesus, Adrienne thought to herself, maybe I am a visionary. Tara laid down her chopsticks.

'You can see this by just looking at me?' she asked.

'Looking at you in the light.'

She reached out and placed her hand reassuringly on Tara's arm and pushed her glasses up on to her hair. Something about the way she leaned forward, oozing concern, seemed to undo Tara.

'Something *has* been happening,' she began haltingly and then burst into tears. 'It's Pete ... he thinks I'm seeing someone else.'

'What?'

Adrienne fished out a packet of tissues. An old reflex. She always had a pack on hand for clients.

'And are you?'

Tara looked as if Adrienne had slapped her across the face.

'Of course not,' she said hotly.

'Well, it wouldn't be the end of the world.'

'It would for me.'

Get yourself free, girl, Adrienne thought. 'No one died of a break-up,' she said instead. *Not true*, a voice inside her insisted, but she tamped it down. Now was not the time.

'Leave him,' she commanded.

She'd done Tara and Pete's joint charts – secretly. It was a disaster area! Their grand crosses didn't just meet, they locked horns. Maybe Pete was great in bed, but Adrienne doubted it.

'I can't,' Tara wailed, 'not when he's so depressed.'

'Depressed people can suck the life out of you,' Adrienne countered. 'If I'd stayed with Patrick, that's what I would have become. A blood-sucker.'

It was a convenient lie. The Pill not taken had sealed her fate.

'I have to fake it all the time,' Tara said, 'but I didn't think he'd noticed.'

'Ah Lovey, you can't go on like that.'

It was the first time, Adrienne had used an endearment with Tara. It felt transgressive. She wondered if Tara had noticed.

'He wouldn't survive without me,' Tara said.

'Everyone survives.' *Really?* the voice inside queried gently.

'Well, *I* just can't do it,' Tara said crossly.

'You'll be amazed what you find you can do when things get desperate enough.'

'What kind of advice is that?'

'It's all I've got.'

Adrienne had never got to elaborate on Tara's aura. Just as well. She'd seen the look of panic in Tara's eye when she'd mentioned it. She was afraid if she pressed it further, Tara would retreat, and she was in too deep now to allow that. What more could she have told Tara, anyway? Someone is draining the life out of you. He's called Pete and he's a vampire.

The following week she made an appointment with Eleanor Tuft. When her marriage broke up, Adrienne had gone for counselling to Eleanor, a glamorous ex-nun who wore dainty Chanel-like suits and court shoes and dyed her high-built hair a treacly blonde. (This must have been the fashion at the time she'd entered the convent, Adrienne thought.) Eleanor welcomed her like an old friend.

'Adrienne! Come in, sit, sit!'

Adrienne settled in. This was like the old times doing home astrological readings – two women gossiping about the abstract future. After exchanging small talk for a while, Adrienne almost forgot why she'd come and was basking in the feeling of being a successful therapy graduate when Eleanor got down to business.

'What seems to be the problem, Adrienne?'

She was back to being a relapsed patient.

'I'm seeing things that aren't there,' she told Eleanor.

'What do you mean, not there?'

Adrienne explained about Tara's aura. (She didn't mention anything about Róisín. Well, she couldn't, because she'd never admitted to Róisín in the sessions with Eleanor.)

'And what do you think it is?' Eleanor said bending forward in her chair and staring at Adrienne intently.

'It's Mercury in my tenth house,' Adrienne said.

'Seriously now, Adrienne, why do you think you're seeing darkness around your friend?'

'I don't know.'

'In Jungian dream work they say that everyone and everything in the dream is you.'

'But this isn't a dream –'

'But if it were, and there was a black shadow all around you, what would that signify?'

Adrienne racked her brains. She'd forgotten how Eleanor was like the host of a live game show. If she were at home watching this on TV, she'd be shouting the answer at the screen but in Eleanor's presence she ended up blurting out the first thing she could think of.

'I would say it meant that there was another version of me trying to get out into the world that was more authentic than I am.'

'And is that true? That you're inauthentic?'

This was the one time that Adrienne knew the answer to Eleanor's question.

After the visit to Eleanor, Adrienne texted Tara and arranged to meet her outside the office. *Green Room, 1 pm*, she wrote. And Tara texted a smiley face back. The Green Room was so cavernous it never filled and they sat in one of its glassy corners, Tara with her skinny white, Adrienne with a cappuccino and some kind of vegan scone.

'Aren't you having something to eat?' Adrienne asked.

'Not hungry,' Tara said.

Oh God, Adrienne thought, she's in one of her sulky moods. At times like this Adrienne felt like the mother of a teenager.

'Look,' she began, 'I wanted to say something about your aura ...'

Tara set her lips into a thin line. 'Not this crap again,' she said.

'No, you don't understand. I wanted to say that –'

'Just stop, Adrienne, I don't want to hear it. I have troubles of my own.'

Adrienne leaned forward. 'What's up, pet?'

Tara left a long silence. Tears were hovering and her chin quivered. She drew several sharp breaths. Finally, she got through one sentence. 'Pete has left me ...'

'Oh well,' Adrienne said, cheering militantly inside.

'Is that all you have to say?' Tara said. '*Oh well.*'

Adrienne felt her temper rising. Here she was, trying to be emotionally honest for the first time in her life only to find herself being thwarted by some adolescent strop.

'I'm sorry, sweetheart, really I am, but you're better off without him, he was only bringing you down.'

'Well,' Tara said smirking bitterly, 'you'll be glad to hear the feeling is mutual. He thinks there's something going on between us. That's why he's dumped me.'

Adrienne let out a mirthful yelp. 'Oh please, Tara, that's absurd.'

'Is it?' Tara demanded and for one moment Adrienne wondered if, somehow, Tara knew what she'd been thinking – that Tara was a reincarnation. Yes, she had to admit it now, a reincarnation of a child she'd had destroyed half a century ago.

She shook her head to clear that thought away. It just sounded too flakey. Even for her.

'It's called female friendship,' she said tartly. 'Hasn't Pete heard of that? Haven't you?'

'Why would a woman who's old enough to be my mother want to hang out with a twenty-four-year-old?'

The voice inside Adrienne started chanting, *I am your mother, I am your mother.* Here goes, she thought, plunge in.

'Because –' she began.

'Because you're gay,' Tara said matter-of-factly.

'I'm not, as it happens,' she went on. 'Not that it matters.'

'Sounds like someone's in denial,' Tara said triumphantly. 'You may not realize it but you've been hitting on me, that's what Pete says.'

'And what do you say?' Adrienne said. 'Since you're the one having the friendship with me.'

'I, I don't know.'

'Don't you feel you know me by now, trust me?' Adrienne could hear the pleading in her own voice. She was fighting to hold on to her girl. 'You're like a daughter to me,' she said feeling tears gather in her throat.

Tara regarded her, hard-faced.

'Like my daughter,' she corrected herself.

'What?'

'I had a daughter who would have been your age now –'

'Funny you never mentioned her before,' Tara said.

That's because she has just come alive to me, Adrienne thought. You did that.

'Very convenient,' Tara said. 'I think you're just old and eccentric and you've been hitting on me. I've a good mind to complain about you to Keelin for workplace harassment.'

And with that she got up and stormed out leaving Adrienne in the glass box, weeping and unable to stop.

She never saw Tara again. She couldn't have borne going back to the Hub. There was literally nothing there for her. She'd followed Keelin's instructions to the letter and left a clean desk behind. Being there had been a mistake. Who was she fooling – she was neither young nor an entrepreneur, she was fifty-seven! She turned her back on Look Heavenly! The break came just before Covid and the Hub was shut down anyway. She drew the lockdown payments while they lasted and regrouped. She took retraining in office management skills. One of the sessions was with a life coach who asked her to fill in a questionnaire, ten pages of multiple choice questions. It was obviously meant for somebody younger because there was that old chestnut about where you could be found at parties. Not going, Adrienne wanted to answer, but that wasn't one of the options.

When the coach had compiled her answers, she told her she was an INTJ, whatever that meant. When Adrienne questioned it, the coach said: 'Well, the acronyms are difficult. We prefer to use descriptors rather than initials to describe your personality type. Think of yourself as an architect – exact, demanding, a perfectionist, a bit of a loner, but there's also a lot of emotion bubbling away under the surface. You're recording an 85% score on turbulence.'

'So I'm a turbulent architect?'

It sounded like the start of a new religion, and this time, Adrienne wasn't buying. I'm already a failed astrologist, she wanted to say.

In the end, the niece of a friend of hers threw her a lifeline. She'd set up a decluttering service and asked Adrienne if she'd do three days a week in the office. The money wasn't much but it was a start. Adrienne saw no more auras. Instead, she helped Laura rifle through strangers' wardrobes and throw things out. And she stopped marking Róisín's anniversary.

DONE DEAL

Even before she saw the seller's name, Eva recognized the dress from the photograph. It was draped on a headless mannequin, a red velveteen torso on a stick, the sateen beaded bodice and feathered skirt exactly how she remembered it. *For Sale,* the ad read, *vintage 1980s flapper dress, suitable for a wedding. E300 or nearest offer to Fin D.*

Between Zoom work calls, Eva would switch over to Done Deal for a break and idly trawl through what was on offer. She was a lurker on the site; she wasn't interested in buying. She simply wanted to be in touch with home in an uncomplicated, passive way. The distance between Australia and Ireland collapsed once she was in that telescoped virtual space. It meant that, theoretically, she could get into her car to pick up a 1950s cocktail cabinet in Enniskerry, a child's buggy from Macroom, a vintage clock from Artane.

Fin D. It just had to be her, didn't it? Fin Dolan.

Fin was Eva's former step-daughter. How weird did that sound, how many times removed? Seventeen years and 15,000 miles removed.

*

Aren't you taking on a lot, her friends had said when she'd told them she was marrying Lar. Their foreheads creased with worry,

I mean, three kids? But Eva had felt invincible. Anyway, she'd already taken them on. She'd been employed by Lar as an au-pair for the twins and in a matter of weeks, she was in love. Eva had never known anything like it. It had pounced on her and become fierce and necessary. She didn't have to check on this love, or measure it. She didn't have to speculate or wonder. Fiach and Con were her darlings. No, it was more than that; not only were they *hers*, but it was as if they always had been.

The twins were identical but Eva had always been able to tell them apart. Fiach had a little laziness in his left eye, Con had more curls. When she wasn't with them, she would close her eyes and have the same image of them, a pair of blond cherubs, their adoring faces looking up at her, Fiach's runny nose, Con's teething drool, eyes the palest blue, their hands clamped to her thighs. Up, up up, they would chorus in unison. She still remembers the feel of them nuzzling into her neck, their milky smell, their crumby breath. She'd already inhaled them, drunk with their trust and their doughy love. By marrying she was simply getting Lar into the bargain. He was besotted with her and Eva had succumbed to his humid gratitude which, if her friends had asked, she'd have told them had its own sexual allure.

'I can't believe my luck, my darling,' Lar had said when she'd said yes. His endearments still unnerved her.

No wonder he can't, her mother said shrewishly, he's a single father.

*

Looking at the ad again, Eva calculated that Fin must be close to thirty now. Older than Eva was when she was trying to be Fin's mother. She felt her feelings curdle at the memory.

Then a more pressing curiosity took over. Why, after all this time, was Fin getting rid of the once precious dress? It had belonged to Lar's first wife, Niamh. Lar's dead wife, that is. If only Niamh had been a pesky, troublemaking ex warring over access, Eva had thought at the time, everything would have been so much easier. But no, Niamh was a martyred saint who'd died of complications after the birth of the twins. Eva had presumed, when she'd first met Lar, that he was divorced and the victor in a custody battle. When he opened the door to her that's what he looked like – a trendy, stay-at-home Dad with long locks tied in a ponytail, wearing an embossed tunic shirt with a Chinese collar over a pair of jeans. The only hint of a child was the towel thrown over his shoulder. He showed her into the living room which had a thick, soft-pile white carpet. A strange choice, she'd thought, for a house with small kids.

Fiach was bedded down on the sofa in a nest of cushions and Lar picked him up in his arms and turned him around towards Eva like an exhibit.

'Say hello,' Lar said.

Eva reached out her hand for the child's clenched fist.

'He's just woken up,' Lar explained as Fiach began to grizzle. 'He's a bit cranky.'

The door burst open at that stage and Fin marched in. Fair, pouty, cross.

'What is it, Finola?' Lar said, 'Can't you see I'm busy here?'

'Con's just barfed and I'm not going to clean it up,' she announced. She flicked her long hair over her shoulder. Then eyeing Eva up and down, she said, 'Is this her?'

When Lar didn't answer, she flounced out.

'And where's Nana?' he called after her.

'Out!'

Lar looked at Eva helplessly. She reached for Fiach as Lar rushed out of the room. With Fiach in her arms, she felt the charge of love immediately, his eyes like liquid pools of hurt.

She could have done the Mary Poppins thing, barged into the kitchen, offering to take charge, making herself indispensable. But she wanted to see what normal was like in this household. And normal was a man who couldn't divide himself in three. And a daughter who was a handful.

When Lar returned, Fiach was asleep in her arms. Another parent might have been charmed by this, but not Lar. It was back to business.

'You have to understand,' he said, 'the children's mother is dead.'

'Oh,' she'd faltered, feeling a bitch for judging him earlier.

'So you see,' he continued, 'I'm looking for someone who'll be more than just the hired help.'

A mother, Eva's mother said, that's what he's been looking for from the get-go.

She'd had no experience of grief – or a grief-stricken man, to be more precise. At first, she noticed nothing different about Lar. He seemed like most older men – friends of her father's were her closest experience – brisk, civil, distant. If you didn't know he was recently bereaved you wouldn't have guessed he was a tragic figure. Eva saw a lot of him. She lived-in five nights out of seven and he worked from home. He was an architect with a successful practice in town but after Niamh's death he'd turned one of the big bedrooms upstairs into his office. Sometimes clients would come to see him, or other architects from the town office would drop by, but most of the time he would talk to them on the phone. He disappeared in the

Done Deal

mornings and he didn't like to be disturbed. But his presence made a difference; it provided authority and perhaps reproof. Eva was acutely aware of the man upstairs, particularly when the twins were cranky or off-colour, when one's wails would set the other one off. To reassure Lar, she would bring him up a cup of coffee mid-morning, as if to say in the midst of the tantrums and chaos, I *am* in control. She didn't know why she felt the need to do this, remembering the day of the interview and how beleaguered he had seemed.

Perhaps it was the calm of Lar's light-filled room which was, by comparison, an oasis of order. Everything seemed white. Lar's desk, the thin screen he worked on, the large copying machine that sat under the window. She needn't have worried about the babies' squawking: she discovered. Lar wore earphones when he worked. When Eva was in the room, he lifted them off and they sat around his neck like a collar of torture.

'Everything alright?' he would always ask and she would nod and sit opposite him to watch him drink, and savour this grown-up place set apart from the rowdy downstairs. It was over these coffees that Lar began to talk to her.

The first time she saw him upset was when she asked about Niamh's photos. Or lack of them. Fin was doing a school project on genealogy and needed images of her forbears. Which made it sound as if we were all descended from grizzlies, Eva thought. But when she went to look, there were no family albums, no framed photos on the mantelpieces or in the children's rooms. Not even a wedding photo. I'll ask your Dad, she'd said.

'I destroyed them,' Lar said shortly.

'What about the children?' Eva had demanded. She'd done a course on bereavement in her early childhood care course.

'I couldn't bear to still see her.' He raised a hand to his forehead, shielding his eyes from her and his shoulders began to shudder. Eva realized with a start that he was weeping. Oh God, she'd made him cry.

'I'm sorry –' she began but he turned his head away. There was something appalling about his disintegration. No man, no adult had ever broken down in front of her like this. It was a bit like watching him come. When she leaned out to touch his arm he was still flapping his hand at her; she couldn't work out if he was fending her off or reaching for her.

'Sometimes,' he said, snuffling loudly, but still shielding his gaze, 'every thought of her is a pain.'

As time went on, he told her intimate things, things she felt she shouldn't know. There'd been a miss between Fin and the twins, he told her. Another boy they would have called Hugh. They'd been trying for years and it seemed like the miracle was finally going to happen. It was late on, Lar had said, and Niamh had been warned it would be inadvisable to have any more. But she was determined that Fin would not be an only child.

Oh, Eva thought, so the twins are here purely for Fin's benefit. She felt a hot bubble of rage against the ever-present Niamh.

Then he announced, without warning, that he'd decided to send Fiach and Con to creche. Just a few hours a week to start with, he said.

'They need the company of other children.'

Eva was crushed. He was taking them away. Didn't he realize?

'Give you a break,' he'd said.

She didn't want a break from them.

'I'll pay you the same, of course.'

'It's not the money, Lar.' She was on first-name terms with him by then.

'What is it, then? I thought you'd be pleased.'

I can't bear to be parted from them, she wanted to say, they're mine.

'I ...'

'What are you trying to tell me?' he asked like a puzzled doctor.

He was standing in front of her and for a moment she thought he was going to have another grief ambush. Then he grabbed her arms as if he was going to give her a good shake.

'Do you feel what I do?' he demanded.

It sounded more like an interrogation than a declaration of love. What she felt she would have found hard to put into words. His confidences – his confessions, more like – had made her feel empowered. Maybe that was what love was – being in charge of other people's secrets. She looked into his hurt blue eyes and thought two things; I can't wound him further and I can't lose the twins.

'Yes,' she said and nodded vigorously. And it was true. Just not for him.

For the time being, the creche plan was dropped.

A couple of months into their marriage, Fin announced that she wanted to go to a fancy-dress disco at school. She catalogued its virtues. It would be highly supervised, teachers patrolling the perimeter of the school gym, a father doing dee-jay. It all sounded a bit lame to Eva who, at Fin's age, was the champion French kisser in contests they had in the youth club and at sixteen had lost her virginity to a boy in Irish college. In a strategic move, Fin had asked Eva first. She'd sashayed into the kitchen wearing her proposed outfit – a sleeveless white dress with a sheer beaded top and a feathered skirt. Eva suppressed a laugh. The dress was made for someone bigger and gaped under the arms. It was surely meant to have an under-slip because Finn's little breast swellings were clearly visible.

'What do you think?' Fin had asked twirling around in her bare feet.

'What's it for?' Eva had asked.

Fin told her about the disco. 'Can I go?'

'I don't see why not,' Eva said, 'but not in that thing! Who are you meant to be? Big Bird?'

There was an uncharacteristic silence.

'This was Mum's wedding dress,' Fin said, her bottom lip wobbling. Oh God, Eva thought. Another faux-pas to add to the list. (Silently she compared this frou-frou confection to what she had worn at her wedding. She and Lar had married in a registry office on the QT with only Eva's mother and Lar's brother as witnesses. It was in February and Eva had worn boots and a winter coat.)

'You'll have to ask Dad,' Eva said to Finn. When she heard herself calling Lar Dad, it made her feel like she was just another of Lar's brood.

Lar was surprisingly strict about child-rearing, particularly where Fin was concerned. Even though he had got rid of all her photos, he kept the memory of Niamh alive in his parenting. If there was a decision to be made, he would always speculate out loud as to what Niamh would have done. Eva wasn't deemed qualified to decide, not with Fin. The twins, yes, but Fin was a different jurisdiction.

'I'll talk to him,' Eva had promised.

When the kids were in bed, Eva broached the subject of the disco.

Done Deal

'She's too young,' Lar said emphatically.

'Oh come on, Lar, it all sounds pretty innocent.'

'Anything could happen.'

'Like what?' Eva demanded. 'It's a school disco for heaven's sake.'

'Finola's too young.'

He always called her by her full name although Fin insisted on everyone else using the shortened version.

'No,' Lar said. 'Niamh had strong feelings about this sort of thing.'

Eva groaned inwardly. Fin had been ten when her mother died; had Niamh already formulated a policy on teen dating?

'She wouldn't have approved of the over-sexualisation of children,' Lar went on.

'Well, if it's a no, then you'll have to tell her,' Eva said.

The following morning Lar called Fin up to the office. She was on mid-term break and loping around the house bored. Eva waited for the explosion. Five minutes later, she heard Fin galloping down the stairs two at a time. She stormed into the kitchen where Eva was feeding the dishwasher.

'I hate you!' she yelled.

'What have I done?'

'Dad said you argued against the disco!'

'What?'

'Dad said –'

'I did no such thing.' Eva could feel her anger boil.

'Your mother would never allow it,' Fin said, mimicking Lar's stentorian tone.

Eva was about to interject – *I'm not your mother, remember?* – until she realized the trap she was in. Since the wedding she'd been trying to get Fin to call her Mum – which she steadfastly refused to do. Now, now when it suited her, when Eva could be successfully scapegoated, suddenly she'd been elevated to mother status.

And Lar! He hadn't meant her when he was talking to Fin; he had meant Niamh.

She considered having it out with Fin there and then, but her anger had boiled over now and she could feel tears sprouting. Foolish, weakening tears. She did a lightning calculation. The twins were at creche; Fin was big enough to look after herself. And Lar ... well, sod him! She whipped the car keys from the bowl on the kitchen counter and stormed out

She needed to be somewhere off the radar. Swan Lake, that's where she'd go. This was the family's name for the lake, a drive-by beauty spot, which nestled on the side of the motorway. She and Lar would take the twins there to feed the swans though Lar was always clownishly looking over his shoulder because he said he was sure it was against the law. He'd said it was like a capital offence, or was that killing them? She couldn't remember. The thought of going there now reassured her, as much for the memory of those happier times, as of the place itself. In fact, Eva had always thought the lake a bit impoverished, with the road right beside it and the cars thundering by full of people too busy to stop. But, look, it was only a couple of miles away and it was a destination; otherwise she was afraid she might just keep on driving and who knew where she'd end up?

As she approached the lake it began to rain. Great paw prints splatted on to the windscreen. She turned on the wipers. As she did she noticed the car ahead of her suddenly buck and judder. *What the* ... Then it did it again. She put the brakes on gently while checking in the rear-view mirror. The last thing she needed was to be rear-ended. The car ahead was slowing too but still veering, plunging over the centre white line, ducking and weaving. Overtaking drivers were blasting their horns, their siren wails fading like lost warnings as they passed. What on earth was wrong? Was the driver drunk, she wondered, or ill? She put on her own hazard lights. The next minute something very hard and white hit the car. Except that the impact was so loud, it could have been a cloud – what keeps clouds up, she thought fleetingly – as she tried to steer blindly towards the hard shoulder. Everything slowed. It was like being snowed-in or trapped in a very sudsy car wash. Was it the airbag? Had something set it off accidentally? But no, this was not something inside the car. Next thing the windscreen splintered with a strange tinselly sound, and there, straddled on the bonnet, like some awful bloody sacrifice, was a swan. One wild eye was staring at her and a wing flapped ineptly. Feathers were raining down and she couldn't see over the lumpen corpse. She clutched the steering wheel but she didn't seem to have any control. Her breath was coming in barking gasps and she thought *I must stop, I must stop the car*. The next thing she crashed through the low barrier at the side of the road and rolled down a bank until the bark of a tree brought her to a halt. Beyond she could see the water. In the eerie silence, the car seemed to tick. It was only when she had come to a complete standstill that the shaking started.

She was afraid to move lest she disturb the corpse. The dashboard was bowed like a sagging shelf and the windscreen was reduced to a milky web. A sharp breeze was coming through the gap where it had sheared away from the roof of the car.

There was a knock on the window at her shoulder.

Leadenly she rolled down the window.

'Are you alright?'

She had a lopsided view of a man in a V-necked jumper, bouncy drills in his hair, and Elvis sideburns. She was about to answer when he raised a calloused hand to his mouth.

'Oh Jesus tonight,' he said when he saw the swan, and turning away, he threw up into the high grass.

Eva hauled herself out with difficulty. The angle the car was at meant the driver's door could only be opened a fraction before getting embedded in the mud of the embankment, but the man in the jumper had helped her, leading her up the bank to the roadside. The guards were called and by the time they arrived a crowd had gathered. Rain was still spitting though it hadn't become a shower. Somebody rang Lar on her behalf. A passer-by shoved a paper cup of scalding coffee into her hand from a nearby petrol station. They'd over-sugared it and she burnt her tongue, but it gave her something to hold on to. An ambulance came though it wasn't needed. Shock, they said, and wrapped her up in a cape of tin foil and took her blood pressure. There wasn't a mark on her.

'She'll be no use to you now,' the man who had got sick said to her and for a minute, Eva thought he was talking about the swan. But he meant the car. It was the last remnant of her old life, her life before the twins. It was a third-hand Starlet which she'd scrimped and saved for when she'd got her first job. Her mother had helped out with funds because, she said, it was important for her work to be mobile. Now she thought of Eva as stuck. Stuck with Lar.

The car was jammed in a damaging embrace with a tree trunk, the bonnet cleaved in two. Someone had removed the swan but stray feathers still wafted in the early autumn sunshine. In the distance on the lake, the living swans had gathered. Did they know what had happened, Eva wondered.

And why did this swan want to get away? She hadn't even known that swans travelled. They mated for life, didn't they? She'd always thought they just stayed put. Well, why wouldn't you, if you'd found your soul mate?

She stole a glance at the bloodied corpse lying spread-eagled on the grass verge like a felled dive-bomber. She had a sudden image of Fin in her finery. Soiled, limping home. Look how easily beauty could come to grief. Lar was right. She *was* too young.

When Lar came to collect her, the twins were strapped in the back seat of the people carrier. Fin was in the front passenger seat but when Lar pulled in and jumped out leaving the driver door open, she got out and meekly joined the twins in the back. All Eva wanted to do was to rush to them to tell them everything would be alright. Imagine if she'd been injured, or worse? How would those poor children survive? Her stomach made a sickening lurch — that was the seat of her feelings, she realized, not her heart. She turned towards Lar. He was whey-faced. His hair hung in lifeless drifts around his shoulders.

'Oh my God,' he said. Then he looked at her. 'I thought I'd lost you.'

Her rage of earlier was spent. She felt a surge of compassion; wouldn't that do? She moved towards him gingerly, adjusting her silver cape. He staggered forward wrapping his arms around her in a crackling embrace.

The years with Lar were a see-saw of indecision, though in her stomach the dread of the inevitable rupture kept on breaking through. Procrastination eased the dread but as time went on by the ferocity of her love for the twins began to feel like self-harm. She kept on making deals with herself. She'd wait until Lar had fully dealt with his grief over Niamh. She'd wait till the twins went to kindergarten, till they went to school, till they made their Communion … but she knew there was no good time to abandon children. They'd no memory of a mother other than her. Not so with Fin. She would always be Lar's girl, and Eva would always be the evil interloper. Perhaps if she'd had a child of her own with Lar, they might have become a blended family, but Lar was immoveable on more children. He blamed himself for letting Niamh try for the twins.

'I'd never forgive myself if ….'

He didn't finish the sentence.

*

She doesn't know what's happened to Lar. Has he married again? Would he risk it, she wonders, after the debacle with her? Men don't stay on their own, do they? When they'd separated, it had shocked her how little she missed him. But the twins! Not seeing them was a knife in her heart. She'd thought foolishly that she would still have access even though she had no legal claim on them, but Lar had refused absolutely.

'You leave me, you leave them,' he'd said on the phone.

It was only then she'd realized how deeply she'd hurt him. And how wrong she'd been about him. He hadn't seen her as a compromise wife, a mother of convenience. It was she who had been compromising all along. In the background she could hear one of the twins crying, unrelated to the spat with Lar. It was probably Con, who liked anything on wheels and had a propensity for crashing into things. Even so, she couldn't bear

Done Deal

eavesdropping on his pain so she'd accepted Lar's ultimatum without protest just to get off the phone. She could have fought it out in court but instead she opted to travel, to a destination that was as far away as she could find from the source of her guilt. Her babies.

She'd spent her first weeks in Sydney slathered in sunscreen and capaciously hatted like an invalid. She *was* an invalid. Even a year after the separation from Lar, she was in a state of emotional carnage. Being in a strange city all alone at the end of the world felt like banishment. But she had done it to herself. She'd considered ignoring advice and going outside unprotected. Having a layer of her pale skin seared off by the sun chimed exactly with what she felt inside. She would look up at the glaring sky and wonder what the hell she was doing here. Penance was the word that came to mind, Van Diemen's Land and all that. But there wasn't penance enough for what she'd done.

And then she met Ryan. They've been together longer than she was with Lar though it doesn't feel like that. They share a dinky terraced house with varnished timber floors, exposed sandstone brick, and furnished with quirky seconds and the white optimism of Chinese paper lampshades in every room. Although Ryan is a cabinet-maker and he's done much of the renovation work himself, the place has a contingent air as if they're students in a short-term share. The house is under a flight path so they live with the permanently thunderous sound of escape overhead. Eva likes that. Ryan has asked her to marry him several times but she's always refused. The last time, he'd put the little leather box back in his shirt pocket with a sighing finality. (It's his mother's vintage engagement ring so he always has it to hand.)

'Okay, okay,' he'd said and he put his hands up as if he were negotiating with a hostage taker and trying to keep her calm. She was perfectly calm.

'But what about kids?' he'd wheedled.

Eva knew he'd wanted them although up to this he'd never said as much. She, on the other hand, was the only woman she knew who was grateful for the biological clock. Bring it on, she would plead, the final tolling of her womb.

'No,' she said, grasping the nettle. 'I can't, Ryan. I just can't. I can never fall in love with a child again.'

When she said it, it made her sound like a sex offender.

She wanted him to strike her or give her a black eye; something commensurate with her refusals. But he just looked stricken.

'Maybe you'll change your mind?' he said.

She couldn't stand the tenderness of his appeal.

'I won't,' she said, 'Don't wait around hoping.'

And yet, he had.

On the internet nothing dies. The dress stayed online for weeks. Every day, Eva would check to see if it had shifted. She wished she didn't know it was there. It was both rebuke and a memorial. Fin reduced the price twice, once to E250, then to E200. Eva practically prayed for someone to buy it. With it gone, the ghost of Niamh could finally be laid to rest. That was clearly the point Fin had reached too. Or maybe she was strapped for cash? For the first time in their lives, she and Fin both wanted the same thing. In the end, Eva thought, why don't I buy it and put us all out of our misery?

She asked her friend Audrey back home if she would be her proxy so her connection to the business could go undetected. She'd had fantasies about talking to Fin – a mobile number was provided – but she realized she had nothing to say to her. Anyway, if they'd spoken, all Eva would want to do was to talk about the twins. Did they remember her? What are they doing now? Are they happy? In her mind's eye, they're still the tow-headed, short-trousered, knee-scuffed boys they were when she left. Still at an age when she was able to kiss everything better.

When it arrived via Audrey, she tore the brown package as recklessly as a child at Christmas. Audrey, or Fin, had carefully wrapped it in tissue paper which after its long journey was like veined marble. She lifted the dress out, unfolded it and pressed the bodice to her nose. She thought it might contain scent traces of Lar's house, but, of course, if it smelled of anyone it would be Fin. As it happened, it didn't smell of anything, or nothing Eva could identify, at least.

She went to the mirror in the bedroom and held it up in front of her, swinging from right to left profile and back again. It was the first time she'd been this close to it, the first time she'd handled it. The dress had been too big on Fin but looking at it now, Eva saw that Niamh must have been a very slight woman. A size 10. It was the first time she'd considered Niamh as a physical being rather than a disembodied ideal. Eva certainly wouldn't fit into it. No matter, she hadn't bought it to wear it. She planned to burn it.

She was still measuring it up against herself when Ryan came into the room. She saw his expression morph in the mirror's reflection. Confusion first, followed by quizzical surprise. Then his face opened out into a broad beam of hope. She turned around to explain, feeling once again the stone heavy burden of a man's happiness.

WEIGHT

Bernard is sitting at Gate 6D in the departures hall at Abu Dhabi, with two hours to spare after the first leg of his journey east. He is so tired that if he falls asleep, which he will – even on these hard chairs with the metal arms digging into his girth – he knows nothing will wake him. There are no public announcements so he can't even depend on a booming PA to rouse him. It is 3 a.m. for him, but mid-morning here. What to do for two hours? Coffee, he thinks. Proper coffee. Not food – he has done nothing but graze from aluminium dog trays for the past nine hours with his knees up around his ears. He needs caffeine – a tub of it.

There's a ground attendant at the counter who has just bundled the last passengers on to a flight to Khartoum – an Indian family, parents, three children and their cling-film wrapped luggage. He sees she is about to close the gate so he hauls himself out of the bucket seat and pads up to her. Her back is turned. He taps her gently on the upper arm. She stops, turns, flinches when she sees him. Oh God, he thinks, is touching a woman in public a transgression here?

But he doesn't get outrage from her, just the full force of her vibrancy. Nutmeg skin set off by a slash of vermillion lipstick. There's a name tag pinned to her lapel – *Amal*. He thinks of George Clooney whom Olivia used to say she was holding out for when her husband left her. Then George's Amal came along and dashed Olivia's hopes. This Amal is wearing a western-style uniform, a tight rust-coloured skirt, a trim jacket in olive green. Swathed around her neck is a veil that emanates from her head gear, a scarf and hat combined. East meets West.

He feels like a whale in her presence, in the loud Hawaiian shirt he chose for coolness. What a laugh! His pale skin is flushed with the misted residue of old sweat. There are pools under his armpits, plus all the discomforts she cannot see – the chafing thighs, the sweat of his loins.

'You speak English?' he asks, cursing himself for sounding pidginy.

She nods minimally. Bored? Superior? Or afraid to crack her make-up?

'A little,' she concedes.

'I'm looking for coffee,' he says, 'is there somewhere near the gates or do I have to go back?' He points to the maze of brightly lit, duty-free outlets that he had passed without interest. There is no one in his life to buy for – except Olivia, and that's a gift that will have to be chosen with the utmost deliberation, as with all his dealings with her.

'Fat white,' she says pointing a finger straight at him. It is said with so little inflection that he cannot believe what he has heard. The heat has made him slow-witted.

'I beg your pardon?'

'Fat white,' she repeats, still pointing.

Oh God, is she one of these #MeToo women who's going to make an example of him? Or maybe that's just what she sees. A pasty, pudgy sixty-two-year-old man trying it on.

Trip of a lifetime he told his colleagues when he opted for early retirement. Always wanted to see the Forbidden City.

Chinks, they said to him, the chinks have taken over the world, why would you want to go there? (When he was packing he realized they were right – half of his shirts had *Made in China* on the labels).

'Communists in capitalist clothing,' Olivia said, 'the most dangerous kind.'

Olivia has always been a bit of a politico. And Bernard should know. He's nursed a low-lying passion for her all his adult life. But in forty years he hasn't acted upon it, because he knows she's never seen him that way. Very few people have.

He and Olivia started on the same day at City Hall, did orientation together and after detours through several other departments had ended up in Rates. They're the only original ones left, the folk memory of the organization is how their department head puts it.

'As if we're a pair of doddery old fiddle players with all the tunes in our heads,' Olivia used to say.

'Or clog dancers,' Bernard would add. Sometimes their verbal riffs went on for days.

Olivia had recently taking up ballroom dancing, which, foolishly, made Bernard wonder – yet again. He's a good dancer, always has been; his Aunt Min taught him when he was an ungainly teenager. Thought it would be his saving grace.

Olivia jabbed him playfully on the arm. Their tenderness was expressed like this, roughly, like a pair of tomboys.

She wasn't playful about China.

'Terrible human rights record,' Olivia prodded, 'remember Tiananmen Square? What about Ai Wei Wei?' That's Olivia's job – to be the voice of his conscience.

Bernard looks at Amal again as if she has repeated Olivia's impassioned accusations. But there is nothing but indifference in her mask-like face. He feels a tide of fury rising.

'What did you say ...?'

Weight

'Fat white,' she says evenly.

So that's it, he thinks, I am here to be insulted. Openly. A dumpy white man who has no finer feelings, the butt of everyone's contempt. Is this how it will be on his guided bus tour of the Great Wall? Except the Chinese won't say it. Not like this. Inscrutable, isn't that how they're supposed to be? But they'll be thinking it, Bernard is sure.

Then, patiently – as if he were infirm – Amal catches his elbow and steers him around to face in the opposite direction, still pointing her finger. She smiles now. It stings, adding insult to injury. Then he sees it. A sandwich board advertising a coffee shop: *Flat White*.

Oh, relief!

He could kiss her, but he won't, of course.

He turns to say thanks but she is gone, strutting off on her rust-coloured heels. All a mistake, he thinks, a linguistic misunderstanding. *You're tired, you're jet-lagged*. That's Olivia's voice in his head. But it's no good. No matter how much he self-consoles, the trip of a lifetime, that precious balloon of escape that has hovered overhead all his life, shrivels with a fart, all the air gone out of it. What was he thinking? There is no escape from the body's stubborn armour.

He will press on with his trip, he will go on all the tours, he will take photographs of the East Glorious Gate and the Palace of Earthly Tranquillity to show Olivia – she'll allow him to bore her and maybe the boys, if they can be persuaded, with a slideshow. But Bernard's abiding memory of China will be the misconstrued slight of a beautiful woman, and he will remember it as if she had meant every word.

MATURE PEOPLE

When Olivia reaches her destination there's a canvas tent outside where she has to show her card to an official. It reminds her of images she's seen on TV of al-fresco voting in some hot country where the people are eager for everyday democracy. She likes the primitive simplicity of it – the tent, well really an awning on stilts, and the atmosphere of doughty war-time solidarity – as the steward jokes with her about the weather. It's July but it's the same grey, he says. He ushers her into a huge basketball arena with a polished wooden floor. She has to register first at a row of tables where staff with lanyards sit in Perspex boxes in front of screens. The first question she's asked is her date of birth. She overhears the man beside her give his – it's identical to Olivia's, and she wants to say 'snap!' or 'what are the odds?' Then she realizes how stupid she is. Everyone here is the same vintage – that's the whole point.

The steward at the start of the roped walkway leading to the vaccination stalls is standing with her back to Olivia, where a number of people are queueing. She's a heavy-set young woman and something about her shape looks familiar. These days Olivia finds it harder and harder to 'see' people in all the hazard gear. When the steward turns, she's wearing a pair of black-framed spectacles, large as goggles. She holds her hand up policing the air between them.

'Marcella?'

'Liv?' Marcella says peering, then flaps her hands. 'Oh, it must be my new glasses!'

Olivia doesn't know if she means that she can't see properly or that they've transformed her appearance. Either way, Olivia thinks, the glasses have nothing to do with it. It's the estrangement that has overtaken the world since they last met that has made them unsure of one another.

'How *are* you?' Olivia asks.

Marcella shrugs. 'You know.'

'Still writing?'

She'd met Marcella on a writing masters in Trinity College, although they called it something posher. An MPhil. It had never made Olivia feel in the slightest philosophical. When she started the course, in fact, she'd been feeling strangely bereft. Bernard had just left on his retirement trip to China. It was the first time they'd been parted for any significant period of time in forty years. Imagine! He'd wanted her to come with him but she'd refused.

'I have my own plans, thank you very much!' she said while thinking *we are not joined at the hip*.

They were like an old married couple. An old married couple without the sex. Or maybe that was the definition of an old married couple; she wouldn't know. The difference was that she and Bernard had never been intimate. Not in that way.

Once they came of age, Olivia's sons refused to believe it.

'Yeah, right!' Charlie said. He's twenty, a tousle-haired beanpole, cheeky and forthright, and so like his long-vanished father that sometimes Olivia has to turn away from him out of fright. Fright and memory. For Charlie and his brother, Mal, Bernard has always been Uncle Ber. They wouldn't have objected to him as a substitute father. He'd have been a hell of a lot better than some of the specimens she had gone out with over the years. But, at least, Olivia had had enough sense not to move any of them in. So Bernard remained the only feasible candidate, as far as the boys were concerned, although they were convinced that Uncle Ber was a closeted gay. In their circular thinking, it was the only logical explanation for why she and Bernard hadn't 'hooked up'.

The writing course was held in the upper floors of a tall Georgian terrace fronting on to Westland Row. The backs of the houses were incorporated into an enormous glass atrium which meant that what had been exterior walls were now interior. That was how Olivia felt most of the time while she was in Trinity – like someone whose mottled insides were on display. Inside this vault, it was clammy as a greenhouse and made the droves of students seem like rare botanical plants that needed this glaring dry heat to sprout.

The workshop room had two long windows that partitioned the skies of several seasons into four takeaway portions. The students sat around the edges of the room in a U-formation. There was a large empty space in the centre that looked like a bull-ring waiting for Hemingway. Olivia remembered reading somewhere that workshops were the blood sports of the literary world. As she sat there on her first day with her eager new writing notebooks and plastic folders, she felt very old and very prominent. If only there had been one other older person. But no, she told herself firmly, it was better this way; she wouldn't be part of some oldies' ghetto.

First item of business was appointing the class reps. Really? After four decades as a council clerk and an active union member, Olivia thought she was done with tedious business like this. This was, at last, her me-time.

'Volunteers?' the lecturer asked testily.

Mature People

He was Theo Bender, a visiting Scandi writer, who spoke English with dental precision. A very tall man in his thirties with Nordic blond hair, he wore jeans and hiking boots and a stone-coloured ski jumper with a rust-coloured pattern scattered across the shoulders. He had the scrubbed complexion of someone who had trudged directly from the Arctic to be with them. (Olivia was disappointed to learn that everyone teaching her was going to be years younger. She wanted white-haired men in academic gowns, she realized, or if they were going to be younger, someone rakish and disreputable like Michael Caine in *Educating Rita*.)

'Anyone?'

This in bureaucratic terms was the equivalent to a drowning person calling 'help, help' as he goes down for the third time.

'Would one of the mature people volunteer?' Theo said, looking directly at her. Technically, she wasn't the only mature student – you only had to be twenty-three to qualify – but she was the only one who looked it.

'Come, come, it is not a chair on the UN Security Council. It is a simple job dealing with people's complaints.'

Oh well, Olivia thought, I can do that.

She looked around the group. Young hip folk who, fashion-wise, looked like refugees from her own disreputable youth – the boys with beards, in collarless shirts and ripped jeans. The girls were sculpted into leggings (another throwback for Olivia; she'd belonged to the first leggings generation) or wore outsize floral dresses or tiny denim shorts. How on earth could she represent them?

'Do you really want someone as old as your mother?' she asked and then silently corrected herself – as your granny, more like.

They all laughed, more out of nervousness than anything else. They didn't find her self-deprecating humour funny, she could see; time was when that would have appealed. Now, it sounded like special pleading.

'So, you will do it? Yes?' Theo Bender said.

Olivia's first misconception was not realizing how much she'd be expected to write. How foolish that sounded in retrospect. She'd written confessional poetry secretly in her twenties – an unhappy marriage will do that to you – but having spent a lifetime in between reading voraciously for escape, she wanted to master the more muscular world of fiction now. Her notion of writing as something languid and elective was severely tested right from the start. They were expected to cough up 500 words at a moment's notice and Olivia was aghast at how mechanical it all was, as if they were wind-up toys that could only be set in motion by a series of prompts. Although, left to her own devices, Olivia would probably have ended up chewing her pencil. Metaphorically, that is. Everything, she learned, was a metaphor.

Ideas were not her strong suit, though she had a certain fluidity from a lifetime of writing memos and fictional sick notes for her boys. *Malcolm is feeling bilious* (a word she'd always wanted to use) *this morning after a sea journey; Charlie has the mumps* (which he had five times in all) *and must be quarantined*. But those first weeks, their practice, as it was grandly called, reminded her of those pasta machines, where you fed a fat piece of dough in one end and it came out in thin strings at the other.

The others didn't seem to mind. But then it wasn't forty years since they'd last been in a classroom. She saw the hesitation when lectures were over and the young ones were drifting off for coffee unsure of whether to ask her along. They belonged to the generation who didn't want to exclude anybody, but they didn't want an elderly gooseberry for company either. She understood their dilemma but she was determined never to exclude herself either. She wanted the full university experience so she accepted all invites – to poetry readings from Fliss and Emer, and to pub quizzes by Dermot and Carl who needed someone for the vintage trivia questions.

Carl was a beautiful, bald, black American (he told her he had Cuban heritage) who wore John Lennon glasses and was still the right side of forty. He could recite Yeats at the drop of a hat. His party piece was 'To A Friend Whose Work Has Come to Nothing'. Olivia had to train herself to stop sizing him up. Really! You're a sixty-year-old woman, stop! Not only is your lust sexist, it's probably racist too. Dermot, on the other hand, was a bashful twenty-one-year-old, so thin he was almost concave. Marmalade-haired, pale, given to furious smoking which made his breath smell terrible. Olivia was working up to telling him this but never did. The last thing she wanted was to come off as motherly.

'Well,' Marcella says 'I *was* writing a speculative historical novel about Jane Eyre's fat cousin, John Reid …'

Olivia doesn't hear the rest of the sentence. She doesn't hear the past tense in Marcella's account, because she's awestruck by the girl's inventiveness. All of those young people, she remembered, were fizzing with ideas. That's why she gave up. That's what she told herself. She just didn't have the agility of mind.

'I'm back in my parents' place,' Marcella adds, nodding glumly.

Twenty-Twenty Vision

Olivia recognizes the grim resignation of an adult child sent back to the crèche. Her Mal had been living an independent life in a shared house before all this. Now he was working from home in the back bedroom.

'And are you getting paid?' she asks.

'For writing?' Marcella says and snorts with laughter behind her mask.

'No,' Olivia says, 'for this?'

'Oh no, this is a volunteering position. Gets me out of the house.' Olivia thinks she can detect a smile in Marcella's tone.

'And are you?'

'Am I what?'

'Still writing?'

'Oh no,' Olivia says. 'No, I knew when I was beaten.'

She was sure Marcella blushed behind all the paraphernalia.

'Look, Liv –' Marcella began. This time it was Olivia who raised her hand.

'It's fine, Marcella, I'm fine with it. It's not your fault.'

Marcella hung her head and kicked at the ground.

Trying to change the mood, Olivia inquired: 'How's Jamie?'

She, Jamie and Marcella were put into a reading group together early in the first semester. They were in their mid-twenties, same age as her boys, so Olivia felt in familiar territory although soon she realized the gaps in her knowledge. Jamie and Marcella hung around together all the time but they were not a couple. Or at least not a declared couple, which seemed to be regarded as the worst possible condition.

Jamie was neat, clean-shaven. He had a short back and sides and a sharp way of dressing. He wore natty waistcoats and dicky bows with pink or lilac jeans. His shirts were always pressed. Olivia presumed he was gay. He was one of the few who made physical contact with her; he would tap her forearm with his slender fingers when he wanted to make a point. He'd greet her with a comradely arm around her shoulder. He had a light touch.

She liked his intelligence, which was cool and methodical. He could quote whole paragraphs of other writers' wisdom, many of them people Olivia had never heard of. He seemed steeped in this world she had only dipped her toe into. She remembered what he said about Don de Lillo's *Underworld*: 'It's a big baggy monster. He tries like Joyce to squeeze the whole world into it. But shouldn't it be more organized?'

'You mean slimmer,' Marcella said.

'Is it even a novel?'

'Do we have to define it?' Olivia asked.

It was a surprise to her to find she didn't have fixed opinions about the fiction they read. She'd been reading like a child, just gobbling it up, but found herself silent as Jamie and Marcella batted ideas back and forth.

'I say yes,' Jamie said.

'And I say no!' Marcella said hotly.

'Isn't she great?' Jamie would say after one of these declarations.

Marcella never batted away his compliments as Olivia would have done at that age. She allowed them, even though her default mode was slightly scathing. A curled lip under a nest of tangled tawny hair, and clothes designed to dispel attention. Ungainly dungarees, plaid pinafores. Olivia longed to take her in hand, but she resisted. She was finished being parental. Anyway, she detected something condescending about the way Jamie talked at her, like he was patting a small pet dog on the head. But Olivia liked Jamie too much to pursue that line of thinking.

Twenty-Twenty Vision

Maybe it was watching him and Marcella together, but in the early weeks of the first term at Trinity, she found herself thinking a lot about Bernard and their history. They had been work colleagues for practically a lifetime; she knew no one else as long. She'd often toyed with the idea of them as a couple – on certain conditions. If he'd lose a few pounds, if he'd be more manly, grow a pair, she would think to herself, as Bernard danced around her. But even in that she was conflicted. Were he to turn into George Clooney overnight, wouldn't her answer still be no? What she valued about him was his discretion, which she derided as pussyfooting when she didn't want to acknowledge that it was borne out of his feelings for her. His unspoken devotion had become her guilty and sustaining pleasure, particularly during those years when the boys were young and there was no one else even remotely interested in her.

She remembered Bernard gratefully then – wearing the silly paper crowns for Christmas dinner, making a fool of himself at the watersports centre, rolling and tumbling down water slides with the boys because Olivia couldn't swim. Christ, he even babysat when she was going out on dates. Sometimes she'd found herself irritated by his loyalty. It made her cruel, as if he was the faithful dog who could be kicked and not react.

Even when she imagined herself and Bernard together, all she could see were the deficits. Wouldn't it be 'settling' at this stage? Settling for less. Then there was his inexperience. What in the world would she do with him? What would it be like being his sexual teacher? On the other hand, she'd be free to mould him into whatever she wanted. Trouble was she didn't know what she wanted because she'd never had it and that was a kind of inexperience too, wasn't it?

She'd even thought of suggesting a white marriage to him. Isn't that what they call it? Like that elderly gentleman she'd read about who married his male carer to ensure property succession, though neither of them was gay. She and Bernard could grow old together. Would that be so bad? But if it worked, would it remind them of all the wasted time, when they could have been together and weren't? And if it didn't work, what then?

'Jamie?' Marcella says. 'Haven't seen him since we left college. Lockdown, you know.'

She's effecting vagueness, but Olivia doesn't believe her. She wonders if that has to do with the mask. Isn't that why people wore masks in the past – to hide behind, to dissemble?

'I think he was planning to teach English in South Korea, but don't know if he ever made it.'

'But you're still in touch, right?' Olivia persists.

Marcella says nothing. Olivia is about to change the subject again when Marcella adds with a strangled sob. 'No. We're not talking.'

'Oh why? What's happened?'

'You were right about him, Liv. He broke my heart.'

Marcella had taken Olivia into her confidence early on.

'He's bi,' Marcella had confided.

'And are you, you know, together?'

Marcella shrugged and pouted resignedly.

'Well, yes and no.'

'So which is it?'

'It's not that binary,' Marcella said and all Olivia could think of was Venn diagrams and computer code.

'Look, the way it is, I like him more than he likes me, I know that, and in the end he'll go off with a bloke, I'm pretty sure, but why not have him while I can?'

'I'd want to know where I stood,' Olivia said. 'People should be one thing or the other.'

'Don't be like that,' Marcella said. 'I like Jamie and trust him, how many people can you say that about?'

This was hard to argue with.

'I hope you're being careful,' Olivia said thinking of contraception.

'It's gone beyond that,' Marcella said. 'I love him regardless how it turns out. There's no shame in that.'

Despite her youth, Marcella could be quite wise.

Olivia had never had a female friend to whom she confided real secrets. She blamed her marriage break-up, early separation and a hectic life of full-time work and looking after the boys. Female friendships seemed like a leisure activity, one you'd have to devote a lot of time to and, those years when the boys were small, she couldn't afford the luxury of a hobby.

When she and Marcella had one of their sessions, Olivia felt like she'd discovered adolescence. Their long mournful talks about romance were what she imagined she should have had as a teenager. She shared about Bernard.

'Tell him what you feel,' Marcella had said.

'It's not as simple as that. I don't know what I feel.'

'Well, tell him that.'

'But I want to be sure —'

'But you can't be. Move in close to him. As long as he's just an argument in your head, you can keep him at a distance.'

'But what if I hurt him?'

'Don't,' Marcella said.

Olivia noticed Marcella hadn't asked what if Bernard hurt her. There was no need. That was something she was sure of about Bernard.

'It's a risk. Everything's a risk,' Marcella said. 'Being here's a risk.'

'You mean Trinity?'

'I mean life.'

'It was after you left,' Marcella says. Olivia feels obscurely to blame as if her leaving had skewed the status quo. 'Theo assigned us to different reading groups and suddenly the whole thing seemed to disintegrate. Jamie literally ghosted me.'

She looks around nervously, then leans forward conspiratorially.

'It wasn't the sex, it was the intimacy. Know what I mean? You have a special place and then you don't and there's no explanation. It wasn't as if he replaced me with someone else. It was just like he'd dropped off the face of the earth. As if my allotted time with him was over.'

Standing there whispering to one another in the middle of the vaccination centre about intimacy makes it seem like a matter of life and death.

'I mean, if he'd explained, if he'd given me warning. If he'd even texted me and told me it was over.'

Imagine, Olivia thinks, being grateful for being brushed off by text.

'But there was nothing and I didn't have the courage to confront him ...'

'Well, he didn't leave much of an opening, did he? Just shutting off like that. And then with COVID –'

'All the same, I should have confronted him. But I was afraid, afraid that he'd laugh it off, whatever was between us. As if that was the way the world worked and he'd see me as a silly romantic little girl trying to make more of it than what it was.'

'Sounds to me like he was the one who couldn't deal with what was between you.'

'But that's not the worst of it …' Marcella begins.

Olivia scans through the possibilities – pregnancy? venereal disease? – then realizes how out of date she is.

'Marcella?' another steward three lanes away shouts at her. 'Can you come here for a minute?'

Marcella scurries off leaving Olivia dangling.

She thought when she printed out 'A Man In Reserve' for the workshop that it would grow, become substantial, but the content just seemed flimsier in typescript. In particular, she was dreading Jamie and Marcella's verdicts. Even though they'd known one another only two months, she felt close to them, bolstered by their opinion of her. She liked how Marcella called her Liv without even asking – it made her feel as if she'd become another person inside the gates of Trinity. She'd given no hint of what she was writing about. Jamie and Marcella talked about their writing all the time but Olivia felt that was taboo. Anyway she couldn't talk about it in the way Jamie did. How could she be articulate about her incoherence? But her worries were unfounded. That first time, the others were kind, if only by omission. Carl had said her story was a bit timid.

'It's pretty formless,' Jamie said, 'I mean it doesn't go anywhere, doesn't lead us to anything but more confusion.'

'But,' Marcella had counter-argued, 'isn't that just like life? It's autofiction, drawn from life and not neatly tied up into some conclusion to satisfy the dictates of an arbitrary fictional form.'

As she listened to them fighting over her, Olivia had felt like the child of divorcing parents.

'It is not a story yet,' Theo Bender said, 'it is a draft'.

She could feel the wind whistling through the thin stuff of her narrative and imagined a piece of Swiss cheese. She was grateful that Theo had been so diplomatic, but she couldn't escape the feeling the others were all soft-pedaling because they didn't feel her work was worth savaging. She'd seen them fillet Carl's magic realism fables, and dismiss Dermot's painful rural coming-of-age stories as tractor fiction. It wasn't like they couldn't be forthright. Olivia felt like they were being kind to the elderly.

'You must try again,' Theo Bender had said. 'And remember this. Fiction is reality transformed.'

After Marcella disappears, Olivia shuffles up two, then three places in the queue. They are lined up in the roped gangway, their prescribed distances marked out with yellow lozenges on the floor. She can see that Marcella is in deep consultation with the other steward who holds a clipboard. Come on, Olivia thinks, hurry, or else I'll never hear the end of the story. She moves up to the top of the queue. This isn't like the checkout line; you can't volunteer someone to go ahead of you, can you?

Marcella comes hurrying back. She catches Olivia by the elbow with her gloved hand as if she's going to steer her away from the queue. Insead she leans in.

'So what, what did he do?' Olivia finds herself whispering.

'He stole my novel,' Marcella says.

Somehow Olivia was expecting something more catastrophic.

'You know the Jane Eyre novel I mentioned earlier? I gave him the first half of it to read and he decided to write his own version, though he never told me.'

So nothing to do with sexual politics in the end.

'My idea was to have Jane's spiteful cousin John Reid attempt to rape her. And that's why she's sent off to that terrible boarding school. Because nobody believes her. Like a historical #JaneEyreToo story. That's as far as I'd got. I was a bit stuck so I asked him to take a look at it.'

There are bright tears in her eyes behind the enormous spectacles.

'I trusted him entirely. I just never thought –'

'Did he use your material?'

'Oh no, just the idea.'

Is it a crime to steal someone else's idea, Olivia wonders.

'He's turned it into a coming-of-age gay story from John Reid's point of view. He's made it first person. He's made it all about himself.'

'How do you know if you haven't been in touch?'

'Oh, he told me after the fact. When he'd finished, he rang up, finally, to tell me what he'd done. That's why he broke up with me. He cut me off *before* he did the dirty on me. It was a pre-emptive strike.'

'Oh Marcella, I'm so sorry.

'And the worst of it is, he doesn't think he's done anything wrong. "It's totally different to yours," he kept on saying. "There's room for two John Reid novels in the world." Except that his is finished and with an agent in London.'

When Christmas intervened, Olivia was relieved to get away from Trinity. Six weeks at home with only the boys to worry about and one measly recalcitrant story to fix felt manageable. She could do that. Bernard was back and she'd invited him for Christmas dinner. He came armed with his pictures of China. Charlie had set up a screen in the living room and put the images on a loop so they could see them in full glorious technicolour. The boys, bless them, entered into the spirit and ooh and aahed in the right places. The images of the Forbidden City, The Great Wall, the Chinese warriors, dappled the living room in pearly light. The screen was visible, weirdly miniaturized, through the serving hatch, as they ate in Olivia's kitchen. Every so often, through dinner, Bernard would halt mid-chew and say – ah this was when we went to Beijing – but although he was full of talk about the other people on the organized trip, Olivia couldn't shake the feeling that the experience had been a disappointment. She wondered if she'd set him up for that, with all her dire warnings about the hypocrisy of new age communism, the human rights abuses, the Uighir Muslims. She'd really wanted to dampen his unbridled enthusiasm; she'd wanted to shake him out of his wilful innocence; as if he believed he could travel without any responsibility for the conditions at the other end. Not for the first time she examined her conscience with regard to Bernard and found herself wanting.

Remembering Marcella's advice, she chided herself all through Christmas Day – stop keeping your distance, move in. (Which sounded like writing advice to her.) Be kind (which didn't.) But she couldn't do it. When Bernard donned his gold paper crown and danced with Mal's new girlfriend after dinner, she could feel a great chasm opening up between them and she could only see him as an unfortunate fat man who'd accidentally gate-crashed their Christmas.

You're a bitch, Olivia Fletcher, she thought, a total bitch.

'You'll write something else though, won't you. You won't give up?'

Marcella looks at her oddly.

'Of course,' she says hotly. 'I won't let Jamie Hickson have the satisfaction of wrecking my career.'

She leans forward, too close for comfort or safety, and hisses in Olivia's ear. 'I hope he catches COVID and dies.'

She'd been accused of being timid; well, no more! You have a lifetime's more experience than any other student in the room, she'd told herself as she redrafted 'A Man in Reserve', use it! But the deafening silence that initially greeted the second draft should have alerted her.

'First thoughts?' Theo asked.

Olivia knew enough to know they were not lost for words – when was Jamie Hickson ever stuck for something to say? – they were with-holding them.

'Anyone?' Theo prompted.

The tense silence was so prolonged, she was tempted to step in herself and apologize for the story, but the rules didn't allow for that.

'It has no literary merit,' Carl said finally. 'It's sub-par romance. There's no depth, no resonance. The lovers – who aren't really lovers – are not believable and the narration just sits there stating its case.'

'You're too far away from your characters so it just becomes Mills and Boon,' monosyllabic Dermot said. 'Sorry, Oliv.'

'Precisely,' Jamie chimed in. 'Janet Malcolm says the fictional character is *a being with no privacy who stands before the reader naked and exposed* but these people – he smacked the manuscript with his hand – these people are flat and opaque and dressed up in full battle gear.'

'I agree,' Marcella said. 'They don't let us in.'

Some of the others, whom Olivia cared less about, offered their opinions. Then the workshop dwindled into silence.

'Why don't they just fuck one another?' Jamie said at last. He seemed exasperated at Olivia and she couldn't understand how suddenly it had become so personal.

'Exactly!' Marcella chimed in. 'I mean why won't this woman – Paulette, Jesus what a name! – put up or shut up? She's so weak and so vain. And so vacillating.'

Olivia felt the stab of betrayal. How could Marcella be so cruel when she'd confided the real live experience behind the story?

'She despises him, what's that all about?' Marcella went on.

Olivia's face was aflame. She was afraid she was going to cry – or leak from the eyes. In her sixties, even her tears were ungenerous.

'Can we not write about weak and vain characters?' Theo intervened, but it wasn't to defend Olivia, it was to take up Marcella's point. But it took the attention off her.

'We can,' Jamie answered, 'but we have to do it with conviction.'

'And without resorting to cliché,' Marcella added for good measure.

Theo Bender had the last word.

'This is writing for therapy, Olivia, but it's not reaching for Art.'

It was always said with a capital A. In Theo Bender's world that was her capital crime.

She remembered filing out of the workshop in a daze. Condemned by a jury of her peers. Jamie and Marcella asked her to come for a drink as if nothing had happened but she couldn't face it. She felt as she had the first day. Innocent and enormously foolish. She didn't belong here; she never had. It wasn't that she hadn't the brains; it was that her ambition wasn't high-brow enough. Years of dulling, necessary work had knocked that out of her. Life and single mothering and bad TV had thinned her emotions. The bad poetry of her youth at least had had heart.

She stayed on for a couple of weeks but she'd already decided. Oddly, she didn't want Jamie and Marcella to feel responsible. Not for their sake, but for her own. She had her pride. She stopped going to classes in February. For a few weeks she sent in a doctor's note – burnout, he'd written – then she stopped doing even that. It was good timing; it meant there was never a day of reckoning. A month later COVID drove everything online and it gave her the perfect excuse; she couldn't have handled the technology. Or the remoteness. After all, she'd wanted a campus experience. It wasn't the boot camp ethos or even the generation gap that defeated her in the end. Nor was it low self-esteem or the lack of a sense of entitlement that seemed to dog women of her age, the second-chance crowd. As an ordinary citizen of Dublin, she'd never once set foot on Front Square. Now, she'd got used to striding around Trinity as if she owned the place. That was something, wasn't it?

But the reason she couldn't continue was Bernard.

Not only was her fiction all about Bernard, but since his return he'd been pestering her to show him what she was writing. (He offered it as a trade for suffering through his Chinese slide show.) She realized she couldn't show him because everything she'd written was about him. Reams and reams of Bernard. She couldn't stop. Every man in her fiction was fat, self-deprecating, entirely loveable in the abstract. Her father figures, her invented husbands, were all the same. Every woman was her – sharp and prickly when anyone came near, still holding out for someone better. Or just holding out for the sake of it? Because it had become habit. There was nothing elevating in what she wrote, nothing transformative. Her plain truth was just too plain. And too revealing.

'Next!' a steward further up the line calls out.

'That's you,' Marcella says.

Olivia wants to reach out and hug her but she'd probably be done for deadly assault attempting an embrace here. Damn this bloody disease, Olivia thinks, that forces us to rely on words. She thinks of offering her phone number. But why? What comfort could she be to Marcella? She'd warned her that Jamie would break her heart and so it had come to pass. Just not in the way she'd anticipated. There was no comfort in being right.

'So long then,' she says and Marcella gives her a miniature wave, like you would to a small child.

If the tent outside reminded her of third-world democracy, then the vaccination stall, one of hundreds lined up in avenues, reminds her of an astrologer's booth. She'd had her fortune told once at a fun-fair. It was when the boys were small and they'd egged her on because they'd wanted to go back to the shooting range on their own. She'd stepped through a bead curtain into a tent bathed in a brothel-red light. The fortune teller sat at a card table draped in a kilim and there was a stack of cards under her right hand. She had very long, false, red fingernails but apart from that she was in normal gear. Olivia was slightly disappointed at her homely look. She had jaded blonde hair, crêpey skin at the neck and had a flat, fleshy, inexpressive face. Embarrassingly, she wore a pale lilac twinset which Olivia had also bought in M&S but had never worn because she thought it was too matronly. So in some weird way it was like looking at herself in a decade's time. Already, her future being laid out. Olivia didn't remember much about the session. There was the dealing and fingering of the playing cards but all she remembered was the woman told her she would meet the man of her dreams in a large public space. She imagined a hospital, an airport terminal, even a university campus. She'd tried them all. No luck.

Her vaccinator has berry brown skin and nut-coloured hair. She gives off a vibrant, healthy glow. How does she manage it stuck inside a vax centre from morning till night? Wild swimming, the nurse tells her. This used to be called swimming in the sea before it was branded into a new activity by the pandemic (which requires a whole new set of paraphernalia – wet suits and dry robes.) She urges Olivia to try it and Olivia doesn't have the heart to tell her she can't swim. As the boys got older, she'd tried her hand at pastimes, but braving the sea was never going to be one of them. Too much immersion for her.

The nurse jabs her so expertly that she is still waiting for the sting even when she begins rolling down Olivia's sleeve.

Afterwards, like everybody else, she's directed to the observation area where she's told she'll have to wait for ten minutes in case of a bad reaction. The folding chairs are set two metres apart and the place looks all the world like an examination hall without the desks. Even though it's full of old people, people the same age as her, people with the same birthdays even, Olivia is assailed by youthful memories. Discos and dances where, who knew, some of these same men and women might have been in attendance. For a minute she feels again the buzz of apprehension, of possibility. How ridiculous, she chastises herself. We're in the middle of a pandemic and you're thinking about youthful sex. Cop yourself on, she tells herself, but she can't shift the resurrected feelings. What has prompted this, she wonders. Seeing Marcella again? Or is it the atmosphere of shuffling uncertainty in the hall, now caused by stiffening limbs, then by emotional ineptitude. She looks at some of these solid, white-haired men and can see the youths they were. The women come in the same types they did in the late 70s – there are the trim flirtatious ones in crisp casuals, except now they have ash-coloured hair or have gone blonde, and the dowdy heavier ones who've left themselves go and are wearing runners for their fallen arches. Even the ones leaning on sticks don't look that old to her, but that's a delusion, she knows that.

The local radio station is piped through the speakers. 'Saturday Night Fever' comes on. Suddenly in the midst of all this patient, biddable old age, she wants to get up and dance. She wants to see all these old men and women up on their bunioned feet with their untamed locks and their tired leisure wear. She wants to see them revert to the lazy sashaying they called dancing when they were young. That won't be a stretch, will it? She imagines them, the walking wounded, joining a conga line and shunting and swaying around the vax centre gathering up strays as they go. They'll work up a sweat and it'll be a good thing, not a cause for alarm. The vaccinators and stewards will join in, applauding their plucky, joyful elders. Her feet start to tap and she thinks to hell with it, I'm going to do it anyway, and she rises, shimmying her hips and fisting the air. It's like the dole scene in *The Full Monty* except no one joins her.

She sees a steward – not Marcella – stalking towards her and she sits down abruptly, just at the point where she can see the others were contemplating getting up. Oh well, too late. Then it strikes her. If Bernard were here, he'd join her; he's a terrific dancer, always has been.

She picks up her phone.

'Are you free?' she texts, all fingers and thumbs

CURRICULUM VITAE

1.

The shutter slaps open.
The hatch is on the return of a dim stairwell and George leans towards you filling the frame. You hand over your tickets. They're cloakroom tickets in two colours, bedroom pink and primrose yellow. George scoops them up and sets them down on his side of the hatch and begins to count them as if he's shuffling cards. He has a fat, moist lower lip and long, heavy, blonde hair tied back in a louche ponytail.

'Twenty-three,' he shouts and the other 'chef' lifts the ladle and dips it into the huge pot that's farting on the two-ring stove.

It's your last table of the night. You set the tray down on the lip of the counter. George lays out the paper plates on his side. His assistant slops out a ladle of stew on each one. It could be chicken or beef. Either way it's a runny brown sludge with only the carrots identifiable. When seven plates have been filled George lifts them on to your tray, tosses down a bunch of plastic cutlery, and you totter down the stairs.

You walk into a cauldron of noise. On the stage a crooner does Elvis, late Elvis with the black sideburns, white suit and the hip rolls of fat. This one looks the part. A live band crashes behind him and he rubs his lips up against the microphone.

Curriculum Vitae

Cabaret night at the Char-a-Bang, a huge barn of a pub with rows of trestle tables, covered with butchers' paper. It's midweek so only a third full but still boomingly noisy. There are three girls on tonight, like careful drivers at the bumpers, steering their large trays of slop between the tables in the dark.

You deliver your first tranche of plates and return to the hatch for a second trip. And then a third.

For the final time, you head for your table, the group of twenty-three well oiled 'ladies', swaying from side to side and clapping their hands. You set the tray down, steering the plates, bowed out of shape by the liquid dinner, onto the table trying to avoid the lethal flash of the women's charm bracelets and their false nails. You despise them, in your adolescent heart. The loud lipstick, the permed hair, the flashy jewellery, the screeching that proves they're having a good time. Their awful taste in music.

Thank God, soon you'll be out of here. You turn away when someone tugs you on the sleeve.

'Miss, Miss, you've left us short – Marie and Joanie didn't get their dinners,' a woman with blonde corkscrew ringlets shouts.

'I only got twenty-three tickets,' you shout back.

Twenty-three tickets, three tray runs.

You try counting heads again. The number at the table seems to have grown. Where did these extra people come from? Did they sneak in during the show without paying their admission?

You head back to the kitchen.

'We're two short on table twelve,' you shout into the hatch. George appears.

'You know the rule,' he says, 'no tickets, no dinner.'

'Come on, George, it's the end of the night.'

'No tickets, no dinner,' he repeats with his fat lip and glum eyes.

'Please, George, what difference does it make? You'll only throw it out, anyway.'

You think of going back to the table and how those women will turn on you, they'll point their fingers and shove their powdered faces into yours. They'll vent their rage because they've seen your disdain.

You turn away from the hatch and trail back down to the floor. But you can't face it. You turn left by the toilets and take the back way out.

There goes your first job.

2.

Charlie Relihan is like a grocer's assistant in a mustard coat. But underneath he's nattily dressed, white shirt speared at the collar, primly knotted tie, a three-piece suit for when he goes out to visit the reps. He's beaky-looking: small, watchful eyes, a sharp nose, thin hair dragged over his pate. Your job is to sit in the storeroom at a desk, filling requisition orders. Charlie's mantra is 'always look busy'. You're surrounded by shelves of stationery and supplies – order books, receipt jotters, typing paper and ribbons, pens, pencils, erasers, staples, paper clips, desk calendars. From time to time the door will open and someone – often a messenger boy or a secretary from the upper floors of City Hall – will enter and hand you a chit. You fill out their order, putting the stuff in a cardboard box, then you stamp the order and file it away in the book, which Charlie checks when he comes back. Sometimes days can go by and no one comes. You learn how slowly time can pass. But on the bright side, you get to read – a lot. You're three-quarters of the way through *David Copperfield* when Charlie ambushes you, coming back early one afternoon when you're not expecting him.

'What are you doing?' he asks.

You can see he's worked up. It's the first time you've seen him like this.

'I'm reading,' you say.

'Oh no,' he says tragically, 'oh no, my dear, you're not here to read. No, no, no. We can't have that at all. What would happen if the City Manager walked in and caught you … reading?'

You can just see it – the City Manager coming down to your basement hidey-hole for a pencil sharpener.

'But there's nothing to do.'

'There's never nothing to do,' Charlie says. He points to the metal shelves that line the rooms, everything stacked neatly and labelled. You eke out twenty minutes every day stocking them.

You want to ask how many times can you tidy the shelves but you realize you're on shaky ground. Charlie has already said you have a future in Stores. You're not quite sure what that means. You're pleasant to the customers, if that's what he means. Hell, you're glad of them, a new face, an idle conversation to parse the day. It's a temporary job, but still you want to keep it till the summer ends. So you say nothing. But you can sense Charlie's immense disappointment in you, even though you think he's pathetic, all dressed up in his Sunday best, when he's just a glorified shopkeeper. He's seen through your fake compliance to your youthful cynicism.

You learn a new skill. Reading in a drawer.

3.

The department store's electrical counter is an obsessive's dream. It is divided into gradated compartments like a tradesman's toolbox, containing fuses, bulbs, fairy lights, batteries, coils of flex, light switch plates and plugs. Mr Nolan is your supervisor. He dresses in a suit and calls all the staff by their surnames. So you become this new creature, a lady who has strayed from prim Victorian literature: Miss Beale. When he's training you in he's very keen to tell you that, in the trade, plugs are considered male and sockets – 'the receivers', he says coyly – are female. He fingers the prongs of a three-pin plug. 'See, Miss Beale, a threesome.'

4.

You see the limitations of being a shop girl. And, if you move again, you see how the merry-go-round of poor-paying jobs will just go on. The painted horses may be different but the ride will be the same. You save. You get a grant. You go to college. You discover a facility for words.

5.

Just say yes. That is the freelance life. You write about bars, catering equipment, drug addicts, traditional musicians, rare medical conditions, job training schemes for the young. You cover court hearings about TV licences and parking fines, waiting for someone prominent to fuck up. You say yes because you're afraid to say no. It's a bit like love that way. You meet a schoolfriend, Sylvia, in the detergent aisle of the supermarket and she asks what you're doing. When you describe the above she says pityingly, 'Could you not get into journalism?'

6.

Your first commissioning editor, older than you by a decade, has policeman's feet, large and flat. He's a mountainy man with big hands and a scored face that registers a narrow range of emotion. From mild surprise to mild disdain. His physique suggests he should be out stalking the fields, threshing hay, manhandling beasts. Instead he's crouched over a typewriter that looks like a toy in his hammy hands. Others tell you he's capable of calculation and cunning but you can't see it. He is the only boss who ever paid you a direct, open-faced compliment. 'You have more talent than anyone I've seen come into this profession.' You remember that in years to come; it gives you solace even though it was probably a chat-up line.

7.

Your flatmate's boyfriend, Vinny, gets a job dish-washing in The Sultan's Cave, a small basement restaurant that serves Indonesian food – little bowls of rice and fish and peanut sauce which goes with everything. Vinny puts his back out after three days and not wanting to lose the job, he asks you to deputize for him. Your freelancing work is drying up, so you say yes, as you always do, to ready money. You stand in the corner of the kitchen on a duckboard in front of the deep aluminium sink with the hose-like tap and you spray and scrub. You wear a white plastic apron and a pair of white wellingtons. You learn to develop tunnel vision; otherwise you'd be overwhelmed by the volume of work beyond your peripheral vision. You look only to the left where the in-tray is, leaning towers of smeared plates and bowls. Spray, rinse, drain; spray, rinse, drain. You hear the tantrums and the merriment of the chefs at your back but you don't turn around from your dank little position. It is the wettest job you've ever done. You go home damp through as if you'd been standing in a rain shower for eight hours.

8.

Another work drought. You slide electoral notifications into brown envelopes, sealing the pre-addressed envelopes with your tongue. You remember the gummy taste, which is impossible to shift, and the sawdusty feel of your mouth. Kissing democracy is short-lived.

9.

The freelance life gives you tunnel vision. One day on a payphone in the hallway of your flat, you're holding for an interview for a piece that's right up against deadline when an emergency operator intercepts the call asking you to get off the line. Your panic boils over into rage. Does she not understand, you're about to do a vital interview, the piece is due in three hours, you won't be able to pay the rent if you don't get this … 'Madam, this is an emergency,' says the operator and the line goes dead.

10.

You start dating your ham-fisted commissioning editor once he has left his wife. He is scrupulous about not playing favourites so your work drought worsens. You decide to down-size and become a proof-reader.

11.

For the first time you have a woman boss. Mrs Wolfe is a small, energetic woman with a smoker's cough. Everything about her seems congested, as if she can't breathe or work fast enough to meet some urgent demand out there. Her bald husband is a cruel-faced man with thick glasses. He could be an ex-con. The lines on his face are deep as scars yet he has kind eyes. He sticks to the background, tending the machines, and smelling of oil. A silent partner. With Mrs Wolfe there's no other way to be. Her exasperation reverberates. On the phone, in frequent dressings-down on the floor. Even when she's alone, there's a constant muttered monologue of incredulity.

It's a small printing company and to get to the office upstairs you have to pass by the assembly line, where Hayley and Donna and a middle-aged matron, Mrs Burley, collate brochures for aluminium windows and pack flyers for jobbing plumbers. Hayley and Donna are your age. Cheerful, good-time girls, who have hairdresser's conversations about boyfriends and holidays and their plans for the weekend.

Mrs Wolfe likes you, which is frightening. Particularly when you make your first mistake. You miss three literals in a boiler instruction manual and the whole job has to be done again. You're called into the office. Mr Wolfe looks at you with lamb's eyes as you go in and you know you're for the chop.

It would be a relief to be let go, to tell the truth. Mrs W's histrionics are predictable only in that you know they're coming, but you never know exactly when. But she has other plans. Against her better judgment, she decides to be merciful. She sees something in you, she says. My God, what is it? You're demoted to the assembly line where you discover Donna is exactly as you thought but Hayley is a painful introvert trying, like you, to pass. You go out with them and get mildly drunk in a rowdy bar. They invite you to go dancing and try to fix you up. You don't mention the commissioning editor. You believe in keeping work and personal life separate. (Where did you learn that?) The assembly line is pleasant, mindless. For the first time at Mrs Wolfe's, you exhale.

She mistakes your placid contentment for a plucky response to reversal, and after a few months, rewards you with your proofing job back. The old order is restored. Hayley and Donna drop you. Before you make another mistake, you leave.

12.

Questions you're asked at the next interview:
    Do you have a steady boyfriend?
    Do you plan on getting married?
    If so, will you have a baby?
    What about your social life with the night work?
    How do you feel about men swearing?

Paradoxically, this was your happiest workplace, where men swore and you learned how to drink in a hurry.

13.

Proofing is teamwork. You work in twos – one to hold the copy, the other to taste it – i.e. to read it aloud. Reading outside the drawer, in other words. You work with Gerry happily for several years until he's promoted to supervisor and suddenly it's all change. What was cheery slapdashery translates into casual contempt when he's in charge. He's always late. He arrives in on the run, throwing his jacket off, rolling up his sleeves, all business, as if you and others who have been covering for his absence are malingerers who need to be barked into shape. He is the circus master and this is a performance. You fixate on the spittle that gathers in the corners of his mouth, something you never noticed before. It's not like he's frothing at the mouth but you will him, silently, to wipe it away. You fear some day you'll fish out a paper hanky and do it yourself. Wiping his eye, Dr Freud would call it. You're amazed at how quickly you come to resent someone you considered a mate. It's because he imposes his chaos on you. You have enough of your own to be dealing with. You have a life outside that is going off the rails. You have moved on from the commissioning editor and now have a marriage shifting on its foundations, two failed pregnancies, a blameless husband who feels blamed.

Luckily, Gerry moves on, up. In seven years, there are four other Gerrys doing that job. Never you.

14.

Obsolence strikes. You saw it once before when printers were subsumed by technology. Next they come for the proofreaders. You've been replaced by a screen and a little key with your function – SPELL CHECK.

15.

You adapt, use your old skills to new purpose. Rebrand. You're a copy editor now and Shirley's your boss. She's rake thin, with vivid lipstick, big teeth, and an exactitude about pronouncing her final dentals. Gushing is her default mode, but very soon she's hauling you into her office to berate you over your attitude. She suspects you don't 'believe' in the publication, a glossy women's magazine peddling fashion, cookery and dissatisfaction to the housebound mother. She doesn't say that, directly, of course. Instead she talks about you being too much of a stickler.

'Wait till you have children, then you won't be such a perfectionist,' she says.

As if pregnancy were the ultimate corrective for whatever is perceived to be wrong with you. You've had your third miscarriage, but Shirley is blithely unaware of this and would probably still feel entitled to say what she does, even if she knew. You gulp and tell her this is what an editor should be – a perfectionist. It's a job she's never done and it shows in what she writes. But, unlike you, she's acquired the skills necessary for the habitat, chief among them a coat of plumed camouflage. Her areas of willed incompetence are legion. She leaves huge, windy gaps and stands back, waiting for the conscientious to rush in. You've despised other bosses, but this one releases a kind of toxic gas slowly like a faulty appliance. You'll choke so gradually that no one will notice you're turning blue.

16.

It's the economy, stupid. This time it's the copy editors they've come for. Once you had a job, now you're corporate fat that has to be trimmed.

17.

You go back to retail. Home of the middle-aged woman who's reared her children, or looks as if she has. The supermarket chain is looking for personable females of a certain age – comforting, maternal presences with dexterous fingers and a passing acquaintance with a keyboard. You're put on checkout.

Curriculum Vitae

The symphony of bips and bleeps enters your brain. You hear it constantly like tinnitus; you wake out of dreams to it, it marks your time for you. Like life support. But apart from the noisescape the job itself is pleasant, undemanding of your emotions, solitary yet social. Inevitably, you meet people you know, most of whom are too polite to remark on what they consider your lowly position. Not your schoolfriend from the detergent aisle, Sylvia, though, who appears again, this time on your checkout queue. She married a doctor and has gone platinum. You're still dyeing your hair because Corporate says the customer doesn't want to be served by someone who could be mistaken for a pensioner. Makes them look like exploiters. Sylvia leans in and asks a version of the question from thirty years previously. Piteously.

'Did you have to give up on the journalism?'

You sat beside Sylvia at school. The nun who taught you had a club foot and a rolling walk like a listing ship. She looked as if she was about to drop into a curtsey, perhaps before an all-knowing God. Sister Doubting Thomas smiled all the time but there was steel in it. Or was it to cover the pain of her short leg? When she was about to skewer you, she'd smile even harder. She notes that you don't put your hand up in class, even while Sylvia beside you is bobbing up and down and hissing 'Sister, Sister!' at her, gagging to answer every question, though nine times out of ten she's wrong.

'Yet,' says Sister Doubting Thomas, putting her hand in the wound, 'you know the answer and won't volunteer, you won't share your knowledge.' And that she says is a sin, the sin of intellectual pride.

You remember the film *The Nun's Story* when Audrey Hepburn, the brightest student doctor in the class, is asked to fail her exam because her intellect threatens her less intelligent colleague. That, she is told, is her Christian duty. Does she fail the exam. Hell no!

Sylvia stands cradling her king prawns and bottle of dry white waiting for an answer. A doctor's wife, she's owed one.

'I'm undercover here,' you hiss, 'doing an exposé on the sordid life of minimum wage workers in a multi-million-euro global franchise.'

'Really?'

'Yes really, Sylvia. Just like Barbara Ehrenreich.'

You know she's never heard of Barbara Ehrenreich but she nods sagely.

'Your secret is safe with me,' she says and taps her nose.

She was always a bit of a fool.

18.

You're offered training to become a supervisor. A glorified floorwalker, in other words. It's snakes and ladders time. One step up before another sliding fall? You are still deciding what you'll do when your ex-husband shows up at the checkout. You haven't met in over twenty years. He lives in another part of the country so you're not expecting him to be in your world. It's a shock. But what's really shocking is not his strangeness, but his terrifying familiarity. Martin is thinner, grey where once he was russet, more melancholy. In comparison, you've cheered up.

'What happened?' he asks and fixes you with a brown gaze.

'A global recession,' you say lightly trying to neutralize the charged intimacy that comes with his question.

The intimacy of failure, or is it the failure of intimacy?

He treats you like you're still his wife and a worry to him. Did I do this to you, is what he's asking.

Your marriage was a see-saw like this. Who's to blame, as if there could only be one. The three babies you didn't have filled up all the recriminatory space between you. He broke the cycle, and your heart in the process, but someone had to. You don't blame him. Not now. He replaced delivery with deliverance, gave you permission not to try again. Or not to fail again. He wept when he said he was leaving you; you had to comfort him. To make it less final, you promised one another that if you were both still free, you'd get back together again when you were old. By which you meant the age you are now.

'How's Angela?' The woman you think of as his new wife.

'Angela died,' he says.

'Covid?'

He nods.

'Oh, Martin,' you begin but he shakes his head and you know not to continue.

A queue is forming behind him. Your supervisor, a sharp young woman with a navy suit, and a cash pouch under her arm, pauses by the till.

'Is there a problem here?'

Not unless you call a fifty-seven-year-old bereaved man with a sliced pan, three apples, a pack of cheese singles and a minute steak who's about to weep, a problem.

You come around to the customer side of the checkout. You steer Martin to a chair that's left out for the elderly to take breathers.

You remember your ancient youthful promise.

Versions of these stories originally appeared in *The Irish Times, The Lonely Crowd, Banshee, The Stinging Fly, Headstuff, Numero Cinq* and *Southword*